The Curious Cases of

Sherlock Holmes

Volume II

By

Stephen Herczeg

Paperback ISBN 978-1-78705-761-6
ePub ISBN 978-1-78705-762-3
PDF ISBN 978-1-78705-763-0

Published by MX Publishing
335 Princess Park Manor, Royal Drive,
London, N11 3GX
www.mxpublishing.co.uk

Cover design by Brian Belanger

To

Derrick and David

Without whom none of this

would ever have happened

Contents

Copyright Notices

Foreword
by David Marcum

Sometimes over the last few years – and especially during the tumultuous events of 2020 (and now 2021) – I've thought about connections that we all have now that simply didn't previously exist. For many of us, not that long ago, our world was very small – family and co-workers and the people we saw in our towns. But with the connections of social media – for good or bad – we now have links to people all over the world that we would have never known otherwise. If the COVID pandemic had hit just a few years ago, I personally wouldn't have had any specific concerns about people outside of my own local sphere – it would have been horrible, but nameless and faceless. Now, by way of connections through mutual admiration of Sherlock Holmes, I "know" many people from around the world – even if we've never met in person (yet) – and my concern over their well-being and safety, and my joy at their triumphs and good news, exists in a way that wouldn't have been possible before.

One such person that I'm very glad to now "know" in this modern sense is Stephen Herczeg, Author.

I first became acquainted with Steve while editing a book of sequels to the original Sherlock Holmes stories. He had previously written a Holmes tale that was included in the Belanger Books collection Sherlock Holmes: Adventures in the Realms of H.G. Wells (2017), and now he wanted to write a sequel to "The Engineer's Thumb". As a diligent editor, I'm always happy to receive new stories, and I'm always hoping that the author will be good – which means to me that the stories are written in the mold of the original Canon in the voice of Dr. John H. Watson – and also that the author will become a reliable repeat contributor. Steve is both of these.

His enthusiasm is notable and always welcome. He always wants to join the party. When he doesn't know something about The Canon, he's always very happy to learn, and he's great to work with.

Whenever I've been involved in editing a new Sherlock Holmes anthology – for either Belanger Books or MX Publishing – Steve always steps up, with stories that are Watsonian and uniquely interesting. When I also began editing new Solar Pons anthologies, he wanted to be part of those as well.

Like many of us Sherlock Holmes pasticheurs, Steve isn't in it to get rich. (In the case of the MX anthologies, he – along with the rest of us – donates his royalties to the Stepping Stones School for special needs children at Undershaw, one of Sir Arthur Conan Doyle's former homes. So far, the nearly two-hundred contributors from around the world have raised over $75,000 for the school, and no end in sight!) We write because we enjoy it – as painful as the process is sometimes – and also to add to the Great Holmes Tapestry. Another benefit of writing for these various Holmes anthologies is that they give us opportunities to produce more stories that we otherwise might not attempt, and after a while, we step back and see that we've written a good many of them.

And that's what has happened for Steve: After being in so many Holmes anthologies, he now has a plethora of adventures with his name on them, ready to be collected into his own book. I'm personally thrilled that this volume now exists, and that people who possibly didn't have a chance to read these stories when they originally appeared in various anthologies can now enjoy them collected in one place. I very much hope that this book will be followed by Volumes II and III and so on . . . .

I'm very glad, in this time of worldwide worry, to know Steve, and to have enjoyed his stories. Sit back and dive in – and let the present fade away for a while as Watson tells us another excellent adventure of his friend, Sherlock Holmes . . . .

David Marcum
February 2021

Foreword

by Derrick Belanger

It was on July 12, 2017 when I was first introduced to the talented Sherlockian author Stephen Herczeg via email. Mr. Herczeg wrote to me, starting off as he always does with a friendly "Gidday!" and asked if I'd consider including his story "The Curious Case of the Sleeper" in my anthology Sherlock Holmes: Adventures in the Realms of H.G. Wells. I read his story, and replied with a strong YES! "The Curious Case of the Sleeper" does a remarkable job of blending the writing of H.G. Wells with that of Dr. Watson's adventures. Add in a touch of Dickens with the ending, and you have a wonderfully imaginative mystery.

That was the first of many stories by Mr. Herczeg which I'm proud to have published. What amazes me with Herczeg's work is how he is able to create an excellent Sherlock Holmes pastiche no matter if he is working in the boundaries of Doyle's traditional Victorian England or if he is pushing those boundaries and incorporating elements of science fiction, horror, or steampunk. Take for example his excellent, "The Body at the Ritz". In this story, Holmes is called in to solve the mystery of a body found in an alley outside the Ritz hotel. The plot follows a traditional Holmesian narrative where Holmes and Watson are their 19th century selves; however, it also has them living in a steam powered world of horseless carriage lined streets and dirigibles covering the skies.

While this anthology focuses specifically on Herczeg's works around Sherlock Holmes, I would be remiss if I didn't also give a shout out to his wonderful writings of the other Sherlock Holmes, the one that resides in Praed Street, Mr. Solar Pons. Herczeg's Pontine works featured in The New Adventures of Solar Pons have Sherlock

Holmes's successor with his partner, Dr. Parker, solving crimes in the early twentieth century, just as August Derleth intended. As Herczeg does with his Sherlock Holmes writing, sometimes he bends the rules a bit with his Pons stories. In "The Rondure of Cthulhu," his piece in The Necronomicon of Solar Pons, the Praed street sleuth is pitted against the monsters from the world of H.P. Lovecraft. The story is an excellent piece of detective and weird fiction. I highly recommend seeking out Herczeg's Pontine work which is just as good as his Holmes writings.

One last point I'd like to make about Mr. Herczeg is how willing he is to push himself to keep writing new pastiches. Whenever I send out a call for new Sherlock Holmes fiction, Mr. Herczeg is always the first to respond, eagerly taking on the challenge of adding more stories to his personal Holmes canon. I'm sure this anthology will be the first of many.

Keep visiting 221 B Baker Street, Mr. Herczeg. We look forward to more thrilling adventures!

Derrick Belanger
February, 2021

The Adventure of the Double Cross

It was a lovely late summer afternoon in 1890 when the shrill cry of our doorbell broke the serenity. I was reposing in our small garden with a cup of iced tea and the Sunday papers. Mary stepped out onto the patio and handed me a folded telegram.

"I think it's from Sherlock," she said, adding with a wry grin, "Should I prepare your travelling case?"

Perplexed, I stared at the proffered telegram and then back at my wife and shrugged.

"Oh, I shouldn't think it will immediately come to that," I said.

Mary chuckled to herself, "No, it never does," and retired back into the house.

I watched her go for a moment then turned my attention to the paper. Unfolding it, I read the words with a touch of trepidation and excitement.

It asked for my attendance at a meeting between Holmes and Lestrade at 221B Baker Street, at ten o'clock on the morrow.

"The game is afoot?" I asked myself in hope. Secretly, I admitted to myself that life had grown a trifle dull these last few months. Any chance of an adventure with Holmes was a chance worth taking.

***

I stepped from the Hansom onto the footpath outside the dwelling that Holmes and I once shared and welcomed the glorious morning sun on my face.

Part of me still missed my time in this house, but another part reminded me of who waited for me in my own home. I smiled at that, proceeded to the front door and rang the bell.

Mrs Hudson's face was awash with delight as she saw me standing there. Forgetting herself for a moment she threw her arms around me and welcomed me inside.

"Oh, I'm so happy to see you, Doctor, his nibs hasn't been himself for so many weeks now. Only the odd bit of adventure for him from time to time, the rest he spends alone up there. I takes him food, but

1

most nights it comes back uneaten. I've been ever so worried," she said.

I comforted her and apologised for my absence. I explained that I had been extremely busy with my practice and had failed to call upon my old friend and cohort. I promised to make amends, starting with this current endeavour.

She smiled and seemed satisfied.

At the top of the stairs, I knocked once and entered.

I found Holmes sitting in the sunlight filtering into the parlour. He was dressed ready to leave at any moment and was perusing the morning paper. I realised immediately that it was more from impatience than interest, as he bolted to his feet and shook my hand as if we hadn't crossed paths in years. In truth, it had been a few weeks, but I appreciated his welcome all the same.

"What ho, Holmes?" I said, "Have you any clew as to the Inspector's request?"

Holmes shook his head.

"No, Watson, nothing. I've read all the papers and there has been nothing reported of note, so I can't imagine it is a high profile case of any sort, which is a little disappointing, but I admit I have been rather bereft of anything of concern for a while now, so I am very interested in what he has on offer."

He stepped across to the coffee table and poured two cups from the steaming pot.

"Coffee?" he asked in hindsight.

"Thank you," I answered, not necessarily needing another, but not wanting to cause any offence or break in concentration on my friend's part.

I blew on my coffee to cool it slightly and sipped. Remembrance filled my mind; Mrs Hudson did make a good brew. As I took another sip, the doorbell rang.

"Ah, that would be the Inspector," said Holmes placing his cup down and pouring a third, adding a single spoonful of sugar and some milk before stirring it while we heard the sound of footsteps climbing the staircase outside.

Holmes stood with the cup in hand as there was a knock on the door and Inspector Lestrade stepped in.

"Lestrade," said Holmes, "Good to see you." He extended his hand and, surprised, Lestrade took the proffered cup.

"And you Holmes," he took a sip, and let out an audible sigh of pleasure. "Perfect."

He turned towards me and nodded, "Doctor."

I returned the motion. Holmes left a pause of silence hanging in the air while we all became attuned to the same level before speaking.

"Now, Inspector, you have a problem," he said, before taking his seat. I mirrored his actions and Lestrade set his cup down, removed his hat and coat and sat on the third corner of a triangle between us.

"Yes, yes, I do," he said, a slight expression of embarrassment or concern crossing his face.

"I presume it's not a Yard request, as there has been nothing reported this morning," said Holmes, waving a hand across the small pile of newspapers nearby.

"No, nothing like that," said Lestrade, picking up his cup and sipping it again. "It's personal."

Holmes brightened, "Oh, yes?"

Lestrade's face grew darker.

"It's about my cousin. Foolish girl," he said.

I stifled a smirk at the outburst from the Inspector, a man I had known for many years and one who held his emotions and opinions in check at all times.

"Go on," said Holmes.

"A couple of years ago, she went off and got herself married again."

"Nothing strange in that."

"To an American," he spat, a hint of inter-country animosity underpinning his speech. I was even more surprised. Holmes's face remained impassive.

"No. It's nothing like that. I don't care that he's from the States, it's just that I don't know anything about him."

"I assume you checked his background," said Holmes with a grin.

"Of course, I did. My family would have been disappointed if I hadn't. I love my cousin. I've known her all my life. Last thing I want is for her to be hurt. Now, this berk has gone and run off, or disappeared at least, according to her."

"Well, it could happen. Many a man disappears in this city over the course of a year," I said in the unknown man's defence.

"Yeah, but, they are usually low-lifes," Lestrade said.

I nodded. It was true, the underworld of the city was a ruthless place.

"Do you have a name?" asked Holmes.

"Goes by the name of William Middleton. Well-built fellar, about as tall as you, Holmes; dark hair, neatly trimmed beard. Runs a tailor shop down Camden way. I couldn't find anything about him. It's almost like he just appeared five years ago. Claims to have come over from Georgia, to ply his trade in the great metropolis. I've always had my doubts. I mean who would leave America to come to this place? From what I hear the roads are paved with gold and the weather's always marvellous," Lestrade said.

"There is a lot to love about London and England for that matter," I said trying to lighten the mood, "It's not all darkness and crime."

Lestrade glanced at me, then turned back to look into the distance while he sipped his coffee.

"Anyway, Francine drags me around and says that Bill was gone. Four days ago. It's too early to bring it up at the Yard, so I thought I'd come here. I've tracked his trail and there's nothing. Like his past, really. Just nothing. I've got a bit saved up so I can pay you."

"Don't be silly, Inspector," said Holmes, much to my own relief, "I wouldn't dream of ever asking you for money."

Lestrade looked relieved as well.

"Finish your coffee and then you can escort us to this man's shop," he said.

Lestrade nodded and drained his cup. He placed it on the tray and stood up.

"Best get going then," he said.

Surprised, I quickly drained my cup and repeated Lestrade's actions. Holmes simply smiled as he sipped and glanced up and down at the agitated vision of the Inspector.

***

The Hansom dropped the three of us at the corner of Camden High street and Pratt Street. Holmes stopped for a moment and peered around. I followed his gaze, which stopped on a young street urchin holding out his cap to passers-by in the hope of receiving a few coppers. The urchin looked across at Holmes, nodded and replaced his cap. Holmes nodded in return and I watched as the urchin hurried off and disappeared into the crowd.

I realised that this must have been one of the Baker Street Irregulars, the little band of urchins and street people that Holmes employed as a sort of spy network spread across greater London.

We walked down Pratt Street and Lestrade stopped before a three-story Georgian terrace. The ground floor was a small shop with the name "The Yellow Rose Tailor" proudly displayed on the front hoarding. A door to the side of the shop indicated that the floors above were dwellings.

Holmes studied the shop frontage for a moment before addressing Lestrade.

"I thought you said that this Middleton fellow was from Georgia?"

Lestrade nodded, "Yes, that's what he told my cousin."

"Why, Holmes?" I asked.

"Well Watson, the yellow rose is a name often given to a young slave girl named Emily West, who was captured by Santa Anna, and taken with him when he invaded Texas in 1835. The stories say that she was a spy who helped the Texan army defeat the Mexicans at the Battle of San Jacinto. She is somewhat of a hero and legend in Texas. I don't believe that her name would even be known amongst the people of Georgia."

"Remarkable what snippets of information you retain Holmes," I said.

"Thank you, Watson."

He stepped towards the front door, "Shall we go in?"

Just at that moment a cry of, "Hello," echoed out from behind.

We turned to see a small group of people hurrying towards us. One taller gentleman stepped forward and addressed us directly.

"I say," he said, "Do you gentlemen have any idea where Middleton has got to?"

Lestrade took the lead and replied, "That's partly why we're here. I'm Inspector Lestrade of Scotland Yard. We are investigating Mr. Middleton's apparent disappearance. Any information that you could provide would be most appreciated."

The face of the man at the front dropped in agitation. He pointed at the shop and said, "I've no idea where the fool has gone, but he's still got my suit in there. I haven't got another, and I needed it yesterday, for Sunday service."

Another man piped up behind him.

"And he owes me money for groceries. I've tried his wife, but she's skint, an' din't know where he was."

Lestrade held up his hands before the mob began baying for blood.

"I am sorry, but we are as mystified as you all seem to be. Our only hope is to trace Middleton's last steps and see where they lead. We can surmise all we like, but until we find evidence there's not a lot we can do."

Holmes smiled.

"I think you are starting to come to my way of thinking," he said before turning towards the crowd. "Might I ask who here last saw Middleton?" he asked.

A woman's voice piped up from the rear, "I dropped off my skirt on Wednesday around two," she said.

Another said, "I saw him leave not long after that."

"Me too," said another man.

Holmes looked at both.

"In which direction did he go?"

"He was headed to the high street," said the first pointing in one direction.

"No, I saw him going towards College Street," said the second pointing in the other.

Holmes stared at both men for a moment and was about to open his mouth to ask something when the woman spoke up.

"No, he was on the high street. I passed him around two-thirty. I asked him when my skirt would be ready, and he ignored me completely and breezed by without a by-your-leave. I was ropeable. Though he did seem very troubled."

"And which way was he headed then?" asked Holmes.

"South, down towards Euston Road," she said.

Holmes smiled. "Thank you all." He pulled out a small notebook and pen and handed it to the man at the front of the group. "Can you all please put your names and addresses down in this notebook? We may need to come and see you again."

The man took the book and quickly scribbled his name inside. He handed it to another who simply stared at the writing implement before the woman grabbed it off him.

"You really must learn to write one of these days, Fred," she said and entered both her own and Fred's details. The other two followed suit and handed them back to Holmes. As they bustled away we turned back to the shop. Holmes barely glanced at the list of names before returning the little pad to an inner pocket.

Lestrade pulled a ring of keys from his pants pocket, selected a large brass mortice key and unlocked the front door. Struggling, he pushed the door, only to have it stick. Lestrade jiggled it back and forth a few times before he managed to push it wide enough to enter. He ducked behind and picked up a pile of mail and parcels that had gathered.

Finally, the door opened fully with Lestrade holding his find.

"That's quite a bit of mail for only a few days," I said.

Lestrade looked at the items. There were two large ones that appeared to be fabric, with a number of envelopes as well.

"It would appear that business is healthier than my cousin lets on," he said.

"Is that something your cousin has mentioned?" asked Holmes, ever alert for clews.

Lestrade looked up at my friend, "She has mentioned it on and off for the last few months. Middleton always seems busy, but there's only ever enough money to make ends meet, never any more for luxuries."

"Interesting."

"Why?"

Holmes peered around the front of the shop. A polished wooden counter greeted all customers, with a set of changing rooms sitting off to the side. The frontage was furnished with exquisite fabrics and drapery, with two dressmakers' dummies sporting elegant suits on view in the front window.

"One wouldn't think that business was slow, given the style used in this area," he said.

Lestrade peered around and nodded in agreement.

I admit that I was quite taken aback by the ornate dressings of the shopfront and would happily have given my business to the owner.

Holmes walked towards a covered area behind the counter and flung back the drapes revealing a doorway leading to the rear of the shop. He pushed through and Lestrade and I quickly followed.

As expected, the rear of the shop was a plainer, more productive environment. Two sewing machines sat on benches to one side. Several dressmakers' models wearing unfinished suits and dresses stood nearby. A large flat table took up most of the middle of the room; this was obviously the cutting and preparation table, as a half-finished garment adorned the surface.

"It would appear that our Mr. Middleton left in quite a hurry," Holmes said, peering around the room and stopping his gaze at the unfinished suit. To me, it looked the type to be worn to Sunday service.

A small desk sat in the corner, next to a sturdy looking safe. A pile of letters and bills of sale sat upon the desk, reflecting Holmes's question concerning the state of the business.

Lestrade dumped his armful of letters and packages upon the cutting table. They spilled across the surface. My eyes were drawn to a small light-coloured envelope that was slightly thicker than the other larger envelopes containing bills and orders.

The sound of a drawer sliding open drew my attention away from the mail. I looked up and saw Holmes rifling through the desk. He pulled out a foolscap leather-bound volume and placed it on the desk. Intrigued I stepped up and looked over his shoulder. The pages within the folio showed columns of figures with annotations as to the source.

"The accounts?" I asked.

Holmes nodded; his attention directed at the figures. He proceeded to flip through to the end and made several murmurs as something gelled in his mind.

"Anything, Holmes?" I asked.

"Yes, Watson, quite." He pointed at the final few figures of the accounts book. I saw that they were quite large. By my simple reckoning, Middleton's business was doing rather well for itself. I peered up the column and noticed several figures in the debit column. The scrawl next to them was a simple repeated line exclaiming, "XF to JC," each was a sizeable figure and reduced the running balance to almost zero at every occurrence.

"Do you think XF means transfer?" I asked Holmes, pointing at one of the entries.

"I would think it is something like that. From what I can tell, the money coming in is substantial. The business is doing well, but almost every month or so, a large sum is transferred out with no real identification as to the destination. This JC seems to be code," he said.

I turned to Lestrade, "Middleton's not a religious man is he?"

Lestrade's eyes widened in surprise, "I don't think so why?"

"Just a hunch," I said, "JC, Jesus Christ, it may have been a tithing payment or some such to the church."

Holmes smiled, "Very good Watson, I like your thinking. This is not a religious donation, but I believe you may be on the money, so to speak, this JC may actually be a person or a group of some sort. Perhaps, they were Middleton's benefactors and these payments are to pay down a debt."

He stood up and looked at the safe.

"Inspector, do you think that ring of keys has one that fits this safe?" he said, bending to peer at the engraved plate above the lock.

"It's a Harold Haworth, 1850C." He moved the small brass cover plate aside to reveal the keyhole. "Ah, yes, it would be a standard double mortice lock."

Lestrade walked over and held the ring of keys before him. Even I could tell there was nothing that qualified for the correct key.

"Hmmm," said Holmes and moved back to rifle through the desk drawers again. After a few moments, he stood and withdrew his lock pick set. I could tell from a slight grin on his mouth that he was hoping they would be required.

He knelt down, laid out the kit on the floor beside him and set to work. Within a minute or two we heard the satisfying click of the lock mechanism and the thick metal door opened silently on its well-oiled hinges.

The interior was littered with papers, envelopes and more books. Holmes examined each in turn, before standing up with what looked like a small bank account book. He flipped through the entries, then stepped over to the ledger. After a moment of reading both books together, he said, "Ah-ha."

"Holmes?"

He turned the bank book around and showed us the entries within.

The bank book simply showed a series of deposits. I peered down at the accounts book and made the same discovery. The amounts and dates were identical with each of the accounting entries marked "XF to JC."

"Who's the account for?" asked Lestrade.

Holmes turned the book around once more and opened to the first page.

"It says, John Calder," he looked up for a moment searching his memories, "I don't know that name, but it's the address that is interesting. This account is with the Bank of Cornwall, Penzance Branch. I assume then that Middleton has been making entries into the account via a local branch, or even a different bank altogether, and they are transferred to this Penzance branch. It would seem his benefactor comes from Cornwall."

"That's news to me, Francine has never mentioned anything about Cornwall or Penzance. I figured Middleton had come straight to London from Southampton or Portsmouth. Well, I never," said Lestrade.

While Holmes checked the safe again, I wandered over to the cutting table and rifled through the mail. As I had expected, apart from the two bolts of material, the rest were bills and invoices. Then my eyes fell on the buff-coloured envelope.

I picked it up and turned it over. To my surprise, it was not an official letter at all. There was no stamp. No postmark. Not even an address. Only a single word was scrawled on the front in a very jagged form of handwriting. I said the name out loud.

"Mudge."

"Who?" asked Lestrade.

I turned and saw both looking at me. I held the envelope before me.

"This envelope was amongst the mail, it simply says 'Mudge' on the front. What or who 'Mudge' is, I have no idea."

Lestrade picked up a letter opener from the desk and joined me. He took the envelope and carefully slit along the top.

"Police business. I'll explain to Middleton when I see him next," he said with a sly grin.

He opened the top of the envelope and upended it over the table. A small folded piece of similarly coloured paper slid out and I gasped when the rest of the contents spilled onto the table. They tumbled out one at a time until five stared up at me.

Holmes looked up and saw my expression of horror.

"Watson?" he asked as he moved across and peered down at the table. He was silent for a moment, then simply said, "Interesting."

The three of us stared down at the small dried objects on the table.

Lestrade said, "Lemon seeds?"

"Orange pips," said Holmes, "Five orange pips."

He reached for the note and opened it. Inside, one name was written in red in the same handwriting: *Calhoun*. Below the name was a crudely drawn glyph with one horizontal and two vertical lines, all within a red circle.

"Not again," I said.

"I think so," said Holmes.

"I'm confused," said Lestrade.

***

It was a whirlwind of action that found me early the next morning sitting in a first-class sleeper across from Holmes wending our way to Penzance deep in the south of Cornwall.

I replayed the last few hours of the previous afternoon in my mind as we pulled out of Paddington station and began the journey westwards.

Holmes explained to Lestrade the significance of the five orange pips. A sign that the nefarious organisation known as the Ku Klux Klan had a vendetta against the addressee of the note. Holmes, however, added that the person of interest was not the name on the outside of the envelope, this Mudge, but the name scrawled inside, Calhoun.

He stated at the time and backed it up once we returned to Baker Street in the early evening, that Calhoun was indeed the Captain of the ill-fated Lone Star, a bark, registered in Savannah, Georgia, that we believed to hold the murderers of Joseph and John Openshaw. They had never been brought to justice as the Lone Star was believed lost at sea not long after the younger Openshaw's death.

Lestrade was now extremely interested. This was no longer just a case of his missing cousin-in-law, but a case of unsolved murder from many years previously.

Back at 221B, Holmes quickly pulled down his notes from the previous case that concerned the unfortunate demise of members of the Openshaw family, supposedly at the hands of the Ku Klux Klan.

Stuck between the pages was a loose leaf of paper. Holmes pulled it out and read. It was the crew manifest for the Lone Star. Three names were underlined in red. James Calhoun (Captain), William Mudge (mate) and George Savage.

The facts of the case came to mind. These three were the only Americans on the ship at the time. The Lone Star was registered in

Savannah, Georgia, but I remember Holmes stating that the name probably originated from Texas, it being called the Lone Star state.

"I thought this was all done and dusted when the Lone Star was lost," I had said.

Holmes held up the small envelope with the pips inside and the note.

"Given the names on this letter, I can surmise, but not prove, that there were at least two survivors of that shipwreck," he said.

"What does the symbol mean?" Lestrade asked of the three-lined sigil above Calhoun's name.

Holmes looked at it for a moment.

"The Ku Klux Klan is known for using a version of the Greek cross, which has a shortened vertical line, with a small picture of a drop of blood in the centre. During the Openshaw case, I sent for a volume related to this newly established group and using that, I found that they also have a version with two vertical stems that signifies vengeance. Simply, a double-cross."

"So, this Calhoun has double-crossed the Ku Klux Klan?" asked Lestrade.

"It would seem that way," said Holmes, "Given our experience with them, I can only hope we find him before they do."

"What if they finish the job for us?" I asked.

"I would rather we brought him to justice, at least only to give closure to the Openshaw family," he said, "What's left of it."

I had nodded in agreement.

Holmes was quiet for the first part of the journey, his mind seemed ablaze, but his demeanour was dour.

He finally turned to me and said, "Facts, Watson, facts and data. I have too little of both to predict an outcome. That frustrates me no end."

His only deductions to date were that Calhoun and Mudge must have survived the sinking of the Lone Star. The "JC" that supposedly received monies from Middleton was most likely the Captain, James Calhoun. The location was interesting, but as it was the most westerly part of the United Kingdom, the survivors probably washed up there. One possibility was also that this Mudge had journeyed to London to set up a business and raise funds for their return to America and was sending money back to Calhoun either to stockpile or as restitution.

I had asked why Calhoun wasn't in London. To that, he had no direct answer but admitted that Calhoun was in his early sixties, and may have been injured or incapacitated as a consequence of the Lone Star's demise.

Holmes admitted that was why he wished to go to Penzance. From the apparent quick disappearance of Middleton and the last known sighting, he surmised that our quarry headed towards Euston station. Either to escape altogether, or more likely, head to his benefactor in Penzance in person, rather than simply send a telegram.

That was our reason for heading with such haste to the far-flung reaches of the country.

In my lovely wife's defence, she has more insight than I could hope to have at times. I returned home late and informed her that I was to be off early the next morning. She presented me with both a late and nutritious supper and a packed valise ready for at least four day's travel.

Her justification was that I had been out for longer than expected, and the fact that Inspector Lestrade had sent a note directly to me. She handed it over with a slight grin.

I read the contents. Lestrade apologised to me for not coming with us but gave me the name of a trusted officer in the Penzance police station.

I slept a little easier than expected with the knowledge we would have some form of constabulary backup.

That relief was dashed with what Holmes said when we had settled down in our compartment.

He simply leaned over and said, "We are being followed."

Shocked, I asked for an immediate explanation; then Holmes's actions the previous day came to mind.

As soon as we exited Middleton's tailor shop, we were approached by a very young street urchin. If not for the caked dirt on his face I would have called him rather handsome or even cute for his age.

Holmes had taken a shine and talked to the boy, before reaching into his pocket and dropping a guinea into his outstretched cap. The boy had scurried off without another word. On the train, Holmes had confessed that the boy was one of the Baker Street Irregulars and had been put on the case.

It was Holmes's belief that the fact we found an envelope with pips in it, meant that the sender was still around and apparently unaware of Middleton's departure.

It seemed likely that the person would be keeping watch on the tailor shop and had undoubtedly seen the three of them enter the previous day. Holmes had told the young urchin to spread the word and have himself, Lestrade and I, watched and followed.

I then remembered another urchin approached Holmes as we made our way into the Paddington Station proper. I smirked to myself that Holmes was a soft touch, recalling how he entered into a long exchange which ended with another guinea changing hands.

Holmes now confessed that he and I had both been followed by two men. One a dark-haired, swarthy gentleman with a large bushy beard, the other a tall, fair-skinned, powerfully built blonde man.

"Good Lord," I exclaimed.

"Yes," he said, "I do hope you brought your service revolver as I requested."

I patted my pocket, one to signify to him, the other to calm my nerves and reassure myself that it was still there.

"Who are they?" I asked.

"They are either members of the KKK, as it is called, who are desperate to know the whereabouts of Calhoun, or, and this may sound very strange, they are other crew members from the Lone Star," he said, "And if I was to make a conjecture, I would say they are Savage and one of the Finns."

My eyes grew wide. "How could you tell that?"

He smiled, "Simply from the facts. We presume that only the Americans on board were in league with the KKK; Savage is the only American we aren't sure about; and the large blonde fellow sounds like someone of Finnish extraction."

I nodded. It made sense but was still a supposition until proven.

15

The sudden jolting of the train snapped me awake. I looked around the compartment and noticed Holmes was missing. The bathroom door slid open and an elderly gentleman, replete with grey hair and large pair of wiry grey sideboards stepped into the compartment.

I almost stood up at the audacious intrusion of the fellow.

"I say, Sir, I think you have the wrong compartment," I blurted out.

The man simply smiled and shook his head.

"Holmes?"

"Yes, Watson, of course it's me."

"Why the devil are you dressed like that?" I realised he was wearing attire more suited to second or third class than the first-class carriage which we occupied.

"I'm going to do a little investigation and track down our friends," he said, "Give me an hour and I'll meet you in the club car. It is time for luncheon, and we can discuss what to do on arrival."

With that, he unlatched the door and was gone before I could say another word.

I checked my pocket watch and realised we had been gone from London for a good two and a half hours. I decided to wait for another half an hour before making my way to the club car. I calculated that I should be able to enjoy a small meal and drink in peace before Holmes joined me.

As it was, I had finished my meal of smoked trout and vegetables and was sitting back with a brandy and reading the paper, which I had saved for such a moment, when Holmes, dressed in his normal attire again, joined me.

I folded the paper as he said, "Watson!"

"Anything to report, Holmes?"

He smiled and was about to speak when the waiter arrived. Holmes ordered the same as I and waited for quiet once more.

"There are two of them, just as my spy reported. I was detained for a while as I sat behind and waited for them to speak. The swarthy bearded man is an American. He has a broad accent, from the south, possibly Texas or Tennessee. The other is definitely a Finn. He has very little English, and a very broad accent to go with his northern European looks."

"Very good, where does that leave us? Obviously, they are following us, which means they are after our quarry."

"If the American is this Savage fellow, then it indicates that our quarry is indeed Calhoun, or at least that's what Savage thinks as well. We will need to lose them on arrival in Penzance."

He smiled.

"I believe another little disguise may be of advantage."

It was then I told him about Lestrade's contact. I had avoided the fact until we knew of what lay at the end of our journey.

"Excellent. I think the constabulary will be of use if we find Calhoun and need him arrested. Until then I would prefer to lead the investigation. I think the best course of action is for you to proceed to the hotel. That way you can lead Savage and the Finn away from me. I understand that there is a café nearby. If you return there and wait, I will approach the Bank to obtain the address associated with this account, then return." He held up the passbook.

I nodded in agreement. "But, won't they be watching? They'll see you approach me."

He smiled widely, "Oh, I don't think that will be a problem."

When Holmes's lunch arrived, we lapsed into silence while he ate. I stared out of the window and enjoyed the sight of the countryside as it passed by. The next thing I knew, Holmes stood by the table in readiness to leave.

"We have an hour before we arrive. Remember all I've said, and I'll see you at the café," he said before leaving the car.

I went back to my paper.

***

I arrived back at our compartment shortly before the train was due to arrive at Penzance. Holmes was gone but had left his valise behind. I assumed it was to allow him ease of movement once the journey was finished, so I voluntarily dragged the bag out, ready to be collected by the porter.

Try as I may, I kept my eyes to myself as I alighted from the train and waited to collect our luggage from the porter's station, but every man with a beard or every tall man that passed by grabbed my attention as our potential mystery spies.

When finally, the luggage arrived, I picked our cases from the porter's trolley and made my way to the exit. There I managed to flag a Hansom and journey on to the hotel. I was unaware of any tail I may have picked up, though I didn't attempt to hide in any way.

When I arrived at the Queen's hotel, I was delighted to find that our telegram had been received and two rooms awaited us. I informed them that my colleague would be along momentarily and asked them to hold his key but deliver his valise to the room. I quickly went to my own room, laid out my things and hurried down to the café.

It was a very European affair, with a number of tables outside in a small courtyard at the front of the hotel, making the most of the fine summer weather.

The patronage was light on, so I was able to attain a table nearest the street itself. I had picked up a local paper and sat back to wait, whilst enjoying an afternoon pot of tea and scones. My eyes searched over the top of my paper from time to time, but I couldn't identify or locate the suspects.

I lost track of time, once again, and when I picked up my cup and found it empty, I realised that a good hour had passed. My pot was likewise empty, and the small plate held a few scattered crumbs.

My paper chose that moment to lose its rigidity and toppled forward revealing the most unpleasant face I've ever had the horror to behold.

I began to fold the newspaper in readiness to swat the man away when he spoke in hushed tones.

"Watson, it is I. Be quiet and stay surprised. I've found Calhoun's address. He's staying in the Tolcarne Inn, a little pub down by the docks. Seems he can't keep away from ships. Go to the police station and bring Lestrade's contact to the inn within the hour. I'll meet you there."

I whispered back, "But what about Savage?"

"I know where he is, I'll make sure he doesn't follow. Yet."

To make our meeting look legitimate, I fished out my coin purse and gave the horrible beggar a copper and then shooed him away.

"Go away you smelly thing," I said, standing up and waving my arms around in an overtly animated gesture. I smiled inside at my own little piece of acting. I caught sight of the grimace on Holmes's face. A harsh critic of actors at the best of times, our Holmes.

He shuffled off and as I went to pay my bill, I caught sight of movement across the street through the front doors. I kept my eyes forward and saw two gentlemen approach the edge of the road. I ducked into the hotel foyer and heard a slight commotion behind me.

As I walked to the front desk, I glanced through the entrance and saw Holmes between the men and the hotel. He was using his stooped bulk to his advantage and overplaying his hand at begging. The men tried to push past, but he had them at a disadvantage.

I quickly asked the Concierge where the police station was. He gave me the directions to an address only three streets away and pointed me to a doorway towards the rear of the hotel. I scurried off before Savage and his Finnish accomplice could break away from Holmes. As I reached the doorway I glanced back, Holmes and the other two were gone.

The police station was a tiny affair, a small entry foyer allowed for only two people to wait. A wooden counter greeted anyone requesting assistance.

I rang the bell and waited. As luck would have it the only officer on duty was the one I was after. I introduced myself and held out the card that Lestrade had left for me. Inspector Ransome smiled as he saw the name. He shook my hand jovially and mentioned that Lestrade and he had started out as bobbies in the East End. Ransome, it seemed, had moved to Cornwall when he attained the rank of Inspector. He laughed that he was done with the rough streets of London and was much happier in the quiet of Penzance.

"The most we have to deal with here is arguments over whose dog has invaded whose front yard," he said a broad smile on his rotund face.

I returned his smile, before signalling that the quiet of Penzance may be about to be broken. I explained what we knew so far, which I admit wasn't much, and that we had an address.

Ransome nodded at the mention of the Tolcarne.

"That's a bit of a rough part of the town. The docks can get a might rowdy on a Saturday night. They usually sorts themselves out, and the publican is a good sort. He don't truck with no trouble," he said.

He invited me through to the back rooms of the Police station. The area opened up into a small office, with a door leading through to what I presumed would be the holding cells. I wondered which members of this little adventure might be held up there before the day was out.

We stepped up onto the front seats of a large trap with a covered wagon at the rear, used for transporting perpetrators of crime back to the station.

The docks area wasn't very far at all, then again Penzance is not a large town by any means, especially when compared to London. The whole place would fit comfortably just in the East End.

Ransome, showing signs of his former street-smart self, parked the trap down a side street, well away from any view from the Inn itself.

We alighted and stepped onto the broad esplanade that ran along the seafront. The inn sat about a hundred yards down the road. It was an old two-storey whitewashed building. There were a few patrons sitting on benches outside enjoying the diminishing sunshine and nursing the dregs of their drinks before last call sang out from inside.

I was pondering what to do next when a voice spoke up behind us.

"Watson!"

We both turned and found Holmes striding up the side street towards us. He held out his hand and took Ransome's in his own.

"Inspector Ransome, I presume," he said, "Sherlock Holmes, thank you for joining us, and for bringing the wagon with you. I hope we'll be in need of it. I assume Watson has filled you in."

Ransome nodded and spoke, "Yes, but I still don't see any crimes committed."

"Ah, yes, not in this matter. But, if things progress as I believe they will, we should be able to indict this Calhoun character with the murder of young John Openshaw, some five years ago, and his father Joseph before that," he said.

Ransome nodded.

Holmes peered around the corner towards the Inn and took in the layout of the land for a moment. He ducked back and said, "I think it would be best if you stayed here, Inspector, while Watson and I enter the inn and determine whether we indeed have Calhoun and Mudge and whether there is enough evidence that your intervention will be required."

Ransome leaned back and patted his formidable midriff and said, "I could always take a table at the inn itself. I would be closer to the action, as they say, and it would be a matter of mere seconds before I could come to your aide."

Holmes smiled, "Perhaps, but we have another pair of miscreants that might be a little unnerved by your presence. I am hopeful that they will play their hand once we have entered the establishment."

"I thought we had lost Savage and the Finn?" I asked.

"You had," he said with a broad smile, "I made sure to re-engender their interest and lead them here on foot. They are skulking nearby."

I glanced around.

"But not if you give away the fact that we know they are nearby," Holmes said, admonishing my actions. I dropped my gaze to my feet, like a naughty schoolboy.

As we walked to the inn, I asked Holmes how he came by Calhoun's address.

He smiled and said, "I went to the bank and found a young, impressionable teller. I showed him the passbook and said I had found it on the seat in the London to Penzance train. Instead, of handing it in to the station master where I believed it would become lost amongst the large amount of misplaced items, I thought it my civic duty to track down the owner and hand it back."

"Did the teller not suggest that you leave it with the bank?"

"Yes, yes he did. I admitted that I thought the same but determined that if the owner realised they had lost it on a train, he would give up all hope and forget about it. The teller did suggest that they could re-issue the passbook. I answered that the effort required to prove identity and create the records once more were worrisome in the least, and besides, it may be days or weeks before the owner came forward."

A slight smirk came to Holmes's face.

"I put on my most innocent air and finally the teller gave in and provided me with the address. I thanked him roundly and asked his name so that I might advise this Calder, as I was sure he would be most appreciative and may even pass on his gratitude to the branch manager. The teller naturally brightened at that suggestion."

"You are wicked Holmes, really," I said.

"Yes. It's the actor in me. I will, however, write to the bank manager myself and commend the teller, especially if this little adventure resolves itself the way I believe it will."

We reached the inn and entered the front bar. There were quite a few patrons outside, but not that many within. The day was nice, so sitting in a dark, smoky room was not high on most peoples' minds.

Holmes walked up to the bar and gained the attention of the burly barkeeper who was drying glasses with his apron.

"I am here to see a Mr John Calder. I believe he is staying in one of your rooms," Holmes said.

The barkeep looked Holmes up and down.

"Why?" he asked.

Once again, the little bank book came into play. Holmes held it up before the landlord.

"I found his passbook and I wish to return it to him," he said.

"You can give it to me," the man said.

"Forgive me sir, but I think I would be more comfortable returning it in person," he said.

The barkeep looked him dead in the eye for a moment. I truly believed he was contemplating whether to wrest the book from Holmes's hands. I hoped it wouldn't come to that.

I was, however, relieved when the man nodded to the staircase nearby.

"Room 2, top of the stairs on the right," he said.

Holmes placed a guinea piece on the bar.

"I thank you, that should pay for two pints of your finest. My colleague and I will have them when we return momentarily," he said.

The barkeep disappeared the coin so quickly I wasn't even sure I'd seen Holmes place it down.

"Right you are then," he said, a smile suddenly crossing his face.

We climbed the stairs and found a small landing that serviced the only two rooms available in the inn. Due to the age of the building, the ceiling was so low that Holmes had to stoop a little to avoid striking his head on the exposed oak beams.

Holmes presented himself before the door to Room 2 and knocked. I took up a position slightly behind him, unaware that my hand had drawn itself to my pocket and clasped the heavy metal of my service pistol.

The door opened, revealing a moderately tall man who, much like Holmes, stooped to avoid the low ceiling. He sported a well-trimmed beard and had the slightly weathered features of a man who had spent time at sea. I realised it was our quarry from Lestrade's description of him. Holmes knew instinctively.

"William Middleton, or should I say Mudge?" he asked.

"Who the hell are you?" Mudge asked, a look of surprise springing to his face, "How do you know me?"

"Your cousin, Police Inspector Lestrade sends his regards. I also have this," Holmes said, pulling out the small buff-coloured envelope with Mudge's name scrawled on the front and holding it forward.

Mudge stepped back in shock.

"It's you? What do you want from us?" he asked.

Holmes took this as an invitation and followed Mudge into the room. I ducked in and shut the door behind me.

Mudge cowered in the corridor, blocking our view of the main part of the room. He finally moved when another voice broke out tinged with a thick American drawl.

"Get out of the way William, I can't see who it is?" the voice said.

Mudge moved to the side, revealing an older man with a shock of grey hair. His face showed deep lines and the skin was tanned a deep brown. He sat in a chair against the far wall, and strangely for the temperature of the day, had a blanket thrown across his legs. Holmes deduced his identity just as quickly as I had.

"Captain James Calhoun, late of the Lone Star, I presume," he said stepping into the room.

"You have me at a disservice, sir. I have no idea who you are," said Calhoun.

"I am Sherlock Holmes, this is my associate Doctor John Watson," he said.

"And that means what to me?" Calhoun said with an air of dismissal.

"Our paths have never crossed, but I was employed by John Openshaw before his untimely death five years ago, to which I lay the blame at your feet," he said.

Calhoun broke out in a fit of laughter and threw the blanket aside. I looked in shock at what the rug had covered. Both of Calhoun's legs were missing below the knee, both ending in ugly stumps.

"Good lord," I said under my breath.

"You can throw what you like at my feet, they're at the bottom of the Atlantic. Lost when that damn ship fell apart and I dragged this big galoot up from below decks. Main mast snapped off and smashed them to nothing. We washed up on the south coast, everyone else went down with the ship."

He looked us both up and down and thought for a moment.

"You don't look like Klansmen, so, why are you sending young William here those orange pips?" he asked, "You've scared the bejeesus out of him."

"And that's where you have us at a disservice. We didn't send them. I think I know who did, though. Your partner in crime George Savage."

He extracted the letter and held up the double-cross symbol so that Calhoun could plainly see it.

Calhoun's face changed to confusion then relaxed back to slight anger.

"That idiot, he thinks I double-crossed him. Last I saw of him, he was diving overboard like the coward he is. You can tell that slack-jawed chowder headed rum gagger that if I sees him again I'll fix his flint for good."

"I don't know the fellow, so I won't, but why would he accuse you of double-crossing him?"

"That I don't know."

"The gold, I reckon," said Mudge.

Calhoun turned and stared daggers at Mudge, shutting him up.

"Gold?" I asked.

Mudge glanced at Calhoun, then at me before overcoming his answering.

"We were smugglers, that's all, I don't know nothing about murder. I only joined the Klan cause the Captain said I should. We were taking a load of gold back to the Klan in Tennessee," he said, letting it all out, his demeanour brightening as he cleared his conscience, "That's what I thought this was all about. I owe the Captain for saving my life, but don't owe the Klan anything."

"Shut your pie hole, you fool," said Calhoun.

He turned towards us.

"You've got nothing on us or else you would have brought the law with you," he said, "Now get out before things go South."

"Fine," said Holmes turning towards the door, "I have proved that you were behind the Openshaw murders. I will return shortly with the police and have you dragged away."

I turned as well but was brought up short by Calhoun's voice from behind.

"Yeah, I don't think so," he said.

We both turned to find the Captain pointing a gun towards us. Holmes raised his hands slowly, I followed suit keeping my right hand lower.

"What are you doing?" Mudge asked Calhoun.

"I didn't want it to come this, but I've lived too long to end up in a noose," he said.

I slowly dropped my right hand towards my pocket.

"Uh, uh, aah, sonny, I don't think so," Calhoun said, indicating my hand with the barrel of the gun. I raised it quickly.

I kicked myself inside for being so foolish and dropped my head slightly. There we all stood silently, while Calhoun figured out who to kill first. The next few moments are still a blur.

Suddenly, the door burst in. A tall, bearded man stepped into the room. He brought up a small revolver and pointed it towards Calhoun. I could see the taller blonde-haired Finn hovering on the landing outside.

"You owe me," he said, "I killed two fellows on your orders, you promised me, so you owe me."

"Savage!" replied Calhoun, a broad smile on his face, "I thought you were dead."

I saw his gun move slightly then an explosion rang out through the room dulling all further sound.

Savage dropped his own pistol and clutched at his chest. A dark stain spread across the dirty white shirt. He dropped to his knees, his face a mass of shocked terror, and fell forward with a dull thud. The thumping of feet on the stairs told me Savage's Finnish partner had given up on the whole venture.

I dropped to my knee and checked Savage for any signs of life. When there were none, I looked back at Calhoun who wore an expression of pure delight. I knew then that this was a man with no scruples. There was only one place on Earth for such as he, and if I lived another day, I would see him hang there.

Calhoun smiled and said, "I told you I'd fix his flints." He turned the gun towards Holmes and said, "You're next."

Holmes simply smiled and replied, "I think not."

Calhoun's face finally dropped. Holmes knelt down, picked up Savage's gun and directed its barrel towards the old man.

"Poor choice of weapon, Captain, that's a Stevens .22 calibre pistol, if I'm not mistaken. A lightweight firearm much favoured by sailors and seamen. Unfortunately for you, it has a single shot, which you have used, and it must now be reloaded to be of further use," he said.

Calhoun's face screwed up as he realised he'd been found out. "Damn you," he said and dropped the pistol.

***

Ransome entered the apartment with remarkable speed for such a large man. I found out later that he had observed Savage and the Finn entering the inn, so had taken it upon himself to relocate to the front bar. He was taking his first sip of ale when Calhoun's gun went off and almost collided with the Finn as he made good his escape.

The Inspector entered the room and with the wide-eyed expression of one unaccustomed to dead bodies took in the scene. I took him gently by the arm, pointed out the gun, Calhoun and the fact that Holmes had the culprit covered. I suggested that he bring the wagon to the Inn door and send for an ambulance to take Savage's body away.

We stayed for two more days to assist Ransome with the finer details before travelling back to London. I was relieved. Holmes had solved two cases in one single moment. I could update my notes on the original five orange pips adventure and had enough fodder for an entirely new adventure.

The first question I raised with Holmes was what to do with young Middleton, or Mudge, or whatever he wished to call himself.

Holmes was circumspect in this matter.

"For all intents and purposes, Middleton has committed no crime. He was an accessory to smuggling, but that would only apply if the gold had made it onto American soil. It now lays at the bottom of the ocean, so technically no crime has been committed. By his own admission, he was not involved in the Openshaw murders. We can only take his word as we have no further evidence to convict him. We heard Savage admit to the murders on Calhoun's orders, so we have the culprits. Middleton is Lestrade's problem now. I will tell the Inspector all I know, and he can keep an eye on him. It is up to Middleton to confess to his wife. Regardless, it should all make for some interesting family dinners around Christmas time," he said a broad smile on his face.

"And the Openshaw family?" I asked.

"Sadly, John was the last of his line. I shall inform the estate, but that will only give them a procedural closure of sorts after all these years. There are only a few scattered cousins left in the family. So, there is nobody emotionally attached in reality. I have probably had the most investiture in this case, so it brings a very high level of relief, I must say," he said, sitting back and sipping his coffee.

I took the opportunity to glance out the window at the countryside rushing past. The day was bright and serene, and I was eager to be back with Mary. By the time I glanced back at Holmes, his head had sunk to his chest and he was snoozing restfully.

I smiled, happy that another successful adventure was finished.

The Adventure at Dead Man's Hole

It was a dreary day in mid-October that found Sherlock Holmes and me standing on the northern bank of the Thames. To our backs the great stone walls of the Tower rose up, blocking out what little light there was, casting us into a perpetual twilight and robbing us of any heat that the sun might provide. To our left, the mighty north tower of the bridge loomed above us.

Although the bridge's construction had officially finished several months before, there was still a certain amount of work that continued to be done. Shouts rang down from above as the workers went about their business. The clanking of metal and striking of rivets rang out across the slowly moving river as the final construction of the bridge went ahead, heedless of our activities.

The object of our visit lay below, the stinking silt and mud of the riverbed. I could see numerous deep holes in the mud, which could only mean that Lestrade and his men had combed the area for clews before we had been called.

I imagined the fuming anger brewing within Holmes's mind as he surveyed the destitution that was the supposed location of a crime. And it was no surprise when he said, "You would think, Watson, that by now Lestrade would understand not to utterly destroy the evidence of a crime before he calls upon me."

"I do agree, but as I understand it, he wasn't even here when the body was removed, so in his defence, he had no control over the matter." My reply met with a solid and angry harrumph, which brought a slight grin to my face.

The body had been found earlier that morning by one of the workers as they arrived for their shift. There had been no surprise or hurry for that matter in recovering the corpse. This area was renowned for trapping anything that floated down the mighty river. The tides of late had ebbed and flowed with remarkable heights as a full moon smiled down on the city at night, bringing with it the waters, but taking them away once morning broke.

In a city of the size and with the vitality of life that London possessed, it was little wonder that numerous cadavers washed up on her banks during the course of a year.

The area was also the daily home to hundreds of workers employed on building the mightiest bridge to ever grace the cityscape. Accidents happened, far too regularly for my liking, which had forced the creation of what came to be known as Dead Man's Hole.

The designers of the bridge had included a small thoroughfare through which pedestrians could quickly circumnavigate the northern tower and gain access to the nearest bank of the Thames. Sadly, as more and more workers succumbed to gravity and other accidents associated with construction on such a large scale, a place needed to be set aside to house the bodies of these unfortunates until they could be collected by the coroner or a mortician. The pylons and footings of the new bridge also provided an unforeseen hazard, whereby they became a catchment area for all and sundry that floated down the river. Many times, that included the corpses of animals and humans. The watchmen who patrolled the shoreline were tasked with releasing animal bodies to the mercy of the river and to ensure that any humans were taken into the Dead Man's Hole to await their fate.

It was to the Hole that Holmes and I had been drawn by an early morning telegram from Inspector Lestrade of Scotland Yard. I was shaken awake by Holmes's entreaties and virtually dragged from my bed chamber and piled into a hansom even before I broke my fast. I think that Holmes had been a little bored of late, and any evidence of a crime worthy of his attention was a singular delight to his mind.

The dour overcast day and chilling breeze did nothing to enliven my spirits, which continued to claw at my conscience with cries for coffee and breakfast.

The hansom had dropped us off near the corner of the Tower, and we'd made our way across the small rutted track that serviced the construction site and towards the North Tower of the bridge.

Lestrade met us, looking almost as tired and worn out as I felt.

"Sorry to bring you out this early, Mr. Holmes," he said, "but this one's got me puzzled."

"I do hope so," said Holmes as we clamoured our way across the mud track and onto the small concourse at the base of the bridge.

The Dead Man's Hole, as I would come to know it, was little more than a covered tunnel, but had been shut off from public access by a series of wooden barricades. I was unsure if they had been there before or were for the benefit of the current occupant.

Inside the temporary room, we met with a young man who went by the name of Byron Smith. He introduced himself as the coroner's assistant and shook each of our hands. Dispensing with any small talk, to Holmes's apparent delight, he showed us five lumps lying on the floor covered in stained white sheets.

Smith quickly explained that they had found four bodies in the last three days, three of which were obviously street people that had fallen into the Thames. He pointed to a fourth body and explained it was an unfortunate worker that had fallen from the South Tower rigging just the day before. The last body was the reason for our visit.

Before Smith could unveil it, Holmes turned to Lestrade.

"You haven't explained why this one has you flummoxed," he said.

"No, I haven't," he said, nodding at Smith, who quickly drew back the sheet. "See for yourself."

"Good Lord!" I gasped.

Holmes simply stared at the body, a hand cradling his chin, and murmured to himself.

Before us lay an extremely sorrowful sight. It was difficult to tell the actual age, but it looked at first sight like the body of a young man or more of a boy, but that would need further confirmation. His skin was sallow and puffed, indicating a prolonged amount of time beneath the surface of the water. It glistened in places from the presence of adipocere, a waxy substance that forms from the fat on bodies in water and protects them from decay. His hair was matted and dark, his eyes closed shut from engorgement. He was completely nude, showing the brutalisation that he had suffered at the hands of the elements. To add to the peculiarity, a thick strand of rope was still tied around his ankles.

I made him to be around five feet ten inches tall. His weight was obscured by the bloating, but my instincts told me that he had been between nine and ten stone.

Holmes dropped to his knee to make a closer inspection of the corpse. I stepped closer, mindful of the dim light in the tunnel, and gasped again when I made out the scarring on the body.

"You see it then, Watson?" Holmes said.

"What do you make of it?"

Holmes pointed to the marks on the body's chest. They weren't deep, merely superficial, made possibly with a knife or other sharp-bladed instrument. The edges had been puckered by the exposure to water. A long line ran from the throat to the navel, a smaller line ran across the chest just below the pectorals.

"That looks like a cross, but the horizontal line is too low, it's unsymmetrical," I said.

"Or inverted," Holmes said.

My eyes widened. I had seen that symbology before, but never in this way. It was then I noticed a single deeper wound on the left-hand side, slightly above the horizontal line. It too was puckered but was certainly not superficial.

"He was stabbed?" I said.

"Indeed he was. These lines were carved before he died. This," Holmes said pointing to the deeper wound, "was what killed him."

I took a deep breath. It was murder then, and not just some poor vagrant who had died of the cold.

I noticed a pattern of cuts on the forehead and pointed to them. "What are those?" I asked.

Holmes pulled out his glass and leaned in closer. I looked around and found a small portable gas lamp nearby. I brought it across and bent down to shed more light on the subject.

"My word," I mumbled in surprise at the strangely intricate pattern.

"Yes," murmured Holmes. "It's a pentagram. Inverted from the traditional Wiccan form."

"Witches?" I asked, a hint of unreality in my voice.

"No, nothing like that," Holmes said. I breathed a sigh of relief. Witchcraft in any form was a strange world, especially if some were now delving into ritual sacrifice, as this seemed to indicate. "This is worse," Holmes finished, before standing up. "This is Satanic."

I almost dropped the lamp in surprise.

"Satanic?" I asked.

Lestrade pitched in, "Satanic?" Even Smith's face dropped in shock.

"I do believe so," said Holmes, "The inverted cross. The inverted pentagram – both symbols of Satanic cults. The deep wound above the heart indicates how this man – " He stopped himself and peered at the corpse for a moment. "How this *boy* died."

"You think he was a boy as well, then?" I asked. He nodded. "My estimation is he was in the water for a good six months."

"I agree," said Holmes, "The level of water absorption, the amount of adipocere, and the lack of overall decay would suggest that sort of timeline."

Lestrade spoke up. "Do you think he's from London?"

"That is impossible to tell," he said as he dropped down to his knees once again and pointed to marks on the corpse's wrists and neck, and to the rope tied around his feet. "These marks are burns from a rope tied around them, just like the type around the feet. They indicate that the corpse was tied and probably weighted to keep it from floating away."

He stood again and turned, gazing off into the distance as if looking through the nearby tiled walls and out across the great river.

"The recent rains and the abnormally high tides have swelled the Thames upriver. Perhaps our friend here resided upstream and his bonds broke, sending him south and towards the sea. I wonder . . . ."

And that was how I found myself observing Holmes as he mudlarked about in the deep, stinking silt of the great river.

We had borrowed long leather waders from the site foreman and long leather gloves. I had to admit to a feeling of foolishness as I stood on the edge of the stone wall that formed the bank of the river.

The waders came up to my chest and the gloves covered my hands and forearms. I felt like an out-of-place farmer or steelworker.

Holmes carefully trudged his way across the little area, stopping every so often to plunge his hand deep into the muck and fish around for any clews on offer. His efforts had elicited nothing but more mud. In fact, as I became more bored and my unsated hunger grew I began to question my erstwhile colleague's actions.

Finally, I cried out, "Holmes, what the devil are you searching for?"

He stopped and peered up at me, a familiar look on his face. "Why I'm searching for clews," he said as if in answer to everything.

"Any clew in particular?" I asked, through my thinly disguised impatience.

At this, he gave me his aggrieved look. "Well, we have nothing to tell us of this boy's origins. Is he from London? Is he from farther afield?"

I nodded, I already knew that, but still wondered.

"We have the rope," he began.

Again, I nodded. The rope was made of plain hemp, available in any store.

"To what was it attached?" he said.

At that, I shrugged. "Some sort of weight, I imagine."

"Yes, excellent," he said, drawing breath to give me time to reply. When I didn't, he continued. "The body had to have been weighed down at some stage, for at least six months. It was so bloated that it would otherwise simply float on the surface, much like a cork or leaf, and not as subject to the tides. But if weighed down a little, the undercurrent would snatch it and drag it swiftly downriver."

I nodded. It made sense – simple physics that I had seen during my own trips to the seaside.

"The weight itself could provide additional information," he said.

"Possibly not," I countered.

"That is also true," he said, a slightly annoyed tone to his voice.

He ducked down and drove his arm up the shoulder into the dirty brown water. He struggled slightly, then peered across to me.

"Watson, I don't suppose that you could assist me," he cried.

Not disguising my look of disgust, I moved towards the thin iron railings that acted as a ladder down to the riverbed. I reached the bottom and gingerly stepped off, my foot disappearing into the putrid mud. I stepped towards him amidst the most disgusting *schlooping* noises. Just as I reached him, he stood upright with his prize in hand. He smiled and turned towards me, surprised to find me only a few yards away.

"Never mind now," he said. "I've found it."

I bit my tongue to suppress any remonstration.

***

It wasn't until mid-morning that we returned to 221b Baker Street. Once she realised that we hadn't eaten, Mrs. Hudson was quick to bring up a sumptuous brunch with coffee. I thanked her effusively over the noise of my grumbling innards and set about demolishing the fare, whilst perusing the morning paper.

A sketch of the latest player on the political scene smiled up at me from the front page. Sir Geoffrey Warrington was a rising star in the ranks of the opposition party. He had previously made a name for himself as an industrialist trading in goods between the Continent and the United Kingdom, and now that he had entered politics, the thinking was that he would soon lead the Liberals into power at the next election in a couple of years. I turned the page over to find something less boring to read and soon lost track of time.

Holmes was concentrating on something in his chemical corner. I brought over a small plate of food and a cup of coffee, which he unconsciously ate and drank whilst studying the object of his attention. To me, it was just a bunch of stones, wrapped in a small hessian sack. A short trail of broken rope was attached, but Holmes had verified that it was the same as that which bound the corpse.

"I don't understand what's so fascinating about that," I said.

Holmes grinned. "And that is a little disappointing," he said. "What we have here is evidence."

He carefully emptied the stones onto the table and spread the hessian sack out next to them. He pointed at the sack and said, "This small sack has been cut from a larger open-weave bag and roughly sewn together with hemp twine. This type of hessian is used for the holding of root vegetables rather than grains – hence the open weave. It is still strong, but won't allow the vegetables to escape. The twine is ordinary, which is a shame."

He reached over and picked up one of the stones. It was round and smooth and consisted of a white stone, marked with specks of black and brown.

"This is interesting in two ways. First, it's smooth," he said, rotating the stone between his fingers, "but not perfectly spherical. It was smoothed by nature, rather than the hand of man. I would suggest from a running river."

He picked up his glass and peered closer at the stone itself. "The specks of black and brown rock within the conglomerate indicate that it is a type of white granite – not a very common stone, but one that is well known in particular regions."

He placed the stone down and moved across to the bookcase. He extracted a large volume of Ordnance Maps and plonked it down on the workbench. He flipped to London and placed his index finger on the Thames.

"We can assume that the body came downstream, probably due to the recent rains in the West Country which have filled the local streams and rivers and flushed them into the great river."

He came to the edge of the map near Hounslow, quickly turned the maps, following the river through Slough, up past Maidenhead, eventually stopped and placed his finger on Reading.

"Reading," I said, "Nothing ever happens in Reading. Why do you think this boy is from there?"

"He may not be from there, but that is where his body came from."

He pointed to the River Kennett and traced it upstream.

"The Kennett is one of the fastest flowing rivers that feed the Thames. It just so happens that the area near Main Lake is home to several quarries that specialise in white granite. One could surmise that the corpse would have been placed into one of the quieter ponds in that area."

"How, exactly?" I asked.

"The poor unfortunate boy has been underwater for at least six months. Therefore, he was placed deep in a quiet body of water." I nodded. "The stones are from a river, probably just picked up from the bank as needed. The hessian material is from a bag used in a more rural area."

I nodded again. It all made sense. "So what now?"

Holmes looked blank for a moment. He stared at me, then his eyes dropped to what remained on his plate. He picked it up and replied, "Food. I think that I need to have a bite to re-invigorate my mind."

***

I was called away in the early afternoon and didn't return until the evening had settled in. I found Holmes and his brother Mycroft in the sitting room, engaged in a deep debate. Holmes looked across at my entrance with a dour expression on his face. I knew immediately that some new piece of information had come to light in my absence.

"You look exceedingly downcast."

Holmes nodded, as did Mycroft, "Yes, we are. Typically two events occurring on separate days would play no part in the same investigation, but when they transpire within hours of each other, the linkages blaze across my mind like fireworks."

"What's happened?" I asked, looking first at Holmes then at Mycroft, who simply raised his eyebrows and shrugged.

"Mycroft," he said, "has come with a request from a senior member of the House of Lords, Lord Howard Moncrieff."

I searched my memories and reminded myself. "Moncrieff? Isn't he the Earl of Dorchester or some such?" I asked.

Holmes nodded, "Well done, Watson. Precisely."

Still confused I pressed for more information, "And what has happened to him?"

"It seems that Alexander," said Mycroft, "the Moncrieff's teenage son, has vanished. Two days ago."

"But that isn't a long time – especially for a teenager. Perhaps he's run off on some lark for a few days with his friends."

"Perhaps. He disappeared from the school grounds of Pangbourne College. No-one has seen hide nor hair of him since."

The name Pangbourne rang bells within my mind. "Pangbourne College. But that's – " Then it hit home. My eyes widened, "That's just outside of Reading."

"Precisely, Watson, precisely."

"What did he look like?" I asked, my mind on fire.

Holmes held up his hands.

"Calm down, old friend. The body we examined is not Alexander Moncrieff. He is blonde-haired, very slightly built, and has crystal blue eyes. Very different from the boy that was pulled from the river. And remember, the Moncrieff boy has only been gone two days, while the other spent six months in the water."

I relaxed but was still very intrigued. "But you think these two are related?"

"I do. At this stage, it is supposition, but the closeness of location, and the age of both, lead me to believe that there may be a connection." He stared at Mycroft for a moment, before saying, "Dear brother, is the Government keeping any files open on the activities of Satanic Cults within England at the moment?"

Mycroft's face remained stoic. "Why do you ask?"

"The boy found in the River had markings that suggest such. He was also killed by a single wound to the heart by a wide-bladed knife. It may have all been a prank gone wrong, but given this second boy's disappearance, I'm leaning towards the conjecture that he was sacrificed and that there may be more."

"I do not know off-hand if there is anything, but I will make some inquiries. If I find anything, I will return. Until then, what do you plan to do, Sherlock?" asked Mycroft. I could tell he was aching to be gone. His face had shown a hint of disgust at the mention of Satanists, but from experience, I knew that he was more than happy for his brother to undertake the more visceral detective side of such an investigation, and would rather hear of the success or failure at a later date rather than be involved in the deliberations.

"In the morning, I feel that Watson and I will away to Reading." He stepped across to his worktable and stared at the maps. "These drawings do not do justice to the physical locations. There should be more data that I can collect that will lead me to a more concrete conclusion. I don't like supposition *per se*, and would rather that my ideas be dashed with evidence than linger in my brain longer than necessary."

"Well, I wish you all the best. Keep me informed. If you find the boy alive, I'm sure the boy's parents will shower you with riches. If not, then at least they shall be at peace."

With that, he left.

***

The constable at Reading Police Station read the letter from Lestrade again, just to make sure that he had our details square in his mind.

He peered up at Holmes, a quizzical look on his face before he surprised both of us with his next utterance.

"What I'd like to know is, how do two gentlemen from London know about the disappearances?" he asked.

I was shocked. Lestrade had said that Moncrieff hadn't mentioned his vanished son to the police.

"Disappearances?" asked Holmes, placing a heavy inflection on the last syllable. I detected a slight tilt of his right eyebrow as the only evidence of his own surprise.

"Yes," said Constable Corden, eyeing each of us again. "Disappearances."

Holmes continued. "I only mentioned the one body found in the Thames. I don't think that I said anything about any others."

Corden realised he'd made a mistake. He stared at Holmes for a moment, possibly running the conversation back through his mind before nodding.

"So you did," he said finally, "So you did." He reread Lestrade's letter, averting his gaze for a moment before re-locating his confidence. "Well, that's settled then." He looked around. The only other person in the station was a drunk, lying prostate in a cell at the rear of the building. I doubted if the man could hear or even if he would have cared, but Corden leant forward and whispered, "There have been four so far. Regular as clockwork, near the end of the month. All young boys, around mid-teens. Their distraught parents or friends come in. They can't find little Johnny – he's run off or

39

something. I've had no evidence of any foul play, and I'm at my wits' end, but I try to reassure them as best as I can."

He moved across to a nearby desk and brought back a thick file, full of loose papers. He opened it and picked up the top page.

"Neville Borthox: Fourteen, five-foot six-inches tall, dark hair, brown eyes, around ten-stone nine-pounds. Went missing one month ago. Last seen on the Abbey School grounds close to sunset."

I look at Holmes, he shook his head.

"Not our boy," he said.

Corden picked up another sheet.

"Reginald, or Reggie, Hyde-Northam: Fifteen, five-foot eight-inches, nine-stone six-pounds, fair hair, green eyes. Missing for two months. Last known location, Leighton Park Public School."

He flipped to another sheet.

"Clarke Greggson: Thirteen, five-foot two-inches, seven-stone nine-pounds, red hair, green eyes. Missing for almost three months. Last seen at St. Josephs College."

He picked up the final sheet, read his own report and nodded several times, whilst murmuring under his breath.

"I remember this one. Garrison Wainwright: Sixteen, big boy, five feet ten inches tall, ten-stone, dark hair, brown eyes. Reported missing four months ago but hadn't been seen for two months before that. Parents thought he'd just run off. Weren't that worried, to be honest."

"Where was he last seen?"

"He was from Farley Field, down south. Out of school. Worked on his father's farm. The parents are salt-of-the-Earth types. Not too bright, but hard working. As I said, they weren't worried. He'd run off before. The father's a bit of a drinker and gets a might handy. When he hadn't come home for two months, the mother started to get worried and reported it."

I said, "It sounds like our boy then."

Holmes nodded. He reached into his pocket and brought out the Ordnance Map of the area. He quickly plotted the last known locations of each boy. They were scattered around the area, but even with five points, they formed a slight ring around the town of

Reading. The location of Pangbourne College was outside the defined area. The Thames ran through the very centre of the ring.

Holmes pointed to a series of ponds and lakes that flanked the River Kennett upstream from its confluence with the Thames near Reading. He peered up at Constable Corden and said, "Could you take us to this area?" Then, after the officer had walked away, he added, "I'll also send a telegram to Lord Moncrieff. I think that we might need to visit him this afternoon."

***

The police station had access to a simple cart that they used for carrying several men to situations when required. Corden enlisted one of the junior constables to drive, and the three of us sat in the rear. The station wasn't far from the banks of the river. We crossed a large bridge and continued to follow the southern bank towards the series of lakes that had interested Holmes so much.

The area near the river was lined with deep thickets of trees, the land opening up to farms and fields on the south, with dry stone walls bordering each allotment. The river still ran quite strongly. I could hear the constant bubble as water washed across the small rapids created by the build-up of rocks and stones. It was a totally different sound to the slow languid pace that the Thames achieved even during an exceedingly wet spring.

Holmes had his Ordnance Map open in his lap and was keeping track of where we were in relation to the geographical points of interest marked by the cartographers. To the south, I could see the large granite quarry that serviced Reading and provided her with stone and lime for building works.

As we approached a point on the river where it split into two, Holmes called out to the driver, "Take the south fork, please."

We turned and picked our way slowly along the disused rutted track. To our left passed a series of large and small ponds. I glanced at Holmes's map and saw that they were all connected by a network of small streams.

Holmes noticed my interest and said, "This whole area is a major wetland consisting of ponds and lakes, all joined by tiny rivulets that become raging torrents during the wet season."

"I don't understand where you are taking us, though," I said.

Holmes pointed to a small pond at the end of this particular branch of the river.

"Here. From the facts I have at hand, my deductions have led me to this spot."

He looked up from the map and pointed. "In fact, we are here," he said. Corden and I looked in the direction of his finger.

A small calm pond sat at the end of the southern branch of the river. The driver circumnavigated the bank and pulled up on the western side. We stepped out of the cart and onto the muddy ground. Luckily, Holmes had the foresight to insist that we both bring heavy boots. Corden knew the area well and had brought his own from the station.

I peered around. The pond was small but very still. A tiny inlet on the northern side was the source of water from the larger branch of the river. The water drained on the eastern side, running down that branch until it re-joined further east.

Holmes glanced around for a moment then headed towards the tiny inlet. Corden, the driver, and I hurried after him, struggling to keep up with his rate of stride through the boggy ground.

"A-ha!" he said once we reached the inlet. It was there I saw the object of his attention. The inlet joined the pond to a sharp bend in the river. The bank of the river was littered with masses of round white stones of the same type as we had seen in London.

Holmes studied the area for a moment before peering across the pond. He glanced down at the muddy ground, shaking his head slightly and making *tsk*-ing noises. He gently stepped along the banks of the pond, hunched over and examining the ground as he moved.

Finally, he stood and let out a small triumphant shout.

I walked up next to him, mindful of staying close to his own footsteps and asked, "What have you found?"

He pointed at the sodden ground and I could just make out several of the small round stones, half-pushed into the mud. Several deep holes, which I presumed to be footprints, ran down to the water's edge.

"I assume you detect the presence of bootprints amongst the mud and grasses?" Holmes asked.

I was astonished all the same but had to nod at Holmes's remarkable find. "How?"

Holmes turned to me with a wide grin on his face. "Simple deduction. This little pond is regularly kept filled from the river itself via that inlet. Normally it is as we see it, extremely still. The flow out of the eastern side is the same as the flow from the north. The current runs across the northeastern section of the pond." He pointed to the area before us. "Anything in this area will remain still."

"But the body in London?" I asked.

Holmes turned to Corden. "Constable, when was the last storm?"

Without hesitation, Corden responded, "Five days ago. A mighty storm it was, too. I had to bring the lads out to assist the fire brigade with a few rescues that night. Shocking it was."

"That storm stirred up this little pond somewhat. The river would have flooded, and the current would have disturbed anything lying within these muddy waters. The body we observed was wrenched from its mooring and taken downriver on the crest of the torment."

I pointed at the impressions in the mud. "But these are footprints aren't they? Surely, they would have been washed away."

"Which means they are much fresher. Possibly only two or three days old. The ground is still so damp that access without leaving any mark is impossible."

"If they are that fresh, then that means – " I said, realising that someone had possibly left something – or someone – behind.

Holmes's expression turned grave. He nodded. "Yes, Watson, I feel that there is at least one more body in these waters. Somewhere in that direction." He pointed towards the outlet and then turned to Corden. "Constable, did you bring what I asked?"

Corden nodded and trudged back to the cart. He returned quickly with a small four-pronged anchor attached to a long length of rope and handed it to Holmes. "I noticed this anchor at the station. It's used by the canal barges that work the river. The constable was good enough to attach a long length of sturdy rope."

I followed as he made his way to the edge of the water. He unfurled some rope, then swung the anchor around in a wide circle before letting it fly out into the middle of the pond.

The water broke up in a large splash, sending ripples out to all sides of the bank. Holmes waited for the anchor to settle on the bottom then slowly wound the rope back in.

His first try resulted in nothing but an anchor full of dense weed and thick mud. After several more tries in different directions, I was about to comment that maybe he was wrong when the anchor stuck fast.

"I have a bite," he said, as would a fisherman with a live fish on his hook.

He struggled with the rope, slowly dragging in both the anchor and its catch. Bubbles erupted on the surface of the lake as the object at the end of Holmes's rope was dragged towards us.

After a few minutes of a tediously slow battle with his sunken prize, Holmes pointed at the pond surface. A pale white object could be seen through the murk. I didn't need to observe it clearly to know what it was.

Corden, the driver, and I stepped into the water as far as our boots would allow and grabbed at the thing, dragging it up to the bank. I let out an exasperated sigh as we stared at the bloated and sodden body lying on the bank.

Holmes dropped the rope and stepped towards the corpse. It was a boy, of that there was no mistake. His hair was filthy, but even so, I could that it was blonde. Two large hessian bags full of stones were tied around his throat and feet. Holmes placed a hand on a shoulder and rolled the body onto its back. The boy was slightly built, possibly around five-foot-six inches in height.

"It's Moncrieff," Holmes said. I nodded.

Corden simply said, "Who?"

"Another boy that went missing a couple of days ago. Son of Lord Moncrieff, up in Pangbourne," I said.

"Oh my," said Corden. "Why didn't they report it to us?"

"They went straight to a higher authority," Holmes said, "Sadly for Alexander here, someone else was trying to do the same thing."

With the boy on his back, we could clearly see a deep wound on the left side of his chest. The two sets of markings on his forehead and chest were the same as those on the body at Dead Man's Hole. With a slight look of disgust on his face, Holmes pointed out across the water and said, "I think you'll need to drag this pond, Constable. If I'm right, there are at least another three bodies in there."

***

We were let into the main entrance of Moncrieff House by the butler and shown into a small parlour off to one side of the elaborate foyer. A maid brought tea and scones and, realizing that we hadn't eaten for quite some time, I tucked in while we waited for the Lord and Lady to arrive.

Holmes stood to one side of the room, examining one of the many paintings, but I could tell that his mood was quite grim.

"Would you like a scone?" I asked, holding a small laden plate towards him.

He turned, the darkness on his face. "Yes, thank you," he replied, moving across and taking the plate from me. Just as he took a small bite, we heard movement outside. He set the scone down and prepared to meet our hosts.

Lord Moncrieff entered first. He certainly was a presence with a stout frame, his piggy face sporting a shock of white hair, and with ruddy cheeks and a double chin. He was followed by a diminutive woman who trailed in his wake and was almost unseen behind her larger husband.

"You'd be Holmes then?" Moncrieff said.

Holmes nodded and shook the Lord's proffered hand. "Yes. I hear that you've met my brother."

"Ah, Mycroft. Yes, good man. I assume you have news then if you're here."

I noticed Lady Elizabeth and offered her my seat. She shuffled across to me and sat down. Her face was a mask of timidity and fear. She stared up at her husband with the haunted look in her eyes of a mother who has lost a child.

"I'm afraid we have nothing concrete at this stage, but a body has been found," Holmes said. Lady Elizabeth let out a gasp and raised a hand to her face.

Lord Moncrieff faltered slightly but caught himself and remained steadfast. "Is it Alexander?" he asked.

"That can only be determined by yourselves, I'm afraid. The poor unfortunate was taken to the Reading Coroner's building. They will need one or both of you to attend and determine whether it is your son."

Moncrieff nodded, his face grave. "An accident?"

"I'm afraid not," Holmes said. "The indications are far worse, but inconclusive. We still have much investigating to do before this can be laid to rest. Which brings me to the main reason that we are here. I understand that your son was last seen at his school. Is that correct?"

Moncrieff's face turned towards anger. "Yes. Damned foolish place. What am I paying for if they just let these boys loose on the local towns?"

Lady Elizabeth looked aghast. "Howard, this isn't the time to be going into that," she said, her eyes bordering on tears, but her heart remaining as stoic as she could.

"I apologise, dear," he said, "but really, this isn't the first time."

"First time for what?" I asked.

Lady Elizabeth peered up at me and said, "There was a boy, two years ago, who left the school one summer's evening and never returned. We heard about it from an acquaintance. It was never reported by the school itself. He was one of Alexander's closest friends. We almost withdrew him because of it."

"And now it's happened to our Alexander," Moncrieff said. "There will be hell to pay when I see that Principal."

He took a deep breath and drew himself up to full height.

"If you'll excuse me, it seems I have a trip to make to Reading," he said and disappeared. "Dear?" echoed back from the nearby hallway.

Lady Elizabeth sprang to her feet, obviously used to being ordered around. She stopped and turned back. "I assume that you were about to ask for permission to talk with the schoolmasters?"

Holmes nodded. "Yes, I was."

"Ask for Mr. Reginald Brown. Alexander liked him." I noticed a tear form and run down her cheek. Her strength was beginning to fade. "Alexander wasn't a strong boy. He inherited my frame and lack of athleticism. He was also a very emotional boy and easily led. Again, my traits."

She took my hand in her own and stared deep into my eyes. "My husband had always hoped that Alexander would be more like him, but that didn't happen. Still, I think that he loved him. I know my life will never be the same. All I can ask is that you find out what happened. It will never relieve the pain, but it may bring us a little bit of peace."

She released my hand and was gone before I could reply.

Holmes stared at the empty doorway, contemplating.

"A trip to the school then," I said.

***

The main building of Pangbourne College was a towering Georgian edifice built with orange-red brick and grey stone. The window frames and guttering were all white and stood out in stark contrast to the walls.

Holmes and I passed through the main entrance and were greeted by a rather ornate foyer. The school had been refurbished in recent years, possibly due to the input of funds from parents such as the Moncrieffs. A matronly woman with severely tied-back grey hair took our request to see Master Brown and disappeared quickly when we added it was to do with Alexander Moncrieff's disappearance.

Soon we were met by a tall man in his mid-forties with thinning blonde hair. Reginald Brown was an affable man, and I could tell that he held a deep concern for his students' welfare. He plied us with questions of his own to elicit details about Alexander. Holmes gave him several vague answers which either caused him to stomach his unease or told him that no further information would be forthcoming.

Upon hearing that Holmes was a detective, Brown suggested that we should examine the boy's bedroom. The master seemed to brighten at the prospect of watching Holmes at work. I was unsure whether he knew of Holmes's reputation or was merely intrigued. As we walked along the shadowed corridors, Brown stopped a young student passing by and whispered to him. The boy took one look at Holmes and me and scurried off.

We finally stopped at one of the non-descript doors that lined the corridor. Brown turned the knob and ushered us inside. The room was small and brought back remembrances of my own during my time in public school housing. I admit now that those remembrances were not always pleasant.

"Good Lord, these boys," said Brown hurrying over and opening a window. Out of the corner of my eye, I noticed Holmes wince in almost physical pain, no doubt imagining the evidence that could be destroyed by such an act.

Brown turned and took a breath of the fresh air flooding the room. "That's better," he said.

Holmes peered around the room. "If you don't mind, sir," he said, looking Brown directly in the eyes. The Master quickly ducked out of the way and joined me near the entrance.

He pointed to the unmade bed on the right and said, "That's Alexander's bed and his side of the room."

Holmes stood stock still, initially only moving his head for a moment. I could only see the detritus of a teenage boy's life in disarray across the area, but I knew that Holmes was searching deeper.

Finally, he reached forward and picked up an open newspaper from the desk. It took me a moment to form the question internally.

Why would a teenage boy have a copy of the newspaper?

I could make out a black outline surrounding a small square of print on the paper.

"What is that?" I asked as my companion read the page carefully.

He simply ignored me and turned the paper over. A small card dropped from within the pages and fluttered to the floor. Holmes quickly bent and picked it up. A small smile crossed his face.

"Interesting," he said, turning to Brown, "Do you have much interaction with the local girls' school, or is there any interaction between these boys and the fairer sex?"

Browns' face became stern. "Certainly not," he said, a slightly angry tone on his lips, "We have a strict policy on that. There are no organised or even casual activities where students can mix. This school has a strict Catholic philosophy and a matching set of policies."

Holmes nodded.

"Why?" I asked.

He held up the paper. "This is an advertisement regarding a group from the Reading Girls' School," he said. "They want to meet up with boys from the other schools. There's an address to forward an acknowledgement." He held up a card. "This has details regarding the consequent meet-up."

"He was always going on about meeting those girls," said a voice from the doorway. I turned and saw a young boy of about fourteen with a shock of curly red hair and a pasty white face covered in freckles.

"He was supposed to meet up the day that he went missing," the boy continued.

Reginald Brown looked shocked, "Hamish, why didn't you say anything?"

"Alex told me to keep it to myself. He didn't know how long he'd be gone. I didn't want to ruin it for him – it seemed to be important to him."

"Well it may have been very important," said Holmes with a slightly sinister tone. "Did he mention anything further?"

Hamish shook his head. "No. He skipped out in the early evening. Said that he was meeting someone outside the gates, and was heading over to Reading, although he wasn't very specific."

"Did anyone else go with him?"

He shook his head again, "No. No one else knew anything about these girls. I just thought it was all a joke, but Alex just kept going on about it, always bragging to anyone that would listen. No-one did. No one thought much of Alex anyway. He was always bragging about something or other. Most people just ignored him when he started talking."

I looked at Brown. He nodded, "It's true. I think that his father was the main problem. Alex tried to be like him, but he was just a braggart with nothing to back it up."

"What do you think?" I asked, looking across at my friend, but his attention was solely on the personal advertisement and the little card. I leaned in and whispered, "Wasn't that the night of the full moon? I was under the impression that was important to these Satanist blackguards."

Holmes lifted one eyebrow and looked at me out of the corner of his eye. I took it to mean be quiet and promptly shut up. After a moment he finally spoke.

"Watson, I think another trip to Reading is in order."

***

The building that housed the offices of *The Reading Chronicle* was a simple two-story Georgian affair, made of blocks of the same black-specked white granite with which we had become all too familiar.

Holmes and I entered the main entrance, which served as both a reception point and a place for dealing with customer enquiries and requests for advertisements. A young woman of about twenty sat behind the long wooden counter and seemed genuinely pleased at our arrival. It was possible that the day had been rather slow, and any interaction was to be welcomed. A small nameplate told us her name to be Bess Frampton.

Holmes produced the copy of *The Chronicle* that we had found in Alexander Moncrieff's room and showed it to Miss Frampton.

"Good afternoon," Holmes said. "My friend and I are interested in the origins of this personal advertisement,"

Miss Frampton read it thoughtfully and was silent for a moment and then began to nod. "Yes, I know this one. We've had similar requests around the second week of the month for the last six."

"Do you have copies of the others?" Holmes asked.

She nodded and disappeared into the large area behind the counter. I peered through a gap in the frosted glass wall and noticed rows of wooden desks with several people were busily writing. After a few minutes, the young lass returned carrying a bundle of newspapers.

She dumped them on the counter and proceeded to open each, laying them out side-by-side.

Holmes and I searched each page for the advertisements and found that they were all of a similar structure, except that the address changed in each.

"It seems as if they are covering their tracks by using a different return address," Holmes said. He thought for a moment before picking up a form and filling it out with his name and our Baker Street address. He pulled out a guinea and placed it on the counter.

"Miss Frampton, if you would be so kind, can you arrange for the delivery of the *Chronicle* to this address?" he said pushing the slip of paper forward, "When the next one of these advertisements appears, and each month onwards until I advise otherwise."

She read the slip and nodded. "I can do that. I'll put it through to deliveries. We already have a few customers in London, but it won't cost a guinea, even if you get the paper every week for a year," she said.

Holmes smiled, "That's fine. You can keep the rest. I don't think that we'll need more than one copy, in any case."

Bess looked delighted and took the guinea from the counter, slipping it into her pocket. "You'll have your paper within a week or two," she said with a wide grin, "if this person is punctual."

"Excellent," Holmes bowed. "And thank you for your service, Miss Frampton."

***

The following weeks were spent back at 221b Baker Street. Holmes and Mycroft had managed to keep the discovery of the other bodies out of the news. In the meantime, we received two pieces of information that were of the most horrid nature.

The first was that Constable Corden and his men had dragged the little pond off the main part of the River Kennett and sadly found not three but four bodies. Three matched the reported boys, but a fourth was unknown. Each boy had the same markings carved into their foreheads and chests and had been killed by a single wound to the heart from a wide-bladed knife.

The second was that Lord Moncrieff had visited the Reading Coroner and identified his son, Alexander. I could only imagine the grief that had overtaken Lady Elizabeth. I hoped that she had someone to support her, as I didn't believe her husband to be that person.

Early in the week after our return, we had received a summons from Mycroft Holmes to meet him in the Stranger's Room at the Diogenes Club, in order to discuss Holmes's findings so far. It was there that my friend explained the five dead boys identified so far and the unknown sixth. Mycroft was appalled by the loss of life.

"Satanism," said Holmes with a dour look on his face.

Mycroft's face was almost as dark as his brother's. "Not good, Sherlock, not good," he said instead, "Britain is too important on the world stage to have this sort of . . . of . . . pagan ritual going on. I would dearly love to put the full force of Her Majesty's law on to this matter, if just to help Lord Moncrieff, but it is a purely civil matter. What do you plan to do about it?"

Holmes sipped his coffee and thought for a moment. I knew that he'd been working hard in the background, formulating some plan, but the details hadn't been forthcoming. I was on the edge of my seat, waiting for him to continue.

"I expect the delivery of a newspaper from Reading within the week. In there, I hope to find a personal advertisement calling for boys of a – How should I say it? – a *virginal* aspect, to make contact with the girls from a nearby college. It seems to be a simple fishing exercise, but the catch rate has been rather astonishing."

"I don't follow," Mycroft said.

"It is my belief that these cultists are using the newspaper to find the young boys whom they use as sacrifices in their detestable rituals."

"Why boys?" Mycroft asked.

"From my research," Holmes said, "it seems that virgins feature prominently in the more esoteric and graphic rituals. They believe that the devil requires them to be pure of sin."

I took a sharp intake of breath. It did make sense.

"But why not girls?" Mycroft asked.

"Boys disappearing at that age is less obvious, and not liable to attract as much attention from horrified or distressed fathers."

Mycroft nodded. I was quite disgusted at the thought of what had been going on.

Holmes continued, "When I receive the advertisement, I will answer from an address in Reading. I've already arranged for one of my young cohorts to spend the next fortnight there. He will make the contact and ensure that he becomes the next object of the cult's obsession."

He turned and indicated me. "Watson and I will journey back to Reading and join the young lad. I would hardly allow any harm to come to one of my Irregulars."

Mycroft nodded. "Good, good. You have it in hand. I may be able to provide a tiny bit of assistance, but it will have to be discreet," he said touching an extended forefinger to his nose.

***

It was early the next month that Holmes's copy of *The Reading Chronicle* finally graced us with its presence. There, as bold as life on the personal pages, was the latest advertisement. It asked for young boys from the local area to meet with the girls of The Reading Girls' School. Those interested were to send a telegram to the listed address, different from the previous six. Holmes read it with a sly smile on his face.

"What do you think?" I asked.

"Marvellous," he said. "The exact same format, but a different reply address. The *modus operandi* is perfect to weed out the chaff, but we need to make sure our response attracts their attention."

Holmes disappeared into his room and returned several minutes later, sporting his travelling coat and hat, and carrying a small valise. He handed a small note to me which had an address in Reading written on it.

"Join me in three days at that address. By then, I feel that the game will well and truly be afoot." He then promptly left, leaving me slightly aghast.

***

When I finally set foot at the Reading abode that Holmes had organized, I'll admit that I had been busy with patients and other trivial tasks for the last few days, but throughout my mind raced with questions regarding events that would unfold.

I was greeted at the front door by a young man of around thirteen years, with neatly combed jet-black hair and dark brown eyes that glinted with recognition when they fell upon me. I was taken aback for a moment as the boy drew no remembrances from my mind – that was until he spoke.

"Dr. Watson?" he said.

I stammered slightly, "Aiden?"

When I had seen him previously, he sported torn and dirty street clothes, with a filthy flat cap hiding his mussed and mud-streaked hair. The boy that stood before me was the total antithesis of that. He was remarkably well-appointed and could have passed for any public schoolboy of good upbringing.

"Yes, sir," he replied politely, before bowing slightly and stepping back to allow me in.

I found Holmes in a small reception room. He was dressed very smartly, and I realised that he was affecting the guise of young Aiden's father, or at least guardian.

"Ah, Watson," he said as I entered, before giving Aiden an order to take my coat and valise to the back of the little house. As Aiden left he simply said, "Just in case anyone calls, we must retain the impression that Aiden and I are family and have been here a while."

I nodded and then asked, "What progress have you made?"

Holmes indicated a small chair and I sat, ready to hear all. "We've done very well," he said, "I sent the telegram prior to arriving here in Reading, and young Aiden and I moved straight in. It was only the next morning that a knock on the door revealed an answering telegram. Aiden has been invited to a *soirée* for members of the girls' school and their guests tomorrow night."

"Do we know where?" I asked.

"They're sending a hansom for him tomorrow at six o'clock. We'll follow in our own cart, parked around the corner."

"Good. Do you know anything else?"

"Of course," he said, smiling in that inimitable way of his, telling me almost as much as anything that he would say. "I went to the address and waited to see who, if anyone, of note, visited."

"And?"

"It was a small house off the High Street. The only occupants that I could see were a young girl of probably Aiden's age, and a matronly woman that may be her mother – or like me, is posing in that role."

"Interesting. Any idea what they are about?"

"Window dressing," he said, "because it wasn't they who were of interest, but those that visited later in the day. We answered their first telegram with a request for more information. I was present outside when it arrived. The visitation occurred later in the day and proceeded the reply with Aiden's transportation details."

"Who was it?"

"A beautifully appointed black brougham pulled up outside, and a tall man in a dark suit and top hat paid a visit to the two women. By the way, he carried himself, I don't believe that he was the owner of the carriage, but rather a servant. I wouldn't be surprised if the same carriage is used to pick up young Aiden tomorrow night." He took a breath before continuing. "I waited until the man had left, then followed the carriage at a good distance, until we left the town and they headed into the countryside. I dropped back and used the dust thrown up by the brougham to track them. After a time, they finally pulled off the road and went up a lane that led to a rather well-maintained manor house."

"Do you know whose?"

"I didn't at the time. They used a side entrance, so I circled around until I found the main gates. The name of the house and the owner were proudly displayed. The house is one you would know – Southcote Manor."

I was puzzled. The name certainly rang a bell. I searched my memories. "You're correct. It seems very familiar," I said.

Before I could find the information, Holmes said, "It's the home of Sir Geoffrey Warrington."

"Good Lord! You don't think that the potential leader of the opposition is involved in this Satanist crowd, do you?"

"I hope not," he said, "but I've sent a telegram off to my brother, who seemed very perturbed by the prospect. We shall have some of that help he promised, tomorrow night."

I snuck my hand into my coat pocket and felt the cold comforting sensation of my service revolver. The fact that we were about to confront a deranged sect that not only worshipped the opposite force of all that is good and wholesome in this world but one that also had powerful political allies, filled me with the deepest dread.

***

Several minutes before the allotted time for young Aiden's transport to arrive, Holmes and I left via the rear door and then through the back fence gate into the service alley, and around to the nearby side street where Holmes had parked his hired dogcart. We brought it around and sat almost fifty yards from the front door to keep watch.

The dark black brougham arrived directly at six o'clock. A tall man with the top hat disembarked, knocked on the front door, and a moment later returned with Aiden. The door to the brougham was opened from within, and Aiden's face lit up with a wide smile. I presumed that the young lass was inside.

When the brougham was over a hundred yards away, we fell into the same pace behind it. We turned towards the southwest and I assumed that we were heading towards Southcote Manor. I amused myself by viewing the houses and landmarks that we passed on the way. Most were of Georgian age, with several newly added terraces, along with many grand neo-gothic buildings from a long-ago age.

I noticed that another carriage had fallen into lockstep with us and maintained a distance of fifty yards from our rear. I turned to Holmes and mentioned it, asking whether it might belong to Sir Geoffrey Warrington.

Holmes smiled, "No, but it does belong to Her Majesty's Service. Mycroft has sent us some help. There will probably be more trailing further behind that one."

I took one quick look over my shoulder and studied the cart. It was a large four-wheeler with a pair of well-built men in dark coats in the driver's seats.

After nearly half an hour of travelling well into the countryside, Holmes spoke up. "We aren't heading towards Southcote Manor."

When the brougham took a left-hand fork in the road, Holmes pulled the dogcart to the right fork and stopped after fifty yards. Several other carts, including the large four-wheeler, pulled up near us.

Holmes spoke to the driver of the first cart. "Jansen, they've headed towards to the Padworth Quarry," he said. "That's slightly unexpected. We'll need to approach with care and surround it. I suggest sending one group to the western side, while Watson and I and the other group go to the east."

The young plainly clothed man nodded and barked orders at the other carriages. They rumbled off past us. Holmes pulled our cart around and headed down the other trail.

Within a few hundred yards we came to another fork and took the left, I noticed that the right-hand trail dipped as it disappeared amongst the trees. Our track soon opened up and I saw the wide expanse of the quarry lying to our right. Holmes pulled up in a small layby, dropped to the ground, and hurried across to the edge of the pit.

I was shocked at the sight before me.

Down at the bottom of the quarry, in a large open, flat space, a circular area was lined with blazing braziers. The bright full moon bathed the circle of people, their faces hidden by hooded robes. They stood surrounding a central figure dressed in a dark brown robe standing next to a wide flat stone, which had all the hallmarks of an altar. The central figure's hood was thrown back and I recognised him immediately as Sir Geoffrey Warrington.

The black brougham stood off to the side, and as I watched, Sir Geoffrey motioned towards it. Two men quickly broke off and hurried to the carriage. They man-handled the supine form of young Aiden from the carriage across to the altar. There they stripped him and lay him on the large flat stone. Sir Geoffrey drew a large wide-bladed dagger from beneath his robes and held it aloft. He began to address the assembly. "Lord Satan, we, your faithful servants, gather beneath the full moon to present to you this poor offering, so that you may bless us with another month of continued success in our endeavours."

I gasped and heard Holmes swear under his breath. Any chance of harm coming to one of his Irregulars was anathema to him. He turned towards Jansen and spoke.

"Get some men down to the entrance!" he hissed and then pointed to the man in the centre of the circle, "I suggest we let the majority of the people escape, as they will want to soon enough, but make sure Sir Geoffrey is detained."

Jansen and his men moved off.

"Why will the other people try to escape?" I asked.

Holmes smiled. "Because of this."

Suddenly, he moved forward and slid and skipped his way down a steep path to the quarry floor. I was taken aback but quickly joined him. He raced towards the circle of adherents, pulled out his revolver, and fired into the air.

The effect was incredible.

The group scattered like a flock of pigeons, running to-and-fro as if the devil that they had so wished to meet had, in fact, arrived. Holmes ignored them and moved towards Sir Geoffrey. The politician simply stood and eyed Holmes, a grin on his face.

"Drop the knife," said Holmes. "This disgusting play-acting is over."

"You have me at a disservice, sir," said Sir Geoffrey.

"I am Sherlock Holmes."

Sir Geoffrey's smile grew. "Ah, Mycroft's little brother. The detective." He waved the knife before him. "What gives you the right to confront a Member of Parliament embracing his religious freedoms? You aren't the law. You are nothing."

Holmes stepped forward. His face was alight with an anger I had rarely seen. He opened his mouth to speak but was cut off as Jansen stepped in front of him, a pistol trained on the politician.

"He may not be the law, but I am," Jansen said. "Inspector Michael Jansen, Intelligence Branch, and you are mine now."

***

It was a dismal day that found Holmes, Mycroft, and me back in the tiny town of Pangbourne for a memorial service. It was a sombre occasion for Lord and Lady Moncrieff to say farewell to their son, Alexander.

The rain pattered on the ground as we gave our condolences to the family, who thanked Holmes for both discovering their son's body and his killer. Lord Moncrieff kept his stoic visage as always, but my heart sang for Lady Elizabeth who seemed on the verge of a breakdown.

The three of us moved to a sheltered patch where we could watch the rest of the assembly and speak.

"What of that degenerate, Sir Geoffrey?" I asked, noting my voice was full of disgust.

"He will hang," said Mycroft, "The Prime Minister is adamant of that. He has placed the full force of the Attorney General's Office onto it."

"What of the others?" asked Holmes.

His face soured slightly. "The Security Service is scouring the country for them. Sir Geoffrey has kept his mouth shut, and will probably take their identities to the noose."

"Damn him," I swore.

"Yes," said Holmes. "I think that's what he wanted all along."

"Why would someone in his position do such a thing?" I asked.

"Regardless of any supernatural connotations," said Holmes, "I suppose it was that inner belief in the Devil's works that gave him a level of inner superiority and confidence which enabled him to achieve such a high office. History is replete with many an evildoer that has possessed such an aura, and I'm afraid that it is in the nature of man to bolster his inner worth through such fictitious means."

I nodded and peered out at the rain pattering down as the last of the mourners disappeared from view.

The Case of Vanderbilt and the Yeggman

As I drew the curtains on another mid-spring evening, I couldn't help but shiver. The temperatures during the day had been mild to warm, but the chills of winter had not yet removed themselves completely from the night.

Turning back to survey the mess I'd made of the day's *Telegraph*, I realised that a stranger could only draw one conclusion from reading its contents: A heatwave was blasting the great city, given the panic contained in every story. Such was the dread that gripped the media and political class over incidents occurring thousands of miles away in Afghanistan.

The outcome of another skirmish between Russian and Afghani forces threatened to bring British forces into play. Such an expansion was too close to the Indian border for the locals to accept.

Coupled with veiled threats emanating from Russia, the events had placed the British Defence Forces, both home and abroad, on notice for immediate deployment to the region. Contracted arrangements to finish several new British Ironclads had been brought forward. The Prime Minister had formed a war committee and was in the process of requesting additional funding for defence spending.

I shook my head as I gathered up the scattered pages of the newspaper. The sabre-rattling affairs of state always brought back flashes of my time in Afghanistan. I tried to dispel such remembrances, but a small squeal of pain in my shoulder answered the siren song.

I stretched to full height, trying to ease the throb through movement. Placing the newspaper on the settee, I paced about the sitting room in an attempt to stop the ache. I put it down to the chill or the silly way I had stooped down to pore over the newspaper.

Holmes was out on a case to which I hadn't been made privy, so I had occupied my time with the news, attempting one of his techniques of cross-matching articles to build a deeper picture of the story –

something for which I now berated myself as I stepped around the room, bringing the fire in my shoulder under control.

I paced past the door to Holmes's bedroom and then the fireplace, and found myself at Holmes's chemical bench. It was there I saw some of His private paraphernalia: Two slim glass syringes were filled with brown-tinged liquid, resting in an open red silk-lined case.

"Oh, Holmes," I said out loud, a hint of exasperation on my lips. I picked up one of the syringes and looked closely at the contents. Pursing my lips, I peered around for any other evidence of Holmes's cocaine habit. Finding none, I replaced the syringe and snapped the case shut.

I've failed to stop you in the past, but at least I can delay any future use for a little while.

I stepped away from Holmes's table just as the door to the sitting room opened. Surprised, I quickly slipped the syringe case into my jacket pocket and promptly forgot about it.

The tall aquiline features of Sherlock Holmes poked through the doorway and glanced across at me.

"Ah, Watson, good man," he said. "Grab your coat. Lestrade needs us at the Yard. *Tout de suite*, it seems."

***

Even though the traffic at that time of night was rather light, it still took the hansom a good twenty minutes to cover the distance to the Yard. I had lost count of the number of times Holmes and I had journeyed along the same route over the last few years. The hansom pulled to a stop outside the front entrance, where we alighted. As always, I turned and paid the driver before joining Holmes.

"What is this about?" I'd waited to ask, as Holmes was disinclined to converse during our journey.

"Lestrade's telegram was non-specific on that point."

He pulled out a small, folded paper and read aloud. *"Come now. Have arrested supposed friend of yours. Will only talk to you."*

"Very strange," I said.

"Hopefully," answered Holmes. I caught sight of a slight smile on his face. He did love a good mystery, and given the amount of information he had to hand, I hoped this one kept him intrigued.

"What friend of yours could he have arrested?"

Holmes turned towards me, that grin still in place, "On that note, Watson, I can honestly say I have no idea. The telegram didn't give me enough information, and I certainly have no knowledge of any friends or acquaintances that have come under the suspicions of the police of late."

I looked up at the imposing edifice of Scotland Yard, the nearby gas lamps casting a pallid glow across the orange-and-grey bricks. We stepped through the great oak doors and stopped in the small reception area. The gap above the small wooden counter provided the only view into the inner workings of the Metropolitan Police.

At that time of night, only a few bobbies were on duty, either moving around with sheafs of paper or sitting at their desks and filling out reports.

We stepped up to the counter and rang the small metal bell.

A young constable looked up and approached the counter. He recognised us straight away and nodded to the door to the side of the counter. Stepping through as he opened it, we followed him through the uniform work area and into a corridor beyond.

"The inspector's down in the basement," he said. "We've got a right strange one this time."

"The basement?" I said to Holmes in surprise. He simply smiled and held up a single finger to silence any further questions.

We went down a short flight of steps just outside the workroom and walked along a long corridor that ran past storage cupboards and finally into the area reserved for small holding cells. From our past experience, I knew that there were also some unfurnished rooms specifically set aside for interviewing suspects.

I'll admit that I've never enjoyed entering this part of the building. It reeks of misery from an older time, almost as if we had entered a medieval dungeon complete with torture chamber. Admittedly, the only criminals brought here are those charged with crimes against the Crown. The Yard's location means that miscreants captured near the Houses of Parliament, or worse, Buckingham Palace itself are most likely to be brought there.

Finally, the young constable stopped and knocked on a solid wooden door. The knob turned and the door opened a crack, revealing the familiar face of Inspector Lestrade.

"Excellent," he said before stepping back and opening the door fully, allowing us to enter. The constable withdrew, and Holmes and I stepped into the sparsely furnished room.

The only other occupant of the room was a rat-faced little fellow who looked to be in his mid-forties. I could add or subtract a decade though due to the light. He sat on a chair in the middle of the room, his hands shackled behind him.

His features were amplified by the fearful look on his face and the way his eyes darted around the room and across both of us as we entered. A hint of recognition dawned on that face as he saw Holmes and he broke into a wide grim.

"Mr. 'Olmes," he said. "God bless you, sir!"

Holmes peered down his long nose and returned the smile. "Hello, Nobby," he said, "What trouble have you got yourself into this time?"

Nobby looked mortified. "Oh, no, sir, I done nuffin', 'onest. I've been tellin' the inspector 'ere just that. It's all a stitch-up."

Holmes turned to Lestrade, whose expression held the look of someone that lived his life being lied to by criminals.

"What is Nobby here meant to have done?" Holmes asked.

Lestrade pulled out a small notepad and made a big deal out of flipping to the requisite page, whilst eyeing the man in the chair with a healthy level of disdain.

"Arnold Brown, known on the street as 'Nobby', was caught coming out of the back entrance of Number Ten Downing Street – an address I'm sure you are familiar with."

I was aghast. My eyes darted back to look at Nobby again. I studied him more closely and realised that beneath his slightly grubby coat, he wore a neatly pressed dinner suit, with a white low-cut waistcoat and matching white bowtie. If I were to have met Nobby in a mansion house, I would have mistaken him for the butler or a simple valet.

Lestrade continued, "Two uniformed constables were on duty patrolling the grounds when they came upon this fellow skulking across the rear lawns."

"I wasn't skulking," said Nobby, "I 'ad an errand to run for my master."

Lestrade harrumphed. He'd obviously heard this before we arrived.

"And who would that master be?" asked Holmes.

"I shouldn't really say," said Nobby.

"Fine, then. It's the cells for you," said Lestrade, fed up with Nobby dodging the question, "You wanted Sherlock Holmes. Well, here he is. If you're not going to answer the questions then you'll spend time in the lockup." He stepped towards Nobby, whose face lit up in fear.

"All right, all right," he said, peering back at Holmes hoping for some sympathy from my friend. When Holmes remained stoically still, Nobby relented, dropped his head and continued. "I'm workin' as man-servant to Mr. Johan Vanderbilt."

"Who?" asked Lestrade.

"Johan Vanderbilt," repeated Nobby, "He's an attaché to the German ambassador. I been workin' out of the London residence. It's a good job, been there for the last six months. On the straight and narrow, me."

"Well that's very good to see, Nobby," said Holmes.

I was quite intrigued. From experience, I knew that Holmes had a large sphere of acquaintances across London, and indeed the country. I assumed that Nobby fell into one of the various coteries that circled Holmes, or vice-versa.

"How exactly do you know Nobby here?" I asked.

"I'd like to know as well," said Lestrade.

"Ah," said Holmes, a wry smile on his lips. He stepped closer to Nobby, stared down at him for a moment before turning back to us. "Nobby here taught me everything I know about safe-cracking. He's been at it for well over twenty years. One of the best in London."

Lestrade's face lit up. "A yeggman, aye." He rubbed his hands together in glee. "Must be good at his job, 'cause I don't know him, but a yeggman caught coming out of the Prime Minister's residence – you might be going down for a long time, my boy."

Nobby cried out in terror, "I done nuthin'! I was working for Vanderbilt, 'onest, I was. Talk to 'im. He'll vouch for me!"

Holmes remained stoic, surveying the scene, searching for clews and digesting all. I'll admit my heart went out to the little man. His demeanour suggested sincerity, but I could tell that Holmes, himself, wasn't convinced. Lestrade was ready to hang the safe-cracker.

Holmes pondered for a while longer, leaving the room in silence, before he turned to Lestrade. "I assume, Inspector, you haven't searched Nobby as yet?"

"No. When he started going on about only talking to you, I thought I'd better wait."

"I've got nothin' on me, 'onest, Mr. 'Olmes. We've known each other for years. I wouldn't ask for you to vouch for me if I'd done somefin' bad, now would I?"

Holmes stood, peering at Nobby's face for several moments before turning to Lestrade. "Inspector, if you would be so kind, could you please undo Nobby's handcuffs?"

Nobby's face lit up. I was taken aback. Grumbling to himself, Lestrade stepped behind Nobby and undid the cuffs.

The yeggman rubbed his wrists to restart the blood flowing. "Thank you so much for trusting me, Mr. 'Olmes. You're a saint, I've always said that," he stated as he stood and headed towards the exit door.

Holmes waited until Nobby put a hand on the doorknob before speaking.

"Ah, not so fast Nobby." The former safe-cracker stopped in his tracks and turned slowly to face Holmes. "It might be prudent to inspect your garments before you head off. Just to satisfy the inspector. I wouldn't want him to think that there was anything untoward about this affair," Holmes said. I felt that there was something unsaid in his statement that would become evident quite soon.

Holmes held out a hand, I could tell he was holding his smile in check, "I'd like to have a quick look at your coat if I may." He shrugged, "Just as a matter of course."

Nobby's face was aghast. He slowly peeled off the coat and handed it to Holmes. My friend took it without taking his eyes off Nobby's expression. My eyes flicked between them, and I finally saw what Holmes saw. As Nobby's eyes dropped to the bottom of the coat, Holmes nodded, turned the coat around, and examined the lining inside. He let out a small, "A-ha!" and stepped over to the chair. Laying the coat across it, with the inner lining revealed, he ran a finger down the stitching in the centre and found a small unsewn section.

"If I'm mistaken, Nobby, I apologise in advance and will repair your coat," he said, before jamming a finger inside and pulling at the thread. It came away easily, revealing a larger section that had evidently been unpicked. The hole created was large enough for his entire hand. Holmes stood and reached into an inner pocket of his own coat and slipped out a pair of fine kid-skin gloves.

Wearing them, he thrust a hand deep inside the lining of Nobby's coat and fished around for a moment. A smile crossed his face and he brought out a folded sheaf of stiff parchment held together with a bright red ribbon. I caught sight of a seal on the outer page. I'm sure that there was a crown, and possibly a lion or unicorn.

"Good Lord!" said Lestrade. "What in the blazes is that?"

Holmes straightened and examined the papers for a moment, mumbling to himself before looking at Nobby and shaking his head.

"Nobby, you've been a very bad boy," he said.

The (now it seemed) active safe-cracker, looking much more presentable in full valet uniform, dropped his head in shame.

***

As Mycroft Holmes looked up from his work, his mouth dropped open in surprise as he spied his brother's silhouette in the doorway. "Sherlock? What in blazes are you doing in here? And how did you get in?"

A pale face at Holmes's shoulder looked past us and addressed Mycroft. "I'm sorry, sir. I did recognise your brother and was about to come for you, but it's what he was holding that made me bring him straight to you."

Mycroft stared at the man, a flush of anger ran across his cheeks. "Fine, Johnson, but that's not the proper process is it?"

Johnson's face went bright red. "No, sir. Sorry, sir." He backed away and virtually ran away down the corridor.

Holmes moved across to the large oaken desk and *plonked* his prize on the desk before his brother's eyes. Mycroft peered at the parcel of parchment wrapped in red ribbon. He looked from the papers to Holmes, confusion writ large his face. Slowly he pulled at the bow of the ribbon and freed it. He unfolded the sheaf of papers and read the opening words on the first page.

His face turned from confusion to horror.

"Sherlock, where did you get this? You could be in serious trouble."

Holmes took one of the chairs before Mycroft's desk and motioned for me to join him. Mycroft watched in silence as I walked over and sat down.

"I'll admit, dear brother, that I didn't open the papers. I realised as soon as I saw the seal, and was informed of the original location, that it would be tantamount to treason. I could have left the papers with the constabulary, but we agreed that it might be best to bring them to someone of your – how should I put it? – *station* within the Government."

Mycroft pursed his lips and read the first page again. He shook his head. "Where did this come from?"

"I think you already know that."

"Yes. I do."

I piped up, "Well, I don't, so please explain to those of us who are still in the dark."

Mycroft glanced at Holmes for a moment, then turned his face towards me. As always, he treated me with respect. "Well, Doctor, I would think you already know this came from the Prime Minister's residence." I nodded. "Neither of you could have known though, that these are the PM's personal notes to be read out in Parliament on Monday morning. Once presented, they will be taken away and typed up to form an appropriations bill to be tabled at Parliament later in the week. The final bill," he patted the sheaf of papers, "is set to rock the country to its core."

"Why?" I asked, leaning forward in an attempt to make out the wording and figures evident on the parchment.

"This country is on the brink of war – with Russia of all places."

I nodded. "It's all through the newspapers."

Mycroft harrumphed. "Reporters," he spat, "Until they got wind of it, there was nothing but a simple border skirmish. It would have resolved itself in a week and England would have had no reason to be involved. Our papers have blown it up to the point that the Russians have been emboldened and are pushing ever further into Indian territory. This," he smacked the papers, "is the result. Our pacifist Prime Minister is suddenly egged on by his constituency and taking us towards conflict. This outlines the amount of money he will request from Parliament and the armaments and troops that it will pay for. All to be sent into Afghanistan and into this conflict."

"But surely we have learnt from the past," I said, imploring Mycroft.

He smiled back at me. "Doctor, you should know better than any of us here the futility of combat – combat that results when our ill-informed superiors begin to rattle their sabres."

Holmes finally spoke up. "I'm surprised, brother. I thought you fully supported the decision-making processes of our Government."

Mycroft sighed, "No, I fully support our Government. It just leaves me a little exasperated when those decisions go awry through unsupported opinions rather than actual facts."

He looked down at the parchment and thought for a moment before peering up at us once again.

"Enough of my own opinions, I can only assume that this parcel came from the safe in Number Ten." Holmes and I nodded. "Given the lack of excitement, I can also assume that it hasn't been found to be missing."

"Worse than that," Holmes said. "It has been replaced." He pointed towards the desk. "It seems that the miscreant that stole the original was also tasked with substituting another set of papers. I haven't seen them yet, but I assume they have revised figures created to mislead the Prime Minister and possibly embarrass him, or at worst, lead us to implement an incorrect regime of military acquisitions."

Mycroft thought for a moment, flipping through the notes and murmuring under his breath before looking back at us. "You may be right, Sherlock, but as to misleading the Government, that won't happen. The PM's figures would have been distributed to the Ministries of Defence and Finance already, plus to the Under-Secretaries to prepare the actual bill for tabling in Parliament. This action could embarrass the Prime Minister if he was to read them out in the House, but I feel that there is something far more sinister behind this." He stared at Holmes for a moment before the younger brother answered.

"Espionage," he said, a slight smile on his face.

"Why are you smiling?" Mycroft asked. "You could have just admitted that you already knew. I assume you know who then?"

"The Germans, it seems, but I'm unsure why. The man who stole these papers was doing so under contract to a member of the German diplomatic corps."

"Who?" said Mycroft, a look of confusion on his face. "I'm quite familiar with the Ambassador, Baron Egor."

"The papers were purloined by one Arthur 'Nobby' Brown, a yeggman from Soho," started Holmes.

Mycroft interrupted, "Sorry, did you say that he was an 'eggman'?"

"No, *yeggman*," said Holmes, placing particular emphasis on the first syllable, "It is street slang for a safe-cracker. Anyway, Nobby Brown was hired by Johan Vanderbilt, an assistant to the Ambassador. Nobby was arrested outside of Number Ten whilst the Prime Minister was entertaining several European ambassadors, including Baron Egor Staal. Nobby went in with Vanderbilt, slipped away from the dining room, opened the safe, switched notes, and exited the building. It was only through sheer luck that a pair of bobbies were checking the rear of the property when Nobby crossed their path."

"Vanderbilt? I don't think I've met him."

"Well, you might have an opportunity tomorrow. He's to meet with Nobby to lay claim to these notes."

"It will be no good if it's on the Embassy grounds."

"With that, we are quite fortunate. Our captive yeggman was to meet this Vanderbilt in a small pub in Covent Garden to hand over the papers."

"What time?" asked Mycroft.

"Twelve-thirty, a half-hour after opening. Good idea, that. They should be able to hide amongst the lunchtime crowd," said Holmes.

Mycroft stood and picked up the parcel of papers and walked around the desk. "I need to get these back into the PM's safe before he becomes aware and – " He stopped and tapped Holmes on the shoulder. " – I don't understand what interest these Germans have in our defence movements, but we should use everything at our disposal to upset their attempt."

"What are you thinking?" I asked, my eyes darting across to Holmes and seeing a familiar sly grin on his face.

"Who would have written up the PM's notes in the first place?" Holmes asked.

"That would be Miss Marsden, the PM's personal assistant," Mycroft said shaking his head, "She would be long gone."

"Do you have anyone else on staff that can draft up a set of mock papers?" asked Holmes.

"Perhaps, but I think we need to keep the number of people within these walls that know about this to a minimum," Mycroft said.

"I believe I may know someone that can help. We'll need to borrow those," Holmes said pointing at the sheaf of papers, "Or at least an example of Miss Marsden's handwriting, for authenticity's sake. We will also, of course, need some official stationery, including some more of that ribbon."

"More than easy to arrange," said Mycroft.

**

Within half an hour, Mycroft had the wheels turning throughout the Houses of Parliament. At Number 10, Mycroft himself led us down a corridor and into the Prime Minister's outer offices. Using his own key, he rummaged through the personal filing cabinet of Miss Marsden and retrieved another batch of the PM's reading notes.

Back in his office, all three of us crowded around his desk to view the spoils.

Miss Marsden's notes were written out in a spidery thin scrawl, very reminiscent of the delicate hand of a woman. The fake notes consisted of similar penmanship but had a slightly heavier look to them.

Mycroft read through the faked papers, murmuring and mumbling to himself as he did so. Finally, he burst out, "Preposterous! Whoever wrote this has no idea about the workings of Parliament, or indeed the Defence force."

"Would the PM have gotten far into the figures before realising?"

Mycroft thought for a moment and shook his head. "Sadly, he would have probably read them all out and only realised once the guffaws broke out from the cross-benches."

"As I thought," said Holmes. He then pointed to the script and commented, "This was drafted by a man. The downstrokes on the pen are much heavier than Miss Marsden's, but overall, it is a very good likeness. The forger obviously had access to a set of notes such as ours."

"I agree," said Mycroft. "That worries me quite a bit."

"Why?" I asked.

"It would appear that the forger is working within these walls."

My eyes opened in surprise and I nodded in response. Such an act by a member of Parliament or the Civil Service was tantamount to an act of treason in the eyes of the law.

Finally, Mycroft sat back and closed the papers. He looked exhausted. I think it was mostly due to the gravity of the situation, rather than any physical exertion.

"Would it have been as bad as you thought?" Holmes asked.

"If the PM had read this out without examining it first, which is most likely, he would have seemed a fool, and would certainly have stumbled within a couple of pages. The scandal surrounding the theft and replacement that would soon erupt would be far worse." Mycroft peered up at his hawk-faced brother. "I can't thank you enough, I really can't."

"It's not us you have to thank," Holmes said, "I think you should send your regards, and possibly something a little more substantial, to Inspector Lestrade and the two bobbies that caught Nobby."

"Yes, yes, you're right. I will see to it. But first – " He pulled a few sheets of paper from his desk drawer and scrawled several lines whilst flipping through the sheaf of fake papers. I looked across at Holmes, a perplexed look on my face. He simply smiled and shrugged.

Mycroft laid down his pen, gathered up his notes and the fake papers, and stood up. He strode from the room with a rare sense of purpose. Holmes kept pace with him easily, but I found myself falling back. Luckily, the journey downstairs and into the sub-basement area was short.

We entered a large room packed with shelves and cupboards. A lone desk sat near the doorway and acted as a counter. A young man of barely twenty years sat behind the desk. He was working away on a sort of long handwritten document when he noticed us. His eyes went wide as we entered, he dropped his pen and shot to his feet.

A nervous voice peeped out of his mouth. "Mr. Holmes, sir. What can I do for you?"

"Ah, Atherton, good lad," he said. "Surprised you're here."

"Um, I took the opportunity to learn more about work, sir," he answered with a smile.

Mycroft returned his smile and nodded, "Good man. You'll go far with that attitude. Now, back to business, I need ten pages of the PM's stock paper, a length of red ribbon, a pen, and ink."

Atherton looked confused for a moment. "I'm only meant to give that out to Miss Marsden," he said.

"And normally that would be fair," said Mycroft, "But I have been asked to prepare some reading notes for the PM on Monday and know that he prefers all his notes to be on the same paper stock."

The young man nodded. "I can't argue with that." He turned and disappeared into the depths of the rows of shelves. The sound of his rummaging filtered back to us.

I pivoted and noticed Holmes taking a special interest in what Atherton had been working on. From where I stood, I could see that it was writing, some large, some small, some heavy, some verging on spidery. It was then I noticed Atherton's jacket hanging on a coat rack near the aisles of shelving. My eye was drawn to the pin on the lapel. It was composed of a small silver bar on a red and green striped ribbon. If I wasn't mistaken I would say it was the Afghanistan medal, I had a similar one myself for services in the war. I thought to myself that the lad was far too young to have served and assumed it was a father's or grandfather's pin.

I was about to comment to Holmes when the young lad returned. He *plopped* the supplies down on the desk and handed a wooden clipboard with an attached sheet of paper to Mycroft.

"Just need you to sign for these, sir. Normally, I wouldn't need to ask, but I've been told to keep a close watch on our more special items."

Mycroft nodded and signed. Atherton took the clipboard away and handed over the stationary. He nodded slightly, before saying, "A good night to you, gentlemen."

"And you to Atherton, and thank you," said Mycroft before ushering us out of the room. I looked back as I exited and noted Atherton's gaze intently fixed on the three of us. I was confused as to his expression – it appeared to be part concern, part fear, and part suspicion.

***

Within moments we had been ushered back into the cold London night. The fake notes, loose sheaf of papers, pens and ribbon – all contained in an official leather satchel.

Mycroft had expressed his concerns about our next steps but wanted to be kept up to date as things progressed. I admit I was still at a slightly loose end. I had faith that the Holmes brothers knew what they were doing, but as always would have liked some inkling of the plan going forward.

Holmes hailed a hansom and as we climbed aboard I peered back to find that Mycroft had already disappeared back inside the building. By the time I turned forward, Holmes had given the driver our destination, so I simply sat and watched as we navigated the virtually empty streets.

After about fifteen minutes of travelling along the edge of the river, we turned right then onto the King's Road. I felt it was time to ask, "Holmes, where the devil are we going?"

"To visit an old associate," he said in that enigmatic way of his.

"Another one?" I asked, the question disappearing into the ether. Grumbling to myself, I sat back in the seat and remained silent. After another few minutes and we turned into the Fulham Palace Road and headed towards Hammersmith. I was certainly intrigued by now, even more so when we pulled up in front of a dark four-storey Georgian building on the Hammersmith High Street. Holmes leapt from the hansom and made his way towards the ground floor entrance, leaving me to pay the cabbie.

"You might want to get him to stay for a while," Holmes said over his shoulder. "Say two hours."

I heard the heavy knocker hammer away as I was negotiating the fee with the driver and managed to join Holmes just as the door was opened by a crook-backed old man who looked to be in his seventies. He peered up at Holmes's darkened face and I saw a grin appear on his face.

"Sherlock Holmes! My word, it's been well over ten years, hasn't it?"

"Yes, Clive, yes it has," Holmes said.

The old man stepped back and allowed us both to enter. He looked me up and down before Holmes introduced me. "Ah, this is my associate, Dr. John Watson. Watson, this is Mr. Clive Trimble."

I held out my hand, but Trimble shied away, preferring to nod instead.

"Ah, yes, Clive doesn't shake hands. Do you, Clive?" Holmes asked as the old man nodded. "He is very protective of his hands. Any damage may affect his craft."

"Craft?" I asked.

Before I received an answer, Holmes strolled down the corridor, followed by the old man. I closed the door and chased after them, catching up in a room at the back of the house consisting of several draughtsman's tables, each with a gaslight situated above them. An ornate table sat at the end of the room, with two lights shining nearby. Holmes and Trimble stood next to a normal flat table. Holmes withdrew the sheaf of parliamentary stationery, notes, and other paraphernalia from the satchel and placed them on the bench. Holmes pointed to the figures that Mycroft had drafted, then the fake notes and Miss Marden's scribbles.

"Clive, I haven't asked for a return of the favour I gave you all those years ago, but tonight I am."

Clive's face dropped into a stern expression. "Nothing illegal is it?" He shook his head and backed away a step. "I don't want to be doing nothing illegal again. I've left all that behind. I'm too old to go back inside Wandsworth. It'd be the death of me."

"It's all right Clive. Nothing about this is illegal. In fact, you would be helping your country." Holmes pointed to the fake notes. "I need you to write up a set of notes like these – " Then at Mycroft's figures. " – using these numbers instead – " Finally, he pointed at Miss Marsden's writings. " – in the handwriting style of this young lady."

Clive looked at each in turn, his eyes lit up at the prospect of what he was to do. "And this is nothing illegal?"

"I assure you, this is all above board. Would I lie to you?"

The old man peered up at my good friend, a small smile crossed his lips and he shook his head. "No, no, you wouldn't lie to me, Mr. Holmes." He picked up the pages and moved across to the ornate draughtsman's board and began to delve into his craft. I was intrigued and watched from several feet away as he practised the strokes from the PM's secretary's scribblings before creating another set of notes with Mycroft's figures.

I almost started when I heard Holmes's voice in my ear. "The man is an artist. He is renowned for recreating historical documents and notations in almost the exact replication of the original's handwriting and calligraphy."

"But that could so easily be seen as fraud or forgery," I said.

"Ah, yes. Sadly, Clive did stray onto the other side of the law on one occasion. We crossed paths when I was asked to help investigate a case of illegal forgery."

I must have looked confused, as Holmes smiled and said, "Oh, before your time, Watson, before your time. Not an overly exciting adventure, but I'd be happy to relate it to you at another time. Anyway, I tracked the original documents and the miscreants that had ordered the work to be done, and I managed to convince the police that our Clive here had been duped into committing a crime. They reduced his sentence by five years, which – given his age – probably saved his life."

"Was he innocent?"

"That question requires further discussion, as there was a lot of additional information that you would need to make your own judgement, and this isn't the appropriate time or place to expand fully."

We went silent as we saw Clive turn towards us with a disparaging look. I wandered away and perused the works on the other draught boards. One towards the far end of the room held a large sheet of parchment upon which were the letters *A*, *J*, and *S*, written in various styles and sizes. As I studied it, I noticed Holmes standing beside me.

"Ah, Clive has himself an apprentice, it seems," he said.

Confused, I asked, "How so?"

"Well the first thing one is taught is to practice your calligraphy using familiar text. The letters of the alphabet, your name, address, things like that. Most students use their own initials the most," he said, before turning away and rummaging through a large pile of seemingly forgotten sheets of parchment in the far corner. Finally, he stood and brought across a single but very dusty page. He placed it on the draught board next to the object of my interest.

It was a similar page, but it was covered from edge to edge with variations of the letters *S* and *H*. As I stared at the lettering, the penny dropped. I turned to face Holmes.

"You were a student?"

He smiled., "Why yes, Watson, I was. Clive never throws anything away. After he was released from Wandsworth, I helped him to set up this shop, and then engaged his services to learn the art of calligraphy and script replication."

"Forgery, you mean."

Holmes chuckled, "Well, yes, forgery if you like, but it was all in the interests of education. One must understand the criminal mind and their techniques to be able to interpret and judge the distinction between real and fake."

Before I could reply, Clive looked up from his work and harrumphed. "I believe I have finished."

We hurried over and glanced at the finished notes. I was amazed. To my layman's eye, the delicate feminine scrawl of the PM's assistant was reproduced as if by the same hand. I glanced at Holmes. A small grin told me that he seemed just as impressed.

"Excellent work, my good friend," he said. "Excellent work."

**

Holmes, Lestrade, and I arrived at The Lamb and Flag pub dead on midday. The wonderfully bright sunny day did nothing to heighten the drab look of the external façade of the building. It was nestled down Rose Street in Covent Garden, a street by name only, as in reality it was little more than a dimly lit back-alley that curved around connecting Floral to Garrick street.

The three of us had affected the look of everyday workers, shunning any trappings of finery and dragging out our oldest, shoddiest clothing. Holmes had any number of costumes from which to choose. I simply picked my oldest clothes that I had kept on hand in case Holmes dragged me off on another undercover adventure. It was Lestrade that looked the most out of place amongst the three of us. He obviously had to delve into the back of his cupboard and drag out some very old and well-worn clothing that must have been in everyday use once due to its wear, but they hadn't graced his body in years.

The interior of the pub was no different from the outside in terms of décor and refinement. It was a simple room with a series of booths along the walls, consisting of hard wooden benches and tables, and a scattering of small wooden tables and stools across the central area. A bar ran along one wall, with the dour-looking landlord the only worker in sight.

This was simply a drinkers' pub, servicing the workers from the nearby markets, and one could assume, at night, the more questionable local trade.

As we sat nursing our pints of watery beer and avoiding the suspicious eyes of the landlord, Holmes and Lestrade told tales of their knowledge of the place.

"There's a room upstairs," began Lestrade, "that they call 'The Bucket of Blood', on account of the bare-knuckle fights they hold on the first Saturday night of every month."

"That's barbaric," I said, "Surely the constabulary should shut it down."

Holmes harrumphed to remind me to stay in character, while Lestrade chuckled. "The local bobbies know well to leave this place alone. The locals keep each other in check. The law only steps in when someone gets well out of line. It's a balancing act, but it works."

I crossed my arms at the thought.

Holmes piped up, "From my reading, this place has an even longer and stranger history. It was once a more genteel establishment attracting some of the local poets, such as Dryden and Wilmott. In fact, poor John Dryden was attacked by ruffians not far from here, supposedly in revenge for a satirical poem he wrote about Charles the Second's mistress at the time."

"I thought you said that it was more genteel?" I asked.

"Yes, but one must not vilify the King or his mistress. The intriguing fact was that Dryden didn't even write the poem. It was John Sheffield, the Third Earl of Mulgrave."

"So, he was assaulted for no reason, except mistaken identity," I said.

"As it would seem. Very difficult to bring a grievance against the King – especially someone held in such high regard as Charles the Second."

My comment was stopped short as the front door opened and in stepped a tall, slender figure. He was immaculately dressed in a morning suit, with a calf-length frockcoat over it. He took off his top hat and tucked it under his arm. His hair was dark and neatly trimmed, as was his full-faced beard.

He took one look around the room, regarding the three of us briefly before stepping over to the landlord. He held up his index and middle finger and placed some coins on the bar, before moving to the rear of the room and taking a seat in a booth that looked directly at the entrance.

Holmes stared down at his beer and spoke under his breath. "I do believe that is our man."

I directed my own comment at Lestrade. "I do hope you have things in hand outside?"

"Don't worry about that. I've got some of the best keeping their eyes on this place – one either end of Rose Street, and one across the road on Floral Street." He nodded towards the man we believed to be Vanderbilt. "Just in case he goes out the back."

"And Nobby?" Holmes asked.

"He has his own minder, making sure he plays his part."

"Good," said Holmes.

"I assume that you have your own helpers well advised," I said.

"Of course, Watson, of course. Wiggins and Tommy are on the case, with a couple of extras thrown in for good measure. They have Nobby's description, and using his depiction of Vanderbilt, they should have no problems picking up the trail, just in case."

"Surely," Lestrade added, "he'll be headed back to the German Embassy."

"That would be the logical choice, but something disturbs me about all this. The whole German connection, for a start. The Germans have had no interest in Afghanistan, or the sub-continent for decades, so I'm confused why they should show interest now." He took a sip of his beer before looking up as the door opened. "Ah, here we are now, I believe."

The small stature and rat-like features of Nobby Brown entered the pub. He stood in the entranceway while his eyes grew accustomed to the gloom before looking around the room. His eyes fell on the three of us and grew wide in fear. Holmes simply nodded at him before resuming his examination of the tepid contents of his glass.

The landlord piped up from behind the bar. "Hello, Nobby! Usual is it?"

I watched as Nobby peered over at him, before spying the man in the corner with the two beers before him. "Nah, thanks Harold," he said. "I have an appointment." Harold simply nodded and went back to drying glasses. Nobby made his way to the smartly dressed man's booth and sat opposite. The man we presumed to be Vanderbilt, and whom Nobby knew, leaned forward and spoke in a tone too quiet to hear. Nobby was galvanised into action and quickly reached into his coat pocket, extracting the sheaf of pages wrapped in the red ribbon and sliding them across.

The man drew the ribbon, unknotted the bow, and quickly perused the documents. I noticed a small smile come to his face before he closed the documents, retied the ribbon, and slipped them inside his own jacket pocket. From the other side, he withdrew a small envelope which he slid across to Nobby. I barely had time to register the colour of the envelope before Nobby had performed a disappearing act with it.

I leaned into Lestrade and spoke, "You might want to make sure to relieve Nobby of that."

"Already on it," he replied.

The two men held up their beers and clinked glasses before taking long draws in celebration. Their rejoicing was short-lived as Vanderbilt rose, put on his coat, and strode towards the entrance.

The three of us remained unmoved until he had left the building, and then we were a flurry of activity. Holmes and I headed towards the entrance doorway, while Lestrade moved towards Nobby, nabbing him by the collar just as the little yeggman was hightailing it towards the rear exit.

"Not so fast, my lad," I heard Lestrade say before following Holmes into the bright sunshine outside.

Vanderbilt was rapidly disappearing down the right-hand alleyway, heading towards the hustle and bustle of Floral Street. I noticed Holmes peer down the left-hand alleyway and cock his head for a moment before striding after the tall German diplomat.

"Intriguing," I heard him mutter under his breath as I struggled to keep up with him.

As we reached Hart Street, we saw the tall figure of Vanderbilt climbing into a hansom cab. Holmes turned to his right and waved. Immediately, a similar vehicle wound its way through the traffic toward us. We quickly climbed in as Holmes addressed the driver.

"Granton, you saw him?" he asked.

The undercover police officer nodded. "Yes, Mr. Holmes. He fits the description that Brown gave us. Don't worry, I won't let him lose us."

"Good man," said Holmes sitting back and relaxing only slightly.

"What troubles you?" I said. "The man grabbed a cab. Nothing unusual in that."

"Ah, but it is, Watson. Prussia House, which now serves as the German Embassy since unification in 1871, is located in St. James Square. It's barely half a mile from Covent Garden. A tall man such as Vanderbilt could walk it easily in ten minutes. I don't believe that's where we're headed," he said.

As I looked out of the cab, I realised we were passing along Piccadilly, well north of St. James.

"Where could we be heading then?" I asked.

Holmes had a broad smile across his face.

"Care to enlighten me?"

"You'll find out very soon," he answered. "It will be more interesting to see how Mycroft takes the news."

Still intrigued, I glanced outside and realised that we were then passing Wellington Arch and heading towards Belgravia. The houses and buildings had an air of elegance and expense about them that was a world away from The Lamb and Flag.

We passed many buildings proudly displaying flags of other nations outside. I recognised Austria, Hungary, and Italy before we turned into Chesham Street and stopped facing an ornate building that displayed a flag with yellow, black, and white horizontal stripes.

"The Russian Embassy," Holmes said before I could blurt it out myself.

We watched as Vanderbilt stepped from his cab and walked to the front entrance. I was shocked to see the two guards, standing at the front, step back and allow him unmolested entry to the building. This was a diplomat from another embassy – surely they would need some form of identification.

"Well, that was interesting," said Holmes, almost speaking for myself.

"They didn't even stop him. It's as if they know him," I said.

"Yes, so it would seem," Holmes agreed. He reached up and knocked on the roof. "Granton, pull up behind that other hansom. We're about to set a trap for this Vanderbilt chap."

As Granton pulled the hansom up in front of the embassy, Holmes and I alighted. Holmes strode over to the other cab and chatted with the driver. The driver peered back at Granton, who undid his coat and showed the police uniform beneath. The other driver needed no more convincing and left quickly.

Holmes and I moved away from the building but stayed within sight of both the cab and the entrance. The two men stationed on either side of the front entrance eyed us suspiciously for a few moments before turning away.

I leaned into Holmes and asked, "Why would Vanderbilt be allowed such unfettered entry to the Russian embassy? He's a German diplomat, isn't he?"

"That seems to be his station, but then we must delve into his history. Something is unknown to us," he said in that annoyingly deceptive way of his, "but becoming quite apparent." Before I could ask another question, Vanderbilt emerged from the building and strode straight to Granton's cab. We peeled away from our position and hurried after him.

"*Dobryy den' Gospodin* Vanderbilt," said Holmes (Good afternoon Mr. Vanderbilt), as we squeezed in either side of the shocked man, "I assume you are more familiar with your native language." Holmes rapped on the roof and the cab drew away and joined the light traffic.

"Vat is the meaning of this?" Vanderbilt blurted out. Holmes and I placed our arms across him bodily to restrict any chance of his escape. "I will call the police. This is an outrage. I am a German diplomat. Let me go at once."

Holmes smiled, "Sit back and relax, my good man. A policeman is already here, driving the cab. As for you being German – we will get to the bottom of that soon."

When Vanderbilt resisted once more, I pushed my hand into my pocket and pressed the barrel of my service revolver into his side. His eyes went even wider, but all fight quickly left him. Resigned, he sat back and awaited the journey's end.

***

The taller, straight-backed figure of Vanderbilt presented a far different sight in that small sparsely furnished room than did the object our earlier attention. Lestrade mentioned that Nobby had been sequestered to his own cell in Wandsworth for the time being. Holmes reminded Lestrade that Nobby had been helpful in snaring our new culprit, and with passing on the forged notes.

Regardless, he mentioned to me in passing that Mycroft would be informed of everything, which would hopefully have more weight with the judiciary.

Vanderbilt eyed us with both disgust and vile hatred. He retained an upright posture, in spite of the discomfort that he must have felt. I sensed it was more of an act to sway our opinion of him than anything.

"Who are you?" Lestrade asked him for the fourth time.

The familiar response followed, "I am Herr Johan Vanderbilt. I am a member of the German diplomatic corps. I ask for diplomatic immunity and wish to speak to my consular attorney."

Holmes, apparently fed up with the misdirection, finally spoke up. "But that's not altogether true is it, Ivan? I assume it's Ivan, as that is the Russian equivalent of Johan."

Vanderbilt's face turned to rage as he stared towards Holmes.

"I am Johan Vanderbilt. I am German. I was born in – "

Holmes cut him off, "Again, that isn't true, is it? I've been patient, but let us look at the facts, shall we?" He counted off on his fingers, deliberately using his thumb to start with. "One, you employed a local safe-cracker, Nobby Brown, to break into the Prime Minister's personal safe and replace private papers detailing troop numbers and financial information for an ongoing operation on the Afghanistan border between English and Russian troops."

He extended his index finger and tapped it. "Two, you personally delivered those papers to the Russian Embassy. Three, you understand Russian. Four, you wear a close-cropped full-faced beard, very rare in Germany, but very common in western Russia at this time. Five, in The Lamb and Flag, you signalled the number two to the bartender using your index and middle fingers. Any purebred German, worth his salt, would use his thumb and index finger for such a gesture. A mistake like that could get you shot amongst the spy community."

Holmes waited for any reaction. When there was none, he continued. "All we're interested in is who you gave those papers to among the Russian staff, who your accomplice is inside the Government, and how long this has been going on."

"I will never speak. I have diplomatic immunity. You can't prove anything."

"To be honest, we don't need to prove anything. Once those forged papers reach Russia, the fallout will unveil the agents within their embassy, and they will deal with them accordingly. As for you, we have accepted your diplomatic immunity and you will be handed over to the German Embassy staff, who I'm sure will have many questions of their own."

At that moment the door opened and two tall, well-built men in ill-fitting suits entered. They had the square-jawed, blonde hair, blue-eyed look of Continental Germans. They took one look at Vanderbilt and stepped forward.

"Ah, they seem to have arrived," said Holmes.

Vanderbilt's eyes widened in fear and his mouth dropped open. He quickly thrust a hand toward his mouth. I was closest and threw out my hand, knocking whatever he'd held to the floor. It was a capsule of some sort. By now two burly men were holding Vanderbilt, but he kept lunging toward the object. Holmes reached down and picked it up. Sniffing it, he quickly turned his head away. Then he held it toward me and I took a careful smell as well. Bitter almonds. *Cyanide.* Vanderbilt had attempted to avoid our questions, but fortunately, he had been prevented.

"Well done, old chap," said Holmes.

***

It was an early morning a few days later that found Holmes and me perusing the papers whilst finishing off another sumptuous breakfast prepared by our wonderful landlady, Mrs. Hudson.

As I sipped my morning coffee, I mused out loud that the last word we had received from Mycroft was over three days previously.

"I'm still a little shocked at the identity of the German agent within the Home Office," I said.

Holmes looked up from his paper. "Well, the lad had a grudge against Her Majesty's Government."

"I can understand, given that his father died in Afghanistan. Losing one's father so early in life leaves scars, as it did young Atherton."

"Sadly, yes. He brooded on it for years. He wasn't working late to improve his prospects – he was copying classified documents, as I saw on his desk when we surprised him the other day. He'd managed to position himself somewhere that nobody would take any notice of him, learning the ins and outs of the Home Office and the Prime Minister's office, because nobody would think twice about talking around the person in charge of stationery. Such a person is always invisible in such an organisation."

"What will happen to him?"

"Hopefully he will only be treated as a dissident, and not charged with treason," Holmes said, "Well, that's to be hoped for anyway. His biggest mistake was falling in with Vanderbilt. Young minds are so impressionable, especially when they bear a grudge against authority. It will be for Her Majesty's authorities to decide." Holmes turned back to his newspaper.

I did the same and began to read *The Times,* coming across an article that smacked of a result of our recent adventure. The headline read *Russia Calls for Talks.* The article indicated that sources within the Government stated that the Russian ambassador to England had visited the Foreign Secretary to begin talks aimed at easing tensions on the Afghanistan-Indian border.

I peered across at Holmes and held the paper so he could read the headline. "It seems as if Mycroft's little ploy worked."

Holmes looked up from his own reading and smiled. "He will be pleased."

Our attention was diverted by the ring of the doorbell downstairs. A murmur of conversation filtered up to us, which gave me the impression that Mrs. Hudson knew our visitor, followed by a series of heavy footfalls on the steps that led from the entrance to our door.

"I believe we will be able to ask Mycroft all about it," Holmes said.

The door opened and admitted Mycroft with a slightly red face, but possessing a very pleased expression.

"Good morning," he said, removing his coat and placing it on a nearby chair. His eyes darted towards the open newspapers on our table and he nodded. "Ah, so you already know then. Remarkable that something so simple could have such an impact."

"What did you write in those notes?" I asked.

"Nothing ground-breaking," he said, "I merely doubled the number of ground troops, and added a second division of artillery to the figures that the Prime Minister was already requesting. His original numbers were drawn from the intelligence gathered on the Russian's available forces in Afghanistan, and I simply made it appear that England was prepared to overwhelm them with troops and engines of war."

"The bluff worked," said Holmes.

"Yes, yes, it did," Mycroft added, "All I really wanted was to paint a picture that said we were prepared for a protracted campaign. It's something that neither side would really want, and obviously, the Russians wanted it even less than us." He shook his head at the futility of it all. "Especially when one considers that there's nothing there. It's all just ground that even the locals don't really care that much about."

"And Vanderbilt?" I asked.

He nodded towards Holmes and said, "Ah, yes. Everything that my dear brother deduced was correct. The Germans were able to sweat a lot of information out of Mr. Vanderbilt. It seems he had been working under a false name with a false identity for quite a number of years. His real name was, in fact, Ivan Letorovski, born in St. Petersburg. He moved to Germany twenty years ago and worked his way into the diplomatic corps over that time."

"Do we have any agents of that type?" asked Holmes, a sly grin on his lips.

I knew he was having a dig at Mycroft, and his brother didn't disappoint. "If I told you that, you would end up in the same place as Vanderbilt," he said.

"And where is that?" I asked, a sudden prickle of fear rising up my spine.

"Ah," said Mycroft, "the Germans told me that once they had finished interrogating him, he was going to be returned to Germany." He paused for a moment. "In the diplomatic bag."

I winced. "That sounds nasty."

I leaned back and took down the great index volume to which he referred. Holmes balanced it on his knee, and his eyes moved slowly and lovingly over the record of old cases, mixed with the accumulated information of a lifetime.

"Voyage of the Gloria Scott," he read. "That was a bad business. I have some recollection that you made a record of it, Watson, though I was unable to congratulate you upon the result. Victor Lynch, the forger. Venomous lizard or gila. Remarkable case, that! Vittoria, the circus belle. Vanderbilt and the Yeggman. Vipers. Vigor, the Hammersmith wonder. Hullo! Hullo! Good old index. You can't beat it . . . ."

– Dr. John H. Watson and Sherlock Holmes
"The Adventure of the Sussex Vampire"

The Adventure of the Second Body

As the years drew on in the lives of myself and my greatest friend in the world, Mr. Sherlock Holmes, it seemed that the gaps between our visits grew as well. Holmes had retired in the early part of the century to a tiny country cottage near Beachy Head in Sussex. There he continued to enjoy his research into all things esoteric, whilst also keeping bees as a form of relaxation. I, however, maintained a life in the busy metropolis of London, though my days of medical practice were well behind me.

It was on one of the rare occasions that I journeyed south to call upon Holmes that he was once more dragged from his self-imposed retirement and into the world of crime.

We had been simply catching up over a sumptuous afternoon tea, with me showering Holmes with questions about past cases in an attempt to fill in some of the gaps in my notes. I still maintained a healthy number of papers relating to our past cases in my tin dispatch box. Though sadly, Holmes had taken it upon himself to put a stop to the publication of his tales, I hoped to at least compile as complete a record as possible, either to be published by myself or to leave them to a potential future biographer.

I could tell that Holmes knew of my intent, but rather than denigrating my exploits played along to his own amusement. He seemed to enjoy my company, and my questions sent him back to a more exciting time in both our lives.

It was during my questioning over the lost details of the mystery of the banker's wife, that a knock on the door broke our concentration. Holmes's housekeeper answered and within a few moments showed a rather young and slightly scruffy-looking constable into the parlour.

The young man just out of his teens, I could tell, held his helmet in his hands and glanced around with an expression of awe mixed with fright.

Holmes simply waited until the man composed himself enough to make his introductions.

"Hello, Sir, my name is Kendrick Kesson. Ah, Constable Kendrick Kesson, that is," the young policeman said.

After a moment, Holmes spoke. "Well met Constable. I assume you know that I am Sherlock Holmes." The man nodded. Holmes held out a hand to indicate me. "This is Doctor Watson."

Kesson's eyes lit up as he looked across at me. He nodded. "A pleasure Sir, I never dreamed I'd get to meet both of you. Together."

I nodded my thanks and let Holmes finish his assessment, which I assumed was coming. Kesson opened his mouth to speak, but Holmes held up a finger to silence him, before steepling his fingers before his face as he observed the young man.

"So, Constable, you have obviously come in a hurry. You have mud splashed on your boots and lower pants leg. Given the weather has been rather dry these last few days, I assume you were in a boggy field or a forested area which shielded the ground from direct sun."

The constable's mouth dropped open and he nodded.

"You have a small twig gripping the back of your coat and two dead, but wet leaves stuck there as well, so I can presume it was a forest."

Kesson nodded again. "Yes, Sir."

"Now, the darkness of the mud suggests a sizeable forest with a lot of leaf litter to break down. The only sizeable forests in the area are Westdean, which is hardly far enough for you to have worked up such a level of perspiration." Kesson's face remained impassive. "Or, perhaps you've travelled quite far from somewhere like Ashdown?" Again, the young constable's eyes widened in disbelief. "Yes. That's it. Ashdown forest." I saw a small smile come to Holmes's face. "You'd be from East Grinstead then? Working for Captain Neafsey?"

Kesson nodded, his mouth still agape and unable to form words.

I turned to Holmes. From his expression, I could tell that Holmes was holding back a slight chuckle. "Alright Holmes, how?"

"I do apologise to the both of you. Captain Jules Neafsey has done this before. He once worked with Lestrade and moved down to East Grinstead about ten years ago. He takes great delight in sending his junior constables to me when asking for my assistance. He confessed that it was to engender in them a sense of wonder at the art of deduction. In this case, that foreknowledge has simply helped me to ascertain the location of our next adventure together Watson."

***

The drive north took us through the edge of nearby Eastbourne, then Halsham and Uckfield before finally turning west towards Ashdown forest. Kesson's slightly nervous demeanour kept up throughout the journey, answering Holmes's questions with barely more than one or two words. He kept very quiet about the purpose of the trip until Holmes posed a taunting question to the young Constable.

"I do assume that the Captain and the Coroner will meet us at our destination?" Holmes asked, a wry grin on his face. "I haven't had the opportunity to talk with Dr. Grey for quite a while, it will be nice."

Kesson turned around, a puzzled expression on his face. "How did you know?"

I glanced at Holmes, the same question on my lips.

"Oh, that was simple. You have been charged to collect me. Therefore, this is a very irregular crime."

Even I nodded at that piece of deduction.

"We are heading to the midst of a great forest. Not the normal site for a robbery, or any form of fraud, therefore I can only assume there is a body of some sort to be examined."

"Amazing," said Kesson, turning back in a nick of time to realign the car with the road ahead, much to my relief.

Holmes continued, "If there's a body, therefore the Coroner, Dr. Grey, will need to be involved at some point."

As Kesson shook his head, I could see a smile grow across his features. A smile I had seen on many a young policeman's face as they became astonished at Holmes's abilities.

"You are simply astounding Mr. Holmes. Yes, yes, Dr. Grey will be there, and you are quite correct. A body was found deep in the forest. I won't say any more as the Captain expressed his wishes for you to form your own opinions once you arrive."

I became increasingly intrigued by these events and could see another publishable story building as we drove. After another mile,

Kesson turned north once more into a small rough trail and travelled for another minute or so before stopping next to two other cars.

We stepped out and found ourselves deep amidst a heavily wooded area. With only small dirt trails providing any navigable pathways.

Kesson indicated a winding pathway leading West. "Along this way gentlemen, please follow me."

The trail led deeper into the darker area of the woods, and within a few minutes, we found a large congregation of people milling about amongst the trees.

The two policemen were easily identified. One possessed a visible level of authority higher than the other. I assumed this was Captain Neafsey. Spying Holmes, he smiled and moved in our direction, thrusting a hand towards my good friend. As Holmes shook the Captain's hand, he introduced me and then asked about the goings-on. "Apologies if I've interrupted anything, but this one seemed intriguing enough to interest you." Neafsey then turned and indicated a balding man, hunched down with his back to us. "Dr. Grey should be able to fill you in on what we know so far."

As we approached the Doctor, I looked around and was surprised at the ages of the other folk scattered around. Only one other was an adult, while the rest, about ten in all, were all children.

Holmes leant in at that moment and spoke softly to me. "I have been wondering about the scout troupe, myself. Looking at the well-worn path through this area, it may be a regular trail that they follow."

Before I could say anything, we reached the Coroner, who stood to face us. A broad smile broke out across his face as he saw Holmes. They shook hands like old friends, and Holmes introduced me as another medical professional.

Dr. Grey had a warm, friendly handshake and spoke enthusiastically about all the adventures of my erstwhile friend that he had read in the Strand over the years. It was then I finally noticed the body, or at least what was left of the body.

Standing near an open grave, the Coroner moved away, to allow Holmes and I, full view of the object of their attention.

Lying, before us, about a foot below the level of the surrounding ground, was a dirt-stained skeleton. The skull and bones of the shoulders and upper chest had been uncovered, the rest still covered in dirt and forest mulch.

"The scouts found this earlier today, as they were on a trek through the forest. Some of the poor mites are still a little shell-shocked by the whole incident."

Glancing around at the young boys, I noticed a couple had that hollow look I'd seen on the faces of boys, not much older than they, coming off the field of battle. Death seen at a young age can have a profound effect on the mind.

Holmes's voice snapped my attention back to the skeleton. "Is this how it was found? Or did somebody unearth more of the body?"

"As far as I know, no one else has touched it."

"Good," Holmes said, stepping closer and hunkering down for a closer look. He pointed at the edge of the hole. "The sharp edge indicates that this was achieved with a shovel or more likely the square edge of a spade. It does leave one main question open."

"What's that?" I asked.

"Was the purpose of this to uncover the body or to bury something else?"

I was surprised by Holmes's question. "What do you mean?"

Standing and moving to the end of the shallow trench, Holmes pointed to the starting point, then at the skeleton. When I realised there was a vacant gap of some three feet, my own mind became confused.

"Good, you see it too then Watson?" said Holmes nodding at my perplexed expression. "Whoever dug this hole either didn't know the precise location of this body or didn't know there was a body here at all." He crouched once more and looked along the edges of the trench. "In fact, I would submit the latter."

"Why?"

Pointing along the edge of the small trench, Holmes indicated the line and made a small deviation to his right when his finger came in line with the skeleton. "This hole has all the hallmarks of someone digging a grave, but then finding it already occupied."

I stepped next to him and glanced along the same direction. Indeed, the trench deviated slightly to the right as it reached the skeleton.

"I would conjecture that our gravedigger began his excavation, possible to bury a body he had brought along given the dimensions of the hole at this point," Holmes said pointing nearest to us, "then unearthed the skeleton. Being intrigued, he continued to uncover more until either, time grew short or he was disturbed, possibly by the scout troupe. Which leaves ..."

His voice trailed off as he scanned the area, before moving deeper into the underbrush. I examined the ground myself, but could not see what Holmes had, so waited until a familiar tone of enlightenment echoed back. Dr. Grey, the Captain and I followed after Holmes and found him standing by a pile of dirt.

"What have you there Holmes?" I asked.

Holding a handful of dirt, he let it run through his fingers and examined the grains as they fell back to Earth. "This is freshly dug. The looseness of the dirt suggests it hasn't had time to settle and become hard-packed once more." He scanned the immediate area, glancing down at a disturbed patch of grass and what appeared to be two ruts leading up to it. "The body was dragged across to this area, then lay here while the culprit dug a new grave. There is a second body here Captain, you'll need to dig out both the skeleton and this one to give us more clews to go on." Holmes continued to walk around the area, murmuring to himself and studying the ground.

"Something disturbing you Holmes?"

As he walked, he thrust a finger up and waggled it in the air. "Yes, Watson, yes there is. This is far too much of a coincidence. An unknown person, chooses a secluded part of a forest, such as Ashdown, to bury a body, only to find another body already buried there." He stopped and stared at me for a moment. "What do you make of it?"

I thought for a moment. "Either a wild coincidence as you say, or this was the most logical spot to bury a body in this location."

"Or?"

I tried to read Holmes's face, but he retained that stoic almost smug look that I sometimes found irritating, but knew it also meant he was well advanced in the solution than I. "It's not the first."

Holmes smiled widely. "Well done Watson, well done."

The Captain standing nearby looked completely puzzled by our dialogue. He didn't possess the pseudo-telepathic link that Holmes and I did. "What? I have no idea what the two of you are talking about."

"You can tell him, Watson," Holmes said as he continued to examine the ground throughout the surrounding area.

I turned to the Captain and his confused constables and said, "This area is well suited for nefarious means. It is secluded, probably rarely visited, and the ground seems quite pliable and easily dug." Their puzzled looks remained, so I finished with, "It would make a prime location to hide a body, as we have already seen. Therefore, there are probably more buried around here."

As I finished, Holmes let out a familiar "Ah hah," from deeper in the trees. We hurried over and joined him as he pulled branches and leaves from another patch of ground. The fresh brown colour of the dirt had faded back to a deeper, less vibrant brown, but the unveiled patch was slightly elevated from the darker, more settled Earth around it.

"I do believe this area marks another shallow grave," Holmes said.

"Blimey," said the Captain, turning to his nearest Constable, "Dickerson, spades, now." The young policeman sped off without another word.

***

The next hour was a whirlwind of activity, with Holmes moving around the area, uncovering two more possible gravesites. Kesson and Dickerson followed him around and gently excavated the area until it was confirmed a body lay beneath each. The constables refrained from unearthing more than was required to determine there was a body buried there. The light was starting to fail, and Holmes wanted to concentrate on the number of sites rather than their contents at that stage.

As fascinating as the uncovering of the mini cemetery was, I did notice out of the corner of my eye that Captain Neafsey took it upon himself to speak once more with the Scout leader and within a few moments the scout troupe left the area and, I presume, headed back to their campsite.

I'm happy to admit that my interest began to wane, just as the light in the forest, it was then that Holmes joined me. "From what I can see Watson, that is all of them." I glanced around and realised there were now five sites that had been found to contain buried corpses.

"Good Lord Holmes. This is horrible. A serial killer I presume?"

"I'm not overly convinced of that Watson. I have asked Dr. Grey to oversee the exhumation of the corpses. I don't believe there is much more I can deduce from their interred state. The ones we have unearthed so far are similar in so much that they are laid out in the same posture. The age of the bodies differs by only weeks or months, giving me the impression that whoever has been using this area to dispose of these bodies has done so for possibly only the last year."

"And the skeleton?"

"Ah, now that's the most interesting. I think that is still the outlier and may be the clew that breaks this riddle apart."

I had no idea what he was on about but considered that to be a return to our time together many years previously. It was at that point that the Captain stepped over to us and suggested he drop us back at Holmes's house.

Holmes agreed but said he wanted to meet with Dr. Grey in the morning to examine the bodies. The Captain motioned for Dr. Grey to join us and explained Holmes's request.

"This many bodies will need to go to the hospital. I simply don't have the room at the morgue. We'll use one of the wards, there haven't been many patients of late, so it should be fine."

"Excellent," said Holmes. Turning to the Captain, he continued, "One thing troubles me Captain, and that is the skeleton. I don't have enough data and hope that an examination of all the bodies will confirm, but something tells me that there should be more poor unfortunates buried here of the same period as that skeleton."

Glancing at me he asked, "Watson, in your opinion, how long would you say that skeleton has lain here?"

I looked back at the first open grave, more as a way of focusing on the question rather than searching for information. "Given the lack of flesh and no obvious clothing, I'd have to say over ten years, possibly more."

Holmes nodded. "That was my deduction as well, which piques my interest even more."

***

The Captain drove us back to Holmes's cottage assuring us that the bodies would be extricated and moved to the hospital by morning. It had been my intent to head back to London the next day, but I decided to change my plans and stay until this little adventure played out.

That evening we enjoyed a sumptuous meal prepared by Holmes's housekeeper, and I had hoped to sit with Holmes and continue our discussions well into the evening, but he busied himself amongst his old files, while I wiled away the hours, until bedtime, reading a novel I'd brought with me.

It was over breakfast the next morning that I asked Holmes about his previous evening's studies. As he sipped his coffee he said, "Our initial idea that this was all to do with a serial killer disturbed me somewhat. I wanted to delve into my files to find an occurrence of any other killers that took means to hide their victims' bodies in such a remote location."

"What concerned you so?"

"Serial killers, by nature, act mostly on impulse. Those that find they need to hide their victims will do so in locations nearby, or highly accessible to them, sometimes by necessity, sometimes so that they can visit their handiwork. The presence of that many bodies in such a location means that there was a large amount of forethought put into the act of murder and disposal of the corpses."

"Perhaps the perpetrator is a local? And the forest is quite close to their home. That would solve both problems."

Holmes thought about my statement for a moment. "That could be it, I suppose. We will need to establish the identity of the victims or at least the area of their origin."

I started to speak again when the phone tingled in the other room. Holmes almost leapt to his feet and hurried to answer. I followed, quite intrigued by his determination to hear from the caller.

The conversation was rather short but consisted of many nods and affirmative mutterings from Holmes. Within a few moments, he hung up. Turning to me, I could see a glint in his eye and a wry smile on his face. I was confused.

"Watson. The game is indeed afoot."

***

It was once we had driven North through the Sussex countryside and onto the growing town of East Grinstead, and finally entered the Hospital that Holmes's excitement began to make sense to me.

As he had suggested, Dr. Grey had sequestered an entire ward to house the unearthed bodies from the forest graveyard. There were six in all. It turned out another skeleton had been uncovered as part of the constables' excavations the previous evening. The other four bodies were all much more intact and to Holmes's earlier observation possibly only up to twelve months old.

My eyes scanned the bodies and skeletons and finally fell upon the object of Holmes's current scrutiny. Although the man's clothes were filthy with the dirt from his unchosen gravesite, I could tell that he wore the deep blue, almost black, uniform of a London policeman. I gasped with the realisation. Suddenly, what had started as a possible localised serial killer was now a case that would attract a much higher level of scrutiny from Scotland Yard.

I noticed Holmes take out his glass and begin a close examination of the policeman and stepped over to observe. A stern voice from behind, caused both of us to stand and glance around.

"I would much prefer if you would leave these bodies well alone."

At the doorway to the ward stood a tall, well-built man in a day suit. The stern look on his face, and the way he stood, betrayed his profession. A smaller man in a constable's uniform stood behind him, his expression was less grim and more full of wonder. A reaction to the display before him, I supposed.

Captain Neafsey stepped between the plains clothed policeman and the bodies. "And you are Sir?"

A greeting card was thrust in Neafsey's direction. "Inspector Jackson. Scotland Yard. I have been sent to take over this investigation."

"On whose authority?"

"Deputy Commissioner Andrew Black. London Bureau."

Neafsey nodded, and I noticed a wry grin come to his face. "Ah, Blackey aye? We go way back, I'll have a word with him later then and sort out the lines of authority."

"And why would this concern you?"

"I am Captain Neafsey. Commander of the local precinct. Until these bodies are identified, this is still my case."

The two policemen locked eyes for a moment. The tension building between them, until Jackson finally spoke. "Understood, Sir." He indicated Holmes. "And why are these civilians here?"

"This is Mr. Sherlock Holmes and Doctor John Watson. They are helping with this investigation and have already provided undeniable assistance."

"Doctor Watson is also assisting me with the preliminary autopsy examinations," piped up Dr. Grey, winking at me as I glanced in his direction. I smiled at the wily old country Doctor's quick thinking.

Jackson looked from face to face, scrutinising each in turn before relaxing slightly. "Fine. Then you can bring me up to speed on what has occurred." He pointed at the dead policeman, starting with him.

Holmes and I backed away from the corpse as Jackson approached. It was then that the young constable accompanying him had his first good look at the body. I expected a touch of horror, but instead, his entire body seemed to deflate as his eyes fell on the dead man's face.

"Oh, God, that's Smithy," he said.

"Out with it man, who's Smithy?" asked Jackson.

The young constable stepped up to the gurney with the policeman's body and stared down at what seemed to be a close friend. "Albert Smith. We signed up together. Smithy was a bit older than me, and a bit more streetwise. He grew up in the East End, so it was only natural they give him that beat." He shook his head in sorrow. "Last I knew he'd gone missing. About a month ago. He'd done it before though, usually turned up again after a week or two. Pissed out of his brain. The Sergeant didn't really care. He'd dock him his pay for the time and then put him back to work. Apart from his drinking, Smithy was a good policeman. Knew the East End docks like the back of his hand."

"Interesting way of running your force up there in London," said Neafsey, his statement directed at Jackson who harrumphed in reply.

"Well that leaves me to wonder then," said Holmes, "Whether we have another killer running around the East End or is this something far more insidious." He turned to Dr. Grey. "Considering this case is still in your hands, good Doctor, I would think it an appropriate time to begin a deeper investigation into the causes of death."

Doctor Grey nodded then spoke to me. "It may speed things up if you could examine the skeletons first, then join me once I've finished with the first couple of fresher bodies."

I nodded and moved across to claim an apron and some gloves before stepping over to the first of the skeletons. Holmes joined me, I thought in part to avoid the tension exhibited between Jackson and Neafsey, but he mentioned in passing that the crux of the matter lay, not with the fresher bodies, but with the older.

To begin I simply stood and examined the remains with my eyes, murmuring some audible notes as I went. "Male. Approximately five feet eight inches tall. Solid frame given the width of the shoulders." There wasn't much else left of the body. The skin and flesh had rotted away, along with the clothing. The skeletal junctures were still in place, but in moving the body it seemed that the constables had caused them to break as one of the arms and a leg lay separated from the main frame.

As I examined the arm I noticed the first peculiarity about the skeleton. All of the distal phalanges were missing. I quickly checked the hand on the attached arm. The same. I turned and called to Kesson to join us. As he approached I pointed to the hand and asked, "Did you find any free bones in the grave? The fingertips are missing."

Kesson's eyes grew wide as he studied the bones, but then he shook his head. "Not that I know of. We can go back out and look though. Take a couple of hours."

Meanwhile, Holmes had retrieved a pair of gloves and was studying the ends of the fingers with his glass. "What do you make of this Watson?" I leaned in and stared at the magnified ends of the finger joints. Small scrapes ran along a couple of the knucklebones.

"I don't know, what do you think?"

"We'll check the other skeleton, but those marks may be consistent with a common carpenter's chisel." He placed the free arm down and picked up the other, checking each middle phalange, and the proximal on the thumb. Again, a couple had distinct score marks across the knuckle, as if something sharp had gouged the surface.

"Why would they cut off the fingertips?"

"To make future identification of the corpse almost impossible, or perhaps as a way of claiming a bounty, or even as a token to add to a collection."

I screwed my face up at the last suggestion. "Oh, that's disturbing."

"Quite so, but it gives us a starting point." Holmes led me by the arm to the second skeleton and we immediately examined the fingers.

"It's the same," I gasped.

"Excellent," said Holmes. "A strong clew." A smile grew on his face, as confusion grew on my own.

"Care to enlighten me?"

"From your observations, you believe these corpses to be around ten years in the ground, yes?" I nodded. "Good. So, we are looking for someone who operated around that time, and perhaps had a signature such as the removal of the fingertips." I nodded again.

"Someone like Mad Dog Murgatroyd?" said a voice from behind us. We turned to find Captain Neafsey looking at the skeletons, with a wry grin on his face.

"Who?" I asked.

"Yes," said Holmes, "James Mad Dog Murgatroyd. He was put away about eight years ago. Hanged not long afterwards, just before the end of the war. His execution was expedited to free up space in Wandsworth, I think."

Neafsey nodded. "Oh, yeah, that it was. The Yard felt that we were going to get a few coming back from Europe that might go straight to Wandsworth, so anybody that wasn't in for a long time was shuffled off, so to say." The Captain stepped around the gurney and approached the left-hand side of the skeleton. "Now, if this is the work of Mad Dog, there's one more piece of evidence to prove it." Motioning for Holmes to join him and smiling at me, he continued. "If you would be so kind Doctor, could you turn this poor unfortunate on his right-hand side?"

As I did so, Neafsey pointed at the skeleton's rib cage and said, "There, do you see it Holmes?" Holmes nodded. I strained to see and was surprised by a pair of deep gouges on the edges of the fifth and sixth rib bones on the skeleton's left-hand side."

"He was a vicious blighter was old Mad Dog. Used to carry around a nine-inch-long dagger, with a one-inch wide blade. Favourite method of attack was a sharp thrust up into the heart from behind. He was left-handed too, made it so much easier for him."

"I actually read the Coroner's reports of the day when Murgatroyd was arrested. He was consistent and quite accurate, each victim had identical scoring on the ribs. Made it so much easier to convict him." Holmes looked across to the first skeleton. "Now, if you are correct Captain, as I presume you are." Moving across to the first skeleton, he let the last word hang, before carefully manoeuvring the corpse onto its right side. "Ah, hah." I hurried across to join Holmes and was greeted with a similar set of score marks on the rib cage. "What say you, Watson?"

I nodded. "Both remains exhibit almost identical injuries. From these marks, I would surmise that a sharp, wide-bladed instrument was driven upwards between the ribs and into the victim's heart. Death would have been virtually instantaneous." Turning to look across at Dr. Grey, I muttered, "Do the modern victims bear the same wounds?"

Holmes, Neafsey and I joined Dr. Grey as he examined the body of the unfortunate Smithy. The policeman's remains seemed fairly intact. No fingertips were missing, and there was no evidence of death by knife wound. Instead, Dr. Grey pointed to severe discolouration and bruising around the man's neck.

"Strangulation?" I asked.

He nodded. "It would seem so Doctor."

"Have you found similar on the other victims?" asked Holmes.

Dr. Grey nodded and pointed to the nearest body. A rather pudgy man in his early fifties. "Yes. Notice the severe bruising on the throat of that man. Our perpetrator was incredibly powerful, with large hands, and with what seems to be an almost animalistic delight in inflicting harm."

"Why would you say that?" I asked.

"The large man's windpipe was crushed, and there are several bruises on the back of his head. He was either forced against a wall as he was strangled, or his head was hammered to engender his compliance in the act. The strangler kept the pressure up well after the man was dead, hence the damage to the internals of the throat."

"But it ain't Mad Dog," said Neafsey, "It wasn't the way he'd do it, plus he was hanged back in 17, so not a copycat either."

Holmes nodded, but I could tell the wheels of his mind were spinning at a fast rate. He stood, staring at the corpses arrayed before him, a hand resting under his chin with one finger extended up his cheek. Neafsey stared at him for a moment, expecting a comment, but when none was forthcoming wandered away. I knew better than to break his concentration and did the same.

***

Several hours later, once we had finished a wonderful meal and were settled in Holmes's parlour, he with a pipe and me with a cigar, that I finally decided to ask his thoughts.

"Holmes, you've been withdrawn and pondering on this case since this morning. What is worrying you so?"

He drew deep on his pipe, then blew out a deliberately long and slow cloud of white smoke. "The facts aren't fitting into the narrative. The new bodies were found over forty miles from their supposed origin. We know this from the lone policeman, who still being in uniform was possibly snatched while on duty in the East End. We will have to wait for the identities of the other three before confirming that assumption." He took the pipe from his mouth and used the stem to punctuate his points. "Only someone who has applied a level of premeditation to their murderous activities would use such a remote location for disposal. But, the style of death indicates someone with an almost palpable psychosis entrenched in their mind." I nodded in agreement. The level of aggression was disturbing. "As to the two older bodies, and I am confident there will be more if the Captain continues to search, they are the end result of a concerted effort at hiding the evidence of crime. Our probable perpetrator, this Murgatroyd, was a known factor, with a repeatable modus operandi, which resulted in his own demise. I presume these bodies were from his work as an enforcer with the Hoxton Mob."

He suddenly rose and moved to a nearby bookcase, extracted a thick volume and walked to a nearby table. I jumped up, quite intrigued and stood nearby as he opened the book. It was a series of news clippings and annotations in Holmes's own spidery scrawl, about the goings-on of gangs and mobs in London. I hadn't seen these pages before and realised they were part of Holmes's later researches and studies.

"This, Watson is a volume of information I've been building that concerns the growth and activities of criminal gangs in London and the surrounding areas. It seems that since the end of the war, the number of recruits has grown with the returning soldiers, and the boldness of activities is increasing as well. As we enter deeper into the new decade, I believe it will only increase further. These gangs have been building in confidence in line with the activities of their spiritual brothers in the United States, ever since prohibition began."

"That seems to be a longbow you're drawing there, Holmes."

He stopped, look at me with a wry smile, before turning back to the tome on the table. Flipping through several pages, he stopped at one with the name Hoxton Mob written boldly across the top. Holmes pointed to a grainy photograph, clipped from a newspaper, at the top of the page. The photograph featured a bald man, in a suit, being helped into a black car. His helpers had been removed by Holmes's clipping.

"This is Ken Porritt, also known as Curly." I chuckled, as the nickname was an allusion to his obvious lack of hair. "Yes, it's cause he's bald, very dry humour these thugs have." Further below were two names, but no photographs. "Porritt has two known lieutenants, Rene Gibbison and Herbert Marginzer. Now, this gang became quite prominent across the East End before and during the early part of the war. They concentrate on running illegal betting rings out of few local pubs, and of course at some of the nearer racecourses."

"I'm assuming then that Murgatroyd was used to reclaim debts, or at least close them out anyway."

"Precisely, he was a little too enthusiastic, shall we say, and hence why he was eventually hanged."

"That perhaps explains the older bodies, but what of the newer ones?"

"And that has been puzzling me also. I dislike the idea of a random killer utilizing the same dumping ground as an earlier murderer out of pure coincidence, especially considering the size of Ashdown forest. For now, I'd like to believe that our new man must have had prior knowledge and perhaps is working in concert with our long-gone Murgatroyd, almost unwittingly."

"You believe he may be employed by the Hoxton Gang?"

Holmes held up a single finger. "That is one theory."

"The open grave then?"

He held up a second finger. "And that brings us to another set of theories. Our mystery man's purpose was to bury a body. He unearthed a second body, but instead of covering it up again, he left it alone." He stood and began to pace around the room. "Was that act on purpose? If so, why? If he were working for the Hoxton Gang, he would not wish to draw attention to his activities." Holmes stopped and stared at me, a wry grin on his face, then stepped back to the table, flipping over several pages until another account of a London gang was shown. "What if our perpetrator wanted that second body to be found? What if he wanted to draw the authorities to that site so that they would end up unearthing the other victims?"

"But why? I'll admit that in hindsight the newer graves were not very well camouflaged, but surely a murderer would wish to remain hidden."

"Yes, but what if this new murderer was working in competition to the original users of that dumping ground?" Holmes pointed at the page before us. It was similar to the Hoxton Mob page but was headed with the name Sabini Gang. A similar photograph sat at the top of the page; the name Charles Sabini written beneath it. "Then there may be more to this whole adventure."

***

The next morning as I entered the kitchen in search of breakfast, I found Holmes sat in the corner of the parlour, listening intently to a conversation on his phone. I refrained from questioning him out of respect and instead helped myself to the simple fare prepared by the housekeeper.

Luckily, there was coffee, toast, marmalade and the morning's paper. Resigning myself to wait until Holmes joined me, I simply ate and read the news. I was slightly relieved to find that nothing of our grotesque find had found its way to any local reporter's ear. I was sure that Holmes would be of the same opinion.

The local affairs reported in the paper were of a very trivial nature, which made for a much lighter read than those generally reported by the London press. I had almost finished the whole thing when Holmes finally joined me at the table.

He quickly poured himself some coffee and buttered some toast. Before I could inquire about his phone call, he said, "I presume you are heading back to London today?"

To be honest I hadn't even thought that far ahead. I had no train ticket booked as I was under no pressure to return. "I am willing to stay with you whilst this adventure is still underway," I answered.

"Oh, that's precisely why I asked. I just spoke with Neafsey, it seems that our Inspector Jackson has returned to London, with three corpses in tow, including the poor unfortunate policeman. The others will be ferried North during the day. I then made a phone call to a former colleague of Lestrade's. Chief Inspector Sheldon Wengert. He is now charged with keeping an eye on the criminal gangs running

105

loose around London. I have arranged to meet with him later this afternoon."

I almost spluttered out my mouthful of coffee. "You're going to London?"

"Oh, yes, that's why I asked whether you planned to leave today. I thought we could journey together, and I was hoping I could reside in your abode tonight, and possibly tomorrow night."

"Well, of course, that would never be a problem. I just didn't realise you meant to leave almost this minute."

"Oh, there's no need for such haste," he said taking a sip of coffee before continuing, "The train from Brighton doesn't leave for another hour."

It was then I noticed that Holmes was already dressed ready to leave the house. I was still arrayed in my pyjamas and dressing gown. "Well in that case." I quickly downed my coffee and left to pack my bags.

***

Many hours later we were introduced to Chief Inspector Shelden Wengert, a tall slender man with blonde hair and prominent cheekbones. He did not look like a policeman in any way, which I assume helped him no end if he was required to assume an undercover identity.

Greeting us both with obvious enthusiasm, but holding his eagerness in check, he expressed his desire to work with us in any small way possible. It was obvious that our reputation had preceded us, a common occurrence especially since Holmes's retirement from active investigations.

"Have you heard about the six bodies found in Ashdown Forest?" Holmes asked.

Wengert nodded. "Yes, the news went through the Yard like wildfire. Jackson's handling that isn't he?" We nodded in unison. "Hmmm. Strange fellow. Very determined." I stifled a small chuckle. "Where do I fit in then?"

"Ah, we have one major clew that needs to be confirmed. The two skeletons show signs of death consistent with the activities of a local gang soldier from about ten years ago."

A shocked expression ran across Wengert's face. "Do you know who?"

"Yes, James Murgatroyd."

"Mad Dog? Good Lord. He was hanged four years ago wasn't he?" Spent most of the war in Wandsworth."

"That's our understanding."

A broad smile crossed Wengert's face. "I heard there were six bodies found, you mentioned two, you can't believe Murgatroyd had anything to do with it? I didn't see him hang, but I know some who did."

"No, no. The cause of death is completely different. My theory, and it's only a theory at this stage, is that another person became aware of Murgatroyd's dumping ground and used it for his own purposes."

"Interesting. I still don't see why I'm important here."

"I wanted to investigate the growing gang activities in London since the end of the war."

"Ah, yes, precisely why I have my own team."

"Mostly I wanted to find out any recent activity amongst the Hoxton Mob or their contemporaries."

Smiling, Wengert led us to a large map of London. Several areas had been marked with different coloured pens. Two small areas were shown in the East End of the City of London, with the adjacent borders coloured in a thicker amount of ink. The Chief Inspector pointed at it. "The Hoxton Mob and the Sabini Gang both lay claim to this disputed area. There have been some assaults, arson and even a murder or two in that area over the last two years."

"Surely you've made a large number of arrests then?" I said.

"Ah, that's the main problem." Wengert's smile slid from his face, as he became more serious. "It's amazing how few witnesses one finds in these matters. And those that come forward shut up or disappear before a trial can be held."

"What about the local bobbies? Do they keep a close eye on things?"

"Yes. Yes, they do, but a lot of them remain tight-lipped as well. We have another team working on that worrying little aspect."

"What about Constable Albert Smith? He was one of the first bodies we found."

Wengert's face lit up in surprise. "Smithy, aye? Now that is interesting. He was high on the list of suspicious constables. I didn't even realise he'd disappeared, but again that's not my area. I'll have to check with the other team."

"What about the soldiers? Are there any in the Hoxton Mob that would be able to, say, strangle a man with his bare hands?"

The policeman laughed. "Oh, most of them. These soldiers or enforcers are chosen for their particularly large build. Though most prefer to resort to their fists or other weapons. For the most part, murder is bad for business. The soldiers' duty is to act as a warning system to the populace."

"I assume the Sabini Gang has a similar predilection for well-built enforcers?"

"Yes. Again, they tend to only concentrate on threats and intimidation. Any violence is generally done through the use of cutthroat razors or knives. Sort of a signature to maintain their posture." He thought for a moment. "Murgatroyd was an interesting case, if I remember correctly, he overstepped the mark on several occasions. It was his boss that finally set him up, I believe, though it was never proven just assumed."

"Interesting," said Holmes, "That's very interesting."

***

Departing Scotland Yard, we caught a cab back to my abode and I settled Holmes into the spare bedroom that my housekeeper had prepared. I took the liberty of phoning her earlier in the day to give her plenty of notice.

I gave Holmes the grand tour of the place and left him to his devices, while I bathed and retired to the parlour for a late afternoon cigar and perusal of any items of mail that had arrived in my absence.

When my housekeeper informed me that dinner would be soon, I realised that Holmes hadn't made an appearance and, presuming him to have fallen asleep, went to his room to wake him. To my surprise the room was empty, the bed made and unused, except for a small depression where Holmes had obviously sat whilst putting on his shoes.

I smiled to myself as memories of old times flooded my mind. He may have retired, but when the smell of an adventure reached his nostrils there was no stopping him.

After a wonderful repast, I once again returned to the parlour to read the papers and write up some notes surrounding our current endeavour, with the full hope that Holmes would fill me in on any future developments. I knew that I wouldn't be able to publish anything but held out hope that I would find a suitable candidate to carry on in my future absence.

I obviously fell asleep in my chair and was shocked awake as footsteps plodded on the wooden floor into the parlour. My eyes fell on the slightly bedraggled figure before me, fear rising within me before I realised it was Sherlock Holmes. "Good Lord, Holmes, you look dreadful." His face looked sunken and sallow, and his normally tall frame stooped from fatigue.

"I do apologise Watson. I wish this was a disguise, but I am getting old and quite unused to traipsing all across this large metropolis like my younger self once did." I rang the bell, mindful of the late hour, but hopeful that my housekeeper had yet to retire. Holmes took a chair near mine and visibly deflated into it.

I waited until he regained his composure before pressing him for details. "Well, was the effort at least worth it?"

He glanced over and smiled. "Oh, yes, it was Watson, it definitely was." He sat up just as my housekeeper entered. I asked for coffee and brandy. She took one look at Holmes and nodded. Holmes waited until she left before sitting a little more upright and relating his tale.

"Watson, my first stop was to an old friend that served as a guard at Wandsworth up until recently. I plied him with questions concerning Murgatroyd. His actions in prison. His cellmates. His acquaintances. Any enemies he may have had. He was very forthcoming and spun a very intriguing story about this Mad Dog, as he was known."

"Yes?" I said, sitting up, my own interest rising.

"Mad Dog Murgatroyd was indeed extremely upset with his employers. It was well known through Wandsworth that he felt stitched up. The boss wanted a few people disappeared, so Murgatroyd murdered and buried them in Ashford Forest. My contact reckons that he only told a couple of people the actual location."

"Did you find out any of their names?"

Holmes smiled, "Oh, yes, yes I did. And one of them left Wandsworth several months ago and now works in the East End, for one of the gangs."

"Not the Hoxton Mob?"

"No. The Sabini Gang. For one of the Lieutenants. That's why I'm so tired and grimy, I spent a couple of hours wandering around the Sabini's territory looking for our possible culprit."

"And?"

"Oh, I found him. A huge man. With massive hands. And from the way he dealt with several people over that time, quite the temper."

It was then that my housekeeper returned with the coffee and brandy. I poured us both a good shot of both, and as Holmes was reviving himself asked, "Where does that leave us?"

"I think once we've finished this wonderful coffee and brandy, and retired for a well-rested night, we can contact the Chief Inspector and see where that leads us."

I was relieved, I half expected Holmes to be off again into the night to confront this potential murderer, but as it seemed age had slight wearied him and made him more mindful of his own limitations.

When I looked back I realised he'd fallen asleep, with his head resting on his breast. Another reminder of days gone past.

***

The following morning was a whirlwind of activity once Holmes's plans were enacted.

Upon awakening, I strode into the parlour to find it now empty. I presumed that Holmes had moved to his room at some stage during the night, only to be taken by surprise when I found him at the kitchen table taking some breakfast, whilst chatting amiably with my housekeeper.

As I sat and partook of my own breakfast, Holmes informed me that our first port of call would be back to see Wengert to take him through the information gathered the previous night. We were given entry purely through the officer on the front desk's recognition of Holmes and me. A young policeman was called to escort us to Wengert, it turned out to be Constable Green, whom we'd met with Jackson. Holmes and he chatted amiably during our walk, with Holmes stopping our progress for a moment to have a more in-depth conversation with Green before we reached Wengert's rooms. I couldn't hear what was discussed but presumed Holmes wanted to know more details about Jackson's investigation.

"You're talking about Duncan Hullar? He's just a minor soldier in the Sabini Gang, works Raymond Mowler's part of the crew, who himself is just a minor lieutenant. They aren't even the main part of Sabini's organisation," Wengert said as Holmes laid out his information.

"And that seems to be perfect for what they have planned."

Wengert moved across to his board with the Sabini Gang's names and hierarchy mapped out. He wrote Hullar's name well below Mowler's, stepped back and studied it, glancing across at the Hoxton Mob board from time to time.

"And you're old friend places Hullar in Wandsworth at the same time as Murgatroyd?"

"Yes, in fact, they shared a cell for a period of three months, before Murgatroyd was moved into isolation in the weeks before his execution. I feel that he would have been at his lowest point at that time and would have vented out as much information about the Hoxton Mob as he could, to all and sundry."

"And that's where Hullar comes into it?"

"Yes. Hullar was released only a year ago. He had been imprisoned for a violent assault, that sort of record would have left him with very few options when he was released."

"Wouldn't he have used his information to gain a higher-level position in the Hoxton Mob?"

"Or, on Murgatroyd's insistence, he used that information to wangle his way into an opposing gang."

Wengert nodded, "Yes, that makes sense. Even though there is an uneasy peace, these gangs wait for the chance to tear pieces out of each other and gain more territory." He glanced around at Holmes. "You want to talk with Raymond Mowler?"

"Oh, I believe we should try to go to the top of the organisation. If nothing the fact we have uncovered this information will unsettle Mr. Charles Sabini and make him think harder before attempting anything like this in the future."

A smile grew across Wengert's face and he nodded. "If I know Charles Sabini, he will be furious. This could be quite interesting."

***

In my long experience walking in the shadow of Sherlock Holmes, I had been exposed to many a criminal element, and at times been fearful for my life. That afternoon, however, was something completely different.

After the great war ended, a void remained in London. A void created by the removal of so many good young men, also an economic void caused by the closure of many businesses due to their owners and employees going off to war, and many not returning. And a more recent void triggered by the number of men and women, who had been diverted to the cause of war, finding themselves suddenly unemployed while the remaining businesses realigned their efforts back to normal service.

As in nature, humankind abhors a vacuum, and that void was quickly filled with a new style of business. One based on various nefarious activities. Gambling, alcohol, drugs, sex, in a more coordinated and focused way than prior to the war itself.

Criminals banded together into gangs to run these new enterprises. The heads of each taking on almost the same allure as movie stars.

One of the most notorious in London was the Sabini Gang, whose leader, Charles Sabini, had grown up in the East End and now ran several nightclubs and oversaw a large number of bookmakers at racecourses across the south of England.

Wengert informed us that, even though Scotland Yard knew much of what the gangs were up to, there was an uneasy accord in place. The Yard's forces had been decimated by the war, and they were still recruiting. Much slower than the gangs it seemed, so a level of tolerance was applied that dictated where the gangs could operate.

I personally didn't like the idea that criminal gangs were basically operating unhindered in my beloved London, but I understood the pragmatic approach that the Yard took.

It was to one of Sabini's nightclubs that Chief Inspector Wengert took Holmes and me. It was only early afternoon, but the place was a hive of activity as preparations for the evening were underway.

The large man on the door knew Wengert and after a quiet word was sent deep into the establishment, we were led to a large smokey room in the back that operated as Charles Sabini's personal office.

I was surprised, as Sabini's reputation hinted at the glamourous, but he was a simple-looking man, albeit well built from the cut of his modest dark suit. The man standing behind and to his right was similarly dressed. I assumed this was his assistant or a bodyguard.

As we entered, Sabini remained seated, but obviously knew Wengert quite well. "Chief Inspector, to what do I owe this pleasure?"

"Thank you for seeing us at such short notice Mr. Sabini. May I introduce my companions."

Sabini cut him off, looked us up and down and said, "Good lord, Sherlock 'olmes and Dr. John Watson, I presume."

Holmes replied, "I'm impressed. I thought the years of my absence would have dulled any recognition."

"It's the 'at and coat, Sir. I 'ave also read every single adventure that Dr. Watson 'ad published in the Strand magazine. I'm quite the fan you known." He leaned back in this chair and took a deep draw cigar, blowing out a pall of smoke in one long languid release. "What can I do for one of my actual 'eroes?"

"I think it might be more of a question about what we can do for you," Holmes said.

"Oh, yeah, and what's that then?"

"The body of a policeman was found in a shallow grave down south in a very remote forest."

A puzzled expression crossed Sabini's face. "And that 'as what exactly to do with me?"

"The policeman's beat was around this area, and across into Finsbury, Hackney and sometimes Hoxton."

I watched Holmes's eyes glued to Sabini's face. I glanced across at the gangster, hoping to see what Holmes sought. Sabini simply shrugged. "Yeah, lots of coppers on that beat, what of it?"

"This one was taking money from one of your lieutenants. Mowler I think his name was."

"I'd 'ate to tell you 'ow often that 'appens." Sabini held his hands out to emphasise his innocence. "It's the way of the game, isn't it? We keep our bobbies 'appy, and they don't make too many waves for us." He glanced at Wengert. "Isn't that right Chief Inspector?"

"We have an agreement, yes. We turn a blind eye, also yes, but not when you murder our constables."

"Woah, woah, murder? You can't blame my organisation for murder."

Holmes piped up. "You have a Duncan Hullar working for you? Do you not?"

Sabini grimaced and spoke towards one of his assistants standing nearby. The assistant nodded and whispered back. A surprised expression broke out on Sabini's face. He smiled and glanced back at us. "It seems I do. 'e just so 'appens to work for Mowler." His face then turned sour. "'ere, what are you suggesting? Mowler put 'im up to it?"

"Perhaps. I don't suppose we could talk with this Huller?"

Shrugging, Sabini picked up his phone, dialled a number and waited. "Doris, can you track down Mowler and tell 'im he needs to be 'ere now and to bring Duncan Huller. Yes, tell 'im I said now." I noticed Sabini lose the thick accent when pronouncing Huller's name. He replaced the receiver and held out his hands. "Well, we'll see won't we."

It took only ten minutes for Raymond Mowler, with Duncan Huller in tow, to enter Sabini's office. During that time Holmes and I were plied with all sorts of questions about our adventures over the years. For the most part, Holmes simply smiled and allowed me to answer those that pertained to points of clarification. Several though were aimed at the deductive methods applied by Holmes and seemed to have relevance to our current situation. I kept an eye on Holmes and realised he was enjoying the intellectual jousting with Sabini.

When Mowler and Huller entered, I was amazed. As had been described to me already, Huller was a large man, towering well above six foot six inches. I glanced at his hands and realised they were of such a size that they could easily surround a man's throat.

Sabini watched the two men enter and held up a hand as Mowler began to ask a question. "All in good time, Raymond. Mr. 'olmes and Chief Inspector Wengert 'ere 'ave some concerns about a particular Bobbie that's come to some 'arm."

"A Bobbie? We don't do nothing to no bobbies. That's bad for business ain't it?" answered Mowler.

"I've already alluded to that point of view, but a dead body's a dead body and the Yard don't like no dead bobbies."

"Who was it?"

"Constable Albert Smith. Known as Smithy. Been around these parts for years," said Wengert.

"According to one of my sources, he was receiving monies from both the Sabini Gang and the Hoxton Mob. Sort of playing both sides," said Holmes.

"Then it must 'ave been the 'oxtons," said Sabini, "Case closed. Good night."

Holmes smiled. "You would think, wouldn't you? Especially when the policeman's body was found in a shallow grave, in an area of Ashdown Forest that was previously used by a Hoxton Mob enforcer."

Sabini held his hands out in surprise, he glanced at Wengert. "Again, case closed." He reached over to pick up the phone. "I can call Curly Porritt for you if you like. 'e'd be just as fascinated as me, possibly a bit more."

Holmes held up his hand. "There are a few more interesting points that need to be said."

Removing his hand from the phone, but keeping his eyes fixed on Holmes's face, Sabini leaned back in his chair. "Go on then."

"There were other bodies in that location. Five more in all. Two were over ten years old, but three were just as recent as the

115

unfortunate policeman. All men. All strangled. By someone with larger than normal hands and incredible strength."

That's when I saw it, and I could tell that Holmes saw it as well. Sabini's eyes flashed to the right, in Hullar's direction. I glanced at Hullar and saw his face take on a worried look.

"According to one of my sources, James Murgatroyd, who was responsible for the older bodies and worked for the Hoxton Mob, shared a cell with a young man for several months just before his death. Murgatroyd instilled in that young man a hatred for the Hoxton Mob, and information about the dumping ground."

Hullar began to grow fidgety as if he would have preferred to be anywhere else other than that room at that point in time.

"That man, I have been told, and after following him around the East End last night, can truly believe he would be capable of such violence, is your soldier Duncan Hullar." Holmes turned and stared straight at Hullar. The man's face dropped in abject horror.

"No. I never." He stared at Sabini, his eyes pleading for support or an alibi. Instead, he received only accusations.

"Is that true Hullar?" Sabini asked. He looked at Mowler. "Raymond 'ave you brought a killer into my organisation?" Then back at Hullar. "Well, what 'ave you to say?"

"You, you told me to kill 'im. I only done it on your orders."

"Oh, come now," he turned towards Wengert, ignoring Hullar's stare, "You know me Chief Inspector, I'm an 'onest businessman. I wouldn't do nothing like that."

I could tell Wengert struggled to contain his mirth at the suggestion, but Holmes added more. "Given that these bodies were placed in a location once used by James Murgatroyd, and the last body was located near a well-used pathway, I put it to you, Sir, that by your orders and Hullar's actions you were trying to implicate the Hoxton Mob as a way of undermining them and gaining territory."

It was Sabini's turn to laugh. "Nonsense. I'd never do that sort of thing. We've got an understanding, the 'oxton boys and me." He glanced back at Hullar. "I don't know what this blighter's been up to, but it 'ad nothing to do with me. If you want 'im Chief Inspector, then take 'im with you."

It was then that everything went crazy.

Hullar howled in rage at Sabini. His face turned to pure frenzy. He stepped forward and brought up those massive hands, grabbing Sabini around the neck and dragging him from his chair before anyone could react. Sabini was thrust against the wall, gasping for air as the tall man crushed his throat.

Mowler leapt at Huller, but a simple shrug saw him thrown aside. Sabini's assistant ran from the room. I presumed he went for help, but it could have been out of simple self-preservation. Wengert moved forward to grab at Huller, but received an elbow to the midriff, knocking the wind from his lungs.

Out of pure instinct, Holmes and I reached for our pistols, but we both realised that those days were gone, and we hadn't brought them with us.

It was the sudden shock of a gunshot in that small room, that stopped us in our tracks. All eyes fell on Hullar's back. The large man's hands dropped away from Sabini's neck and he slumped to his knees before collapsing to the ground.

Sabini held a small revolver in his right hand, a slender trail of smoke rising from the barrel. He looked from myself to Holmes. "I always keeps this on me, you just never knows when you'll need it. I picked that one up from you and the good Doctor."

***

Back at my house, Holmes and I reposed in the parlour with coffee and a mid-afternoon brandy, something I think was well deserved after the day's events.

"That didn't quite go as planned, did it?" I asked Holmes.

Taking a sip of coffee and placing the cup down, he smiled in my direction. "No, frankly Watson, it didn't, but the outcome was as expected."

"How so?"

"Sabini is no fool. He may not have damaged the Hoxton Mob's hold on any territory as he hoped, but he did remove a troubling element within his ranks. Both Hullar, who verged on the uncontrollable due to his anger problems, and Smith who was playing him against the Hoxtons."

"But, Sabini got away with murder."

"Did he?" Holmes said. "We believe he did, but we only have circumstantial evidence to tie him to the murders. In the eyes of the law, he is free. Hullar's death was self-defence. All the murders can be attributed directly to him. The Sabini Gang is renowned for the use of knives and blunt force trauma via hammers, but never strangulation, therefore there is no direct correlation to their methods."

"I still feel a little unnerved by all this."

"As you should Watson, as you should. Theoretically, we uncovered a strange plot to undermine one criminal gang by another gang and put a stop to it. We found a murderer and he found his just deserts. Sabini and his crew are well in the sights of Chief Inspector Wengert, so will have to play it safe for a while yet. Overall, actually a quite successful adventure."

"If you say so Holmes if you say so." I thought for a moment and asked anyway. "I don't suppose I can write this up for the Strand then?"

"No, Watson, you may not. I'm still retired. This was but a momentary reprieve, and to be honest, a most enjoyable if not a tiring one."

The Tranby Croft Affair

It was mid-morning on a quiet Saturday in September of 1890 that I sat silently in my study, perusing my latest pile of medical journals, when I heard the doorbell chime. The ring was followed by the sounds of my wonderful wife Mary shuffling down the hallway, unlocking and opening the door.

I could hear the sounds of surprise at first, followed by a muted conversation before two pairs of footsteps moved down the hallway towards my study. My concentration ruined, I simply stared at the door leading into my private sanctuary as the footfalls came to a stop just outside.

The door opened and, instead of the wayward patient I had expected, in stepped my good friend Sherlock Holmes.

As he laid eyes on my dressing gown and pile of unread journals, he said, "Sorry to disturb your personal pursuits on this fine morning, Watson, but I have received a rather intriguing telegram." Stepping forward he slid the closed paper towards me.

"Good to see you too Holmes," I answered, still a little stunned by his presence. Opening the telegram, I read its contents. It was addressed directly to Holmes. The message read.

"Sherlock. I need your brilliant mind. I am host to a royal guest for the Doncaster races. At night we play Baccarat. I suspect a guest of cheating. Not normally a real problem, but worried about involving HRH. Arthur Wilson."

Reading through the message again, I refolded and handed it back to Holmes. "This Arthur Wilson, a friend of yours?"

"Oh, yes, our families have been intertwined for generations."

"He's from Yorkshire then?"

"Yes. With his brother, Arthur co-owns the Thomas Wilson shipping company. They inherited it from their father and operate out of Hull. Arthur owns the Tranby Croft estate outside of the city, where it seems he entertains many high-profile guests."

"I assume you know who he speaks of in this missive?"

"Oh, yes, the *royal* and *HRH* references, when coupled with the name Doncaster, which can only mean the race meeting, leads me to surmise that my friend is playing host to the Prince of Wales and his coterie."

"A very fortunate acquaintance on the part of this Wilson fellow, I would think, and one that he would wish to protect at all costs."

"Quite so, Watson, quite so. As the media play it out, the Prince is drawn to any manner of suspect activity. Baccarat is technically illegal in this country and given the company the Prince is known to keep; I presume that the amounts of money involved in these nightly card games would be rather impressive. With such amounts, any form of cheating by any party would be seen as both criminal behaviour and grounds for social exclusion."

"Surely it's not the Prince himself?"

Holmes held up his hands, "I can't say, Watson, I can't say, but never eliminate a suspect until you have all the facts."

"My word," I said, thinking that such a trivial little puzzle had the potential to be explosive, especially if the papers were to find out about it. Standing and moving around my desk, I asked, "Can we make it to Hull by this evening?"

"Yes, if you make haste and get changed. The next train from Kings Cross leaves at twelve," consulting my mantle clock, Holmes continued, "Which gives us less than an hour."

Flustered, I headed for the door, muttering to myself, "I'll have to consult with Mary." Flinging the door open in my haste I was met by my lovely wife holding a heavy-looking valise.

Mary took one look at my reddened face and said, "Well hurry up John, there are travelling clothes laid out on the bed for you, and this case contains two day's change of clothes, plus a dinner suit. You may have to have your shirts laundered by the staff if you are to stay for longer."

I was stunned but assumed that Holmes had pre-warned my wife, who in her infinite patience and acceptance of our lives had taken an active stance. Kissing her on the cheek, as I passed, I muttered, "Thank you."

"Never mind that, begone," she replied, a wry grin on her lips.

***

Despite our concerns, we made the train north with plenty of time to spare. Our luck ran true as we were able to procure a first-class compartment and quickly settled our luggage in place before setting off for the club car for luncheon.

Our time on the train was mostly spent catching up on our own recent doings, plus discussing other items of interest from the news of the land.

I probed Holmes on the possible identities in the Prince's entourage, but he was both unsure and unprepared to surmise.

After our post-lunch coffee, we returned to our car and settled in for the last couple of hours. I returned to the unfinished journals from my morning, whilst Holmes took the opportunity to catch some rest in preparation for whatever awaited us.

It was as we were wending our way East along the Humber River that I noticed the rolling green fields give way to the city itself. Although I knew Hull, or Kingston on Hull as it was properly named, was a bustling port city using the natural shelter of the Humber River inlet to access the trade routes into the North Sea, it still retained the spread-out look of a small village rather than the densely, nestled buildings of the capital.

Our exit from the train at Paragon Station was quick due to the volume of passengers having disembarked in Sheffield and Doncaster, and we soon found ourselves outside the sandstone façade of the station building. As I searched for a hansom or carriage capable of taking us the relatively short distance to Tranby Croft, a tall gentleman in a morning suit stepped towards us.

"Mr. Holmes. Doctor Watson?" I gaped at the man, shocked that anyone would have known us by our appearance, or even that we would be there. Seeing my discomfort, the man bowed slightly before continuing to speak in his deep, commanding voice. "I do apologise, I am Smithers, Mr. Wilson's butler. He asked me to meet you and bring you to Tranby-Croft." Smithers held a hand out towards a beautifully crafted Brougham, replete with a similarly dressed driver who hopped down and snatched up our bags before we could reply.

"Thank you, Smithers. It's been a while," said Holmes as we stepped into the covered part of the carriage.

"That it has Mr. Holmes, that it has. Mr. Wilson was very effusive about your imminent arrival," said Smithers before closing the door and climbing up next to the driver.

"But you didn't reply did you?" I asked Holmes.

"No, I didn't, but Wilson knows that I would never think of disappointing him."

***

As the sun was starting to dip below the horizon, we turned into the drive that ran to the front of Tranby Croft. The manor house was a three-story edifice built-in white brick, though the sun at that hour set the building aflame in a yellow glow. The size of the house and its surrounding grounds suggested the owner was affluent and my own knowledge of Wilson's business pursuits told me he was indeed doing well.

Such a person was a natural magnet for the Prince of Wales, who enjoyed the company of the rich and powerful and had a strong preference for the more enjoyable pursuits in life, some of which, as rumour had it, his mother looked upon with sharp disdain.

Stopping near the main entrance, Smithers stepped down and led us straight in through the front doors and into a private study on the ground floor. There a slightly stoop backed man in his fifties, with a well-groomed head of faintly greying hair, paced back and forth.

Upon seeing Holmes enter the room, the man's face brightened, and he strode across the room and took my good friend in a firm embrace.

"Sherlock, so good to see you. Thank you so much for coming. I know it's a long arduous journey, but I will be forever in your debt."

As they parted, Holmes simply patted him on the shoulder and said, "Arthur, you would never be in my debt, such is the bond between our families." Motioning to some chairs near the fireplace, Holmes continued, "Should we discuss what has happened. I presume we only have a short while before your guests return."

"How? Oh, never mind, I've never understood how you do it."

Smiling, Holmes couldn't help but explain. "Simple really. You were here awaiting our arrival, so therefore you were alone. You mentioned Doncaster in the telegram, so I can only assume that the Prince and his entourage have attended the races and will return tonight for dinner and other pursuits."

Wilson nodded, "Yes, precisely."

"Who are the other members of the Prince's group? That may give me more information to peruse."

"Apart from his three servants, he is only travelling with his good friend Lieutenant Colonel Sir William Gordon-Cumming."

"Ah, the Baronet, formerly of the Scots Guards. The papers make it that they have become quite good friends over the last year," I said. At which point Wilson laid eyes on me as if for the first time. I could only assume it was because his mind was preoccupied with the goings-on and with Holmes's presence.

"Did I not introduce my friend?" asked Holmes, "I'm so sorry, this is Dr. John Watson, my close associate on my many adventures over the last few years."

Wilson shook his head and held out a hand for me to shake. "I'm so sorry Sir, I have been so preoccupied with this little problem, it has so consumed me all day and all last night that I haven't slept and cannot concentrate on anything else."

"No need to apologise, I completely understand," I answered.

Holmes took the reins and led the next phase of the conversation. "Now, Arthur please explain in precise detail, don't leave anything out, what has happened."

Wilson took a deep breath and began his tale. "It started the moment we had word from the Prince that he had chosen Tranby Croft as his residence for the Doncaster races this year. My wife, bless her, went all into a tizzy over the preparations. I think I have been dragged along in her whirlwind of activity, such that my own nerves and emotions are heightened beyond the norm."

It was at that moment that the door opened, and Smithers entered with a tray holding a coffee pot and three cups. "I thought you gentlemen might need refreshment after your journey." Placing the tray on the small table before us, Smithers leant in towards Wilson and said, "Might I remind you, Sir, it is past five o'clock. His Highness is expected soon, and dinner will be served at seven, with drinks in the parlour at six-thirty."

Wilson nodded. "Thank you, Smithers, you are a blessing." With that, the butler left. I poured out three cups, Wilson blowing on his before taking a long draw. Placing his cup down, he took another long slow breath before continuing his story.

"Yesterday was the Prince's first day here. As you can expect the whole place was on tenterhooks. A Royal visit does not happen every week. All went well, and if I was to be honest, I don't think the Prince has the level of pretension that is expected. He is a simple man, used to a lavish lifestyle, but one who is more interested in Earthly pleasures and pursuits rather than pomp and ceremony. The cook prepared a wonderful meal. My wife was cognizant enough to organise for several young ladies to attend the dinner, to provide a level of distraction for the Prince above and beyond simple conversation, shall we say. It was later, once the post-dinner entertainment was underway that he became bored and looked for more serious distraction. It was Gordon-Cumming that suggested we play cards. The Prince had grown to enjoy Baccarat, even though it has been illegal by High Court decree for several years."

"I can only surmise it is that fact that makes it more appealing to the Prince," said Holmes, "Given his documented proclivities."

"Quite so, anyway, there were eight of us in all that moved into the smoking-room where a table had been set up. I, the Prince, and Gordon-Cumming, included. I had also invited several of the Prince's friends, such as Lieutenant General Sir Owen Williams and Lord Somerset. Knowing that Gordon-Cumming was to be at dinner, I invited another Scots Guard, Lieutenant Berkeley Levett as well. My own son Stanley joined them at the card table, as did my wife Mary. I wasn't interested in cards, but I stood nearby, intrigued by the game."

"What happened during the game that convinced you someone was cheating?"

"I hope it wasn't the Prince," I said.

"No, no it wasn't," assured Wilson, "It was that Gordon-Cumming scoundrel. Or at least I think it was. He led the way, betting more than any other, and I was sure that at one stage, the number of counters before him increased after he had won the hand."

"Ah," said Holmes, "The French call that *la poussette*. Many a man has found himself in dire straits on the continent attempting such a fraud."

"But I can't prove it. I kept my eyes on him for the rest of the night, but I could see nothing untoward. It just seemed that my eyes were playing tricks on me. Afterwards, I took some of the participants aside and asked their opinion. A couple of other guests agreed with me, but most others simply thought he had a lucky night. I believe he walked away from the table with several hundred pounds, mostly obtained from the Prince."

"And that is the main problem here? Not just the cheating, but the target of that cheating?"

"Yes. I know the Prince would not miss the money, but such an act against the probable future King is something that just cannot go unnoticed."

Holmes thought for a moment, his hand on chin, a single finger raised along his jawline. A wry grin came to his mouth as a plan formed in his mind. "I think tonight, we should increase the numbers at the table, if possible. That way more eyes can be kept on this Gordon-Cumming. If you are fine with it, I will sit in on the game."

Wilson looked a little confused, "If you think so, but I don't understand the reasoning."

Holmes simply waved his concerns away. "Oh, don't worry about that, leave all to me."

***

Smithers took us to our rooms where we had just under an hour to dress before drinks in the parlour downstairs. When Holmes and I returned to the ground floor, we found the parlour virtually deserted.

The stoic expression on the butler's face told us nothing, but a few questions informed us that the Prince's retinue had returned only just shy of six o'clock. Wilson finally arrived with his lovely wife Mary, followed by several other guests over the next few minutes. Holmes and I were introduced to several of Wilson's friends, including those from the previous night, and some newcomers including another Scots Guardsman Lieutenant Lycett Green and his wife Ethel, and Lord and Lady Coventry.

I immediately fell in thick with the uniformed officers and exchanged notes on our postings overseas and any shared acquaintances we might have. Holmes quickly became the attention of several guests, just from the virtue of being Holmes.

It was well past seven o'clock when the Prince and his party finally entered the parlour. The Prince had a beaming smile on his face, which turned out to be due to his horse winning the Clumber Stakes. The assembled guests unconsciously formed themselves into a line against one wall, awaiting the Prince to greet each in turn. He simply waved a nonchalant hand at all of us and said, "Don't be silly. I'm not the King yet, this is a simple informal affair. Treat me like a friend, not a ruler."

With that, the dinner gong was rung in the dining room and we filed through to take our seats. I found myself between Stanley and Mary Wilson, and Lieutenant and Ethel Lycett Green, Holmes became positioned near the Prince and Arthur Wilson.

The fare on offer was of excellent quality, but in my opinion gone much too quickly, even though I felt my waistband straining in appreciation.

After dinner, we retired to the parlour once more where Ethel Lycett Green serenaded us for several songs after a period of quiet conversation between the guests. My eyes fell on the Prince who seemed quite flushed, possibly from his delight at winning the horse race, or more likely from too much wine consumed at dinner. Even though he talked with a young girl whose acquaintance I had not made, he fidgeted and squirmed in his seat. It was only when Gordon-Cumming stepped across and whispered in his ear that he became motivated.

The Prince called for Arthur Wilson and spoke while motioning around the room. Wilson replied and pointed to a door that I knew led to the drawing-room.

It was then that Holmes stepped up next to me and said, "I feel that the game is on, Watson."

Surprised, I couldn't work out what clews Holmes had found to lead to any furthering of our little mystery, but soon realised he meant little more than the approaching game of cards.

Several of the guests remained in the parlour, while over a dozen of us moved into the drawing-room. Several tables had been pushed together and covered in green baize, in preparation for the card game. A dozen players quickly drew their chairs from beneath the table and sat. I deliberately held back, so that I could observe unmolested. Arthur Wilson stood nearby me as well.

The players that sat were, the Prince and Gordon-Cumming, the Lycett Greens, the Coventrys, Lord Somerset, Mary Wilson and her son Stanley, General Williams, Lieutenant Levett and Holmes. Money was quickly exchanged for small, coloured counters by all players, and the game began.

I must admit that I only had a passing idea about Baccarat, but quickly picked up the idea. In the form played, each person played against the banker who also dealt the cards. The person playing the bank shuffled the decks of cards and proposed a stake that they would play for. The bank stayed with that player until all cards had been dealt, or their stake ran out.

It was up to individual players to choose how much they wagered against the banker on each hand, but it seemed that the Prince and Gordon-Cumming were outbidding the rest of the players by a considerable amount.

The game itself was simple. Two cards were dealt to each player and to the bank. The total of the cards was their face value, except court cards or ten which were worth zero. The player tried to get closest to nine with those two cards, they were then allowed to draw another if desired. The bank was similar but had more complicated rules as well.

As I watched the first few rounds, I noticed that the Prince and Gordon-Cumming were both winning and losing at the same rate. Their piles of chips seemed to remain stable.

It was when the Prince became banker that things changed. Gordon Cumming's rate of winning and losing remained the same, but he seemed to have more counters before him on hands he won, than on those he lost. Within a few hands, this caused the Prince's stake to diminish rapidly.

Glancing at Holmes, I noticed his eyes fixated on Gordon-Cummings as well. It was then I saw that the small pile of counters before Holmes had grown markedly, which was helpful as Holmes was next in line to be banker, when the players decided to take a break.

Coffee and port were served, and the group of card players milled around with those of us who had chosen to observe. I sidled up to Holmes and had a word. "Have you determined whether he's the one?"

Holmes replied, but even now, his eyes were fixed upon Gordon-Cummings, who was in polite conversation with the Prince. "Oh, yes, he's definitely cheating. But he is mainly targeting the Prince for some reason."

"How is he doing it?"

"I believe I know how, but I need to be sure. He is utilising some of the best sleight of hand that I have seen in a long while. Even Maskelyne would be envious of his talent."

"What do you plan to do?"

Smiling at me, he patted my shoulder. "Now Watson, that would be telling, wouldn't it?"

I shrugged and followed as he strolled across to where the Prince and Gordon-Cumming chatted. Standing to his full height, ramrod straight, he deftly butted into the conversation. "I do beg your pardon, your Highness, but I don't believe we were formally introduced earlier."

A stern look crossed the Prince's face as he stared at Holmes. I became nervous that perhaps Holmes's impertinence had offended the Prince but was relieved when a broad grin split his countenance and a hand was thrust towards Holmes. "Mr. Sherlock Holmes. I am absolutely delighted to meet you. Your exploits are legendary." They shook hands like old friends, the Prince then indicated me. "And I believe this is your associate Dr. Watson." I took his proffered hand and bowed slightly as I shook.

"Your Highness."

"I have read many of Mr. Holmes's adventures, thanks to your deft writing hand. I do hope there will be nothing worth sending to the Strand from tonight's little soiree."

"So, do I, your Highness, a quiet night in Holmes's company is a rarity in itself."

Turning to Gordon-Cumming, Holmes held a hand out. "Sir William, you play an admirable game of cards."

"Of what I have observed, so do you, Mr. Holmes. A challenge in itself and you present as a very worthy opponent."

"Thank you. Though these simple parlour games do tend to be a little on the conservative side, with a lack of any real contest."

"Oh, I'm sure we can see whether that can change in the next half. At least between the two of us, hey?"

"I think that would be marvellous," Holmes finished as he moved away and reclaimed his seat at the card table.

"Good Luck," I said over his shoulder before moving back to my own seat.

"Oh, there's nothing here that involves luck," he quipped, shuffling the cards before him as the other players returned to the table.

Then the game really started. With Holmes as banker, his stake was considerably larger than many of the others at the table. Dealing out and playing the first two hands, he was on a steady win-loss ratio, with Gordon-Cumming winning each against him. It was on the third hand that I noticed something interesting.

Gordon-Cumming drew a king and a three on the first round, then a five, giving him a total of eight. Virtually unbeatable. Before him stood a small pile of six counters, equivalent to around thirty pounds.

Holmes dealt out the other hands until it finally came to his turn to reveal his cards. I glanced back at Gordon-Cumming and noticed his pile of counters was now eight. The rules of the game state that a stake cannot be changed once the player's hand has finished. I kept my emotions in check, but I did notice Holmes's eyes glance down at the chips, a small grin leapt to his lips.

He turned over his own cards, revealing a four. The rules were that he should draw another card. Watching his hands, I noticed a peculiar movement of the fingers, which amounted to a five of spades appearing on top of his two cards. He had nine. Unbeatable.

A gasp went up around the table. Gordon-Cumming's face dropped in horror, even more so as the two piles of counters was raked in by Holmes.

"Frightfully bad luck there William," said the Prince, "I thought you had him."

The Baronet's face remained passive, his eyes boring straight into Holmes's.

The next two hands were without incident. Gordon-Cumming winning one and losing the other. It was the next that proved more eventful.

Gordon-Cumming, once again, drew a handy four and a five, giving him nine straight away. This time, I counted eight counters before him. He had opened with a higher bid and I was unsure if he was confident or just plain foolhardy.

Turning his cards, Holmes revealed a queen and a three. By the rules, he was forced to take another card. Glancing at the spot before Gordon-Cumming I was shocked again to see more counters than before. This time twelve red disks sat before the Baronet. Sixty pounds. Twenty more than I had already seen.

I noticed Holmes's eyes flash across to the pile. His hand hovered around the deck, before a deft movement once more drew a card and flipped it over onto the top of his hand.

It was a six. Holmes and Gordon-Cumming had tied. A gasp rose around the table once more. They would require a playoff. The discarded cards were quickly raked in, and Holmes dealt two to Gordon-Cumming and two to himself. The Baronet's cards amounted to five.

"You may raise your stake, I believe," said Holmes.

His lips twitching slightly, Gordon-Cumming replied gruffly, "My stake stands, I draw one."

"Very well," said Holmes, flipping a card over. It was a jack, worth nothing in this game. The Lieutenant Colonel remained on five.

Holmes quickly flipped over his own cards. He had drawn a two and a six. Giving him a total of eight. He did not need to draw another card.

"Bank wins, it seems," Holmes said, reaching across and picking up the pile of counters.

Gordon-Cumming stood up.

"Why William, what is the matter?" asked the Prince.

It was then I noticed that the green baize before the Baronet's place was empty.

"I must retire, I have exhausted my funds," looking around the room, his eyes fell on me, "Perhaps the good Doctor would like to replace me." I took one look at Holmes, who nodded slightly.

"Thank you, Sir," I said, quickly taking the Baronet's seat and exchanging several notes for counters. As Holmes was substituting my money for counters, I glanced over my shoulder and saw Gordon-Cumming making for the drawing-room exit. His face was red. I was not sure whether from rage or embarrassment. He stopped momentarily and motioned towards Wilson, who followed him from the room.

After another hand, Holmes passed the bank to his left. His excuse was that he'd held it for far too long, and it would be unfair to keep it. Just as I was starting to enjoy myself, the Prince yawned widely and stated that he was going to retire for the evening. The party had one final day of races on the morrow, and he wanted to enjoy every minute.

As the guests cashed in their counters and left the drawing-room, Wilson stepped up to Holmes and spoke. "I have only just finished a long and heated discussion with our dear Lieutenant Colonel. He wishes to make accusations against you."

"Against me? Whatever for?" asked Holmes, feigning innocence, but wearing that sly grin.

"He has suggested that you cheated him out of almost a hundred pounds," Wilson said, "I pleaded ignorance, stating that your good name is enough for me and that he would need solid proof."

"Well, he is correct, though I would suggest that tonight he has cheated the Prince out of much more. Perhaps I should talk with him?"

"He wanted that. I have him waiting in my study and have consoled him with a brandy for the time being."

"Good, good, then let's away."

***

Gordon-Cumming stood up as we entered the large study. His face was flushed red, and I was in no doubt that it was anger. He slammed the empty brandy glass down on a side table and stalked across the room towards Holmes.

"Now look here Sir," he said, almost shouting and pointing an accusatory finger at Holmes, "I demand an apology, and you're damn lucky I don't expose you to the entire household, his highness included."

Smiling sweetly, Holmes held out his hands to express his innocence. "I do apologise, Sir," he said, reaching into his jacket and removing his pocketbook. He fished out five twenty-pound notes and placed them on Wilson's desk. "I make it one hundred pounds, forty for the first hand, sixty for the second."

Stunned, Gordon-Cumming stared at the money before quickly snatching it up. "Yes. What in the blazes? You go to all that trouble and then simply pay it back." A smile stretched across his face as he glanced around at Holmes. "You must really value your reputation if you are so fearful and try to hide the facts so easily."

"Well, that may well be, Sir, but I think it would be you that should be afraid for his reputation," said Holmes.

"What do you mean?", asked the Baronet, a suspicious expression crossing his face. He glanced at the money as if to make sure it hadn't disappeared.

"I should think that the money I took from you pales into insignificance compared to the amount you have swindled off of the Prince over the last two nights."

"What?" shouted Gordon-Cumming, "How dare you, Sir? The Prince is a very good friend of mine, and as such, there is no reason that I could even contemplate what you suggest."

"The Prince is as you say, a good friend, but I think it is that friendship that has driven you down a dark path."

"I don't follow."

"No, you wouldn't, but might I suggest that since falling in with the Prince, your service pension and your other investments have not furnished you with a level of income that maintains a lifestyle reflective of your circle of newfound friends."

"How dare you, Sir? My income is none of your business."

"True, very, true. Normally that would be so, but it is my business in this case. The evidence is there, such as your evening suit, though expensive and fashionable, has grown beyond its time."

"What? How?"

"The ends of the sleeves are scuffed, showing a touch of white at the very edges. A sign of age and wear. The jacket's seams have been let in and out on several occasions, causing multiple creases down the sides. That jacket has seen you grow and shrink on far too many occasions. In fact, I'm sure that same could be said for the pants. Even your shoes are suffering from age, only the most diligent level of buffing can cover the multiple scuff marks on the toes and heels. Normally a man in your position would never allow himself to be seen in such a state."

"So, I have an old suit. I wasn't sure how long I'd be away."

"But it's not just that is it? You haven't any servants, in fact, you have been using one of the Prince's men as your own valet. A sign that you may not be keeping a full-time staff at home."

"I...I didn't wish to add to the overall entourage. The Prince has never complained."

"No, well he wouldn't even realise, would he?"

Staring down at his shoes for a few moments, Gordon-Cumming seemed to build up his courage again before puffing his chest out and blasting Holmes once more, "This is foolishness. You are the cheat, Sir, not me."

"Ah, well that may be what you believe Sir, but I have not only my observations but many other witnesses. Dr. Watson here, Mr. Wilson as well, plus I'm sure any number of other members at the playing tables either tonight or last night would be willing to confess

133

that there were irregularities in your betting. I must admit it took me a while to work out how you did it."

"Did what?"

"Oh, come on Sir, don't play the innocent fool," said Wilson, obviously losing his patience, "I saw on numerous occasions, your stack of counters change in size once the play had passed you by. Mostly when the Prince was banker. A most distasteful display."

"I never. You have no proof."

"Ah, but that's where you may be wrong," said Holmes, "As I said, it took me a while, but I have studied with some of the best illusionists in the business. They each have their methods, but I believe you have studied with some of those in the United States while you were there on a hunting trip perhaps."

"Why would I do that?"

Holmes stepped forward, reaching for both the Lieutenant Colonel's hands, he flipped them over and bent them down. Suddenly, a small mechanical arm slid out from beneath his left shirt sleeve, it held a small red counter in the tiny claw at the end. As it reached the end of its track, the counter popped out of the claw and dropped to the carpet.

My eyes grew wide at the startling evidence on show. Wilson gasped and took one step forward. Holmes held out a hand towards him and spoke, "Because the illusionists in America have developed the use of mechanical gimmicks, rather than using simple sleight of hand, to add a level of mystery and showmanship to their tricks. Something that you have brought back with you from there, it seems."

The accused man simply stared down at the exposed machinery. Relaxing his hand, the mechanical arm withdrew until it disappeared into his sleeve. Lifting his head once more, his face wore the expression of a beaten man. "You don't know what it's like you know. Edward has the world at his feet, but he simply takes it all for granted and lets his life pass by without a care. He may well be crowned King one day, but I don't believe he will ever actually be ready to rule. I may have inherited my title, but I served my country in numerous theatres of war. When I returned, several of my businesses collapsed, robbing me of my family's heritage."

"But you maintained your relationship with the Prince?" asked Wilson.

A slight hint of rage came to Gordon-Cumming's voice as he answered, "Well, yes, I am a Baronet. I have a station in society to maintain, and I have been Edward's friend for many years."

"Even though you have stolen from him."

"Pfft, as I said, he wouldn't miss it. He has the riches of Croesus at his command."

"Envy is a poor reason to act as you have," Holmes added.

"Especially from a member of the Scots Guards, one of the most honourable regiments in Her Majesty's army," I felt compelled to include.

Indeed, it was my comment that struck at the heart of the man. He deflated upon being reminded of his service to Her Majesty, even if he was not as honoured by his association with her son. Hanging his head in shame, he mumbled, "You are right Doctor. By cheating the Prince, I have cheated his mother, someone I served in earnest overseas." He drew breath in a long sigh, lifting his eyes to look at his host. "What would you have me do Sir?"

His voice wavering with its own controlled anger, Arthur Wilson replied, "Sir, you have brought dishonour not just upon yourself, but also upon this house." He strode around, waving his hands to the side as his rage built, but he withdrew it inside and calmed down. "I am seriously considering bringing the law into this. We aren't that far from Hull they could be here within the hour."

At which point, Holmes intervened. "May, I suggest something Arthur?"

"By all means Sherlock, but if I don't like it then I'll send Smithers to fetch the local sergeant."

"As is your choice, but would it be more expedient to allow Sir William to repay his debt to the Prince, and possibly sign an affidavit, witnessed by your good self, that states he shall remove himself from any future gaming. Would that meet with your approval?"

"I don't see how?"

135

"Well, that approach would limit any possible damage to the Prince's reputation and would allow Sir William to save face himself."

"Hmmm," replied Wilson, still mulling over Holmes's suggestion.

"I agree," said Gordon-Cumming, "And I do appeal to your good nature, Mr. Wilson. I can only apologise so many times but would be forever in your debt if you would allow what Mr. Holmes has suggested."

Staring at Gordon-Cumming for quite a long time, Wilson finally nodded before opening the door to reveal the stoic figure of Smithers. He spoke to the butler who quickly moved away, before striding across and sitting at his desk. Pulling out a sheet of parchment, he dipped a pen in his inkpot and scribbled several lines on the page, before glancing up and motioning for the accused man to approach him.

"If you wish to end this tonight, then sign this paper."

Gordon-Cumming read the note aloud. "In consideration of the promise made by the gentlemen whose names are subscribed to preserve my silence with reference to an accusation which has been made in regard to my conduct at baccarat on the nights of 8th and 9th of September at Tranby Croft, I will on my part solemnly undertake never to play cards again as long as I live." He paused for a moment as he reread the missive to himself before reaching for the pen and signing his name below.

It was at that point that Lieutenants Levett and Lycett Green appeared in the doorway. Wilson greeted them and appraised them of the situation before turning to face Gordon-Cumming. "Both Levett and Lycett Green expressed their own suspicions last night and earlier this evening. They have consented to add their own testament." As all three approached the desk, I noticed dark looks of distrust, upon the faces of the younger soldiers, directed at their older colleague.

Wilson bent over and added his own name below Gordon-Cumming's before handing the pen to Levett. Within seconds the two names were appended. Looking up at Holmes and myself, Wilson thought for a moment. "I think the leverage that our three names have should be enough to ensure this will pass muster in any court of the land."

Holmes nodded. "I agree. Something such as this should remain within the auspices of Sir William's peers."

With one final look at Gordon-Cumming, whose eyes dropped to the floor as they met Holmes's gaze, my good friend exited the room. I hurried after him, not wanting to intrude on Wilson's next words.

As we made our way back to our rooms, none other than the Prince stepped from his room and into our path. Upon seeing Holmes, a wide grin broke out across his face. "Mr. Holmes, my word, fancy bumping into you at this latening hour. Not tracking down any miscreants among us, I hope."

"No, your Highness, nothing as exciting as that. Watson and I were just confirming our transport back to the train station in the morning, we will be returning to London tomorrow."

"Well, that's a shame, I had hoped to find some time to pick your brains over some of those wonderful adventures you've had. Never mind, now that I have made your acquaintance, I think it may be prudent to invite you over to Marlborough when I'm back in London. It would be so stimulating to talk with someone of your intelligence. Some of my entourage can become serious bores after a while."

"I thank you, your Highness, and would be delighted to attend at any time."

"Of course, only when you aren't saving England from some nefarious cove from across the channel, that is." Glancing across at me, the Prince continued, "Of course, Doctor Watson would be more than welcome as well."

I bowed slightly and said, "Thank you, your Highness, I would be just as deeply honoured as my friend here."

"Very good, very good," the Prince said, "Now if you'll excuse me, I have some things to attend to myself before I turn in for the night. I think her name is Elsie or something. Goodnight gentlemen." He shuffled off down the hallway.

I think I could feel my face redden as I realised what he'd just said. All I could manage in response was to murmur a goodnight.

Holmes waited until the Prince was out of earshot before chuckling to himself. "I think we should keep that little titbit, amongst the same stash of secrets with everything else that has happened tonight."

I gaped a little, but added, "I think you are quite right, Holmes."

***

It was a week later as I sat at my breakfast table and opened the morning copy of the Times that I almost spat out my coffee. The headline on the front page read *The Royal Baccarat Scandal*. The article related almost every aspect of the events that had played out at Tranby-Croft the weekend before. Thankfully, Holmes and I had been left out of the details, as it seemed to have been drawn from a corrupted version of events as if told by someone protecting themselves. As I finished the article I realised it was from an interview with Gordon-Cumming himself.

I excused myself to Mary, dressed and hurried to 221B Baker Street, where I found Holmes sitting quietly in his parlour with the same newspaper in hand. A smile crossed his face as his eyes fell on my exasperated expression.

"Hullo Watson, why so flustered?"

I held up the paper and said, "I see you've read this article, surely you must understand my perturbation."

"I do, my friend, but I also think you have nothing to really concern yourself with."

"But this Gordon-Cumming cad has basically blamed everybody but himself."

"Yes, yes he has. He has even called upon the Prince to be questioned over the matter. I must admit I am a little aggrieved by his stance but can only see his own status crashing around him."

"Do you understand why he would do such a thing?"

"Well, the fellow admitted that he enjoyed the station that his Baronet and association with the Prince brought him. He has stated that his reputation has been tarnished because of the whole affair, and especially because of the paper that he was made to sign by Wilson. At one point he said that the details of which were disclosed to the public. I honestly think that point is a fake claim to overshadow his own guilt."

"He is taking Wilson to court to clear his name. That's where he said the Prince may be called to give evidence."

"Yes. Again, I can only see this as folly on his behalf. He has clouded his own judgement with a false sense of innocence."

"What if we are called to the stand?"

Again, that enigmatic smile came to his face. "I think we would be the last people his lawyers would wish to have speak. I would only tell the truth as I see it, and you would be there to back me up in every detail. As we know, the truth is damning in this case."

I nodded. It was all too confusing and smacked of senselessness.

As history would tell, everything Holmes stated came to pass. Gordon-Cumming filed a writ of slander against Wilson and the other players on that night. The Prince was called as a witness, the first such occasion since the fifteenth century that an heir to the throne had been requested to appear to give evidence in court.

After a rather short trial, the jury found against Gordon-Cumming. His downfall was quick. The next day he was dismissed from the army, and within a short period of time found himself ostracised from polite society. The very thing he had feared all along.

Holmes and I never again crossed paths with Gordon-Cumming, all indications are that he retired to his Scottish estate after marrying an American heiress.

We did however accept several invitations to Marlborough House at the pleasure of the Prince. On each occasion, he plied us with both coffee and stronger drink, and many questions about Holmes's exploits. He seemed highly knowledgeable about all that I had written, and I would not be surprised if a large stack of issues of *Strand Magazine* could be found in pride of place amongst his possessions.

The Adventure at Castle Metzengerstein

After so many years spent documenting the various escapades of my good friend and close associate, Sherlock Holmes, I was still surprised by the way that an unexpected visitor would be the catalyst for yet another adventure.

One such day occurred when I was visiting Holmes on the way to my surgery. I didn't have any patients due for the morning, so spent a quiet moment with my friend talking about recent events and enjoying a lovely tea prepared by Mrs. Hudson.

A ring on the doorbell was followed by Holmes's brother Mycroft entering the parlour. His appearance was extremely unusual as he generally sent for Holmes by way of telegram and had him meet at the Diogenes Club, one of Mycroft's favourite haunts.

He appeared very dour and a little down in the dumps. I attributed it to his need to cross town and visit Holmes rather than the news he carried.

Seeing that morning tea was on offer, he quickly sat and availed himself of a cup of coffee and a scone smothered in jam and cream. Holmes and I simply watched until he had satisfied his hunger and was finally prepared to talk.

After wiping his hands on a napkin, Mycroft reached into his jacket pocket and withdrew a telegram. He passed it over to Holmes who immediately read it.

"Hungary?" Holmes muttered as he read, "It's been many years since I visited there."

He looked up at Mycroft and continued.

"I assume you can't be drawn away from affairs of the state?" he asked.

"No. Sadly, I'm at a rather delicate juncture on some precarious business. I think it best if you travel and represent the family," he said.

By this time, I was beginning to become quite confused.

"Would someone wish to let me in on the news?" I asked.

Holmes smiled and passed the note across. I quickly read it.

The telegram was from a Mr. Istvan Herzog, representing the estate of the Baron Metzengerstein. The message was a short notification that the funeral of the Baron and his wife would be held a week from today in the grounds of the Keszthely cathedral in Hungary. I read it again but could gather no more information. I looked up at the brothers who immediately saw my confusion.

"The Baron was an old family friend. The relationship between the Holmeses and the Metzengersteins goes back many generations," said Mycroft, "Though my brother and I, being the last in the patriarchal line, have rarely visited or engaged with anyone from the family."

"But we do have a duty to uphold tradition. A member of the Metzengerstein family has attended all of the funerals of our forebears for many generations," said Holmes, "It's also a lovely time of year, so a little trip would be most welcome."

"So, you'll go then," asked Mycroft.

Holmes pulled up a similarly folded note from his jacket pocket and held it up. "Mr. Herzog has already contacted me directly. He also asked if I could review the facts of the Baron's death, to ensure that everything is above board from a legal perspective." Turning toward me, Holmes asked, "Would your Mary allow you the extravagance of a little trip to the continent?"

"To Hungary?" I blurted out.

"Don't worry Watson, the Metzengerstein estate is on the western side of the country, not far from the Austrian border. The residents generally speak a rudimentary form of German, much like your own," Holmes replied, a slight smile on his lips.

"If I can ask you one favour, John," said Mycroft nodding his head towards his brother, "Please keep this one's level of geniality to a maximum. Some of our family still carry out a lot of business with the Metzengerstein companies and I'm sure they would like to keep doing so for many years to come."

It was my turn to smile.

"I will do all I can," I answered.

**

We were away in the early morning two days later. Mary was outwardly supportive, but I could tell there was a slight tinge of either envy or anger behind her façade. I located a locum to cover for me at the surgery as well, but once all was prepared I was more than eager to be on our way.

The hansom dropped us off at Victoria station where we were to take the first train to Dover. We managed to make the lunchtime ferry to Calais and were well on our way to Paris by mid-afternoon in a four-passenger carriage.

It would have been marvellous to have had some time in the city of love, but as always our time was precious. We arrived at the Gare du Lyon, and barely had time to purchase tickets before the Orient Express let out a loud whistle to indicate its immediate departure.

Luckily, we were able to procure a first-class sleeper for the twenty-seven-hour journey to Vienna and managed to unpack before the porter announced that dinner was to be served in the dining car.

The night passed without incident and it was whilst sitting in the club car the next day that I finally asked Holmes about the Metzengerstein family.

"Well, to be honest Watson, I've not had a lot to do with the family. Mycroft, being somewhat older than I, has met them on several occasions. My last interaction with them was over twenty years ago," he said staring out the window at the rapidly passing countryside.

"I do know they are a very old family who has lived in the South-Western area of Hungary for generations. They have familial ties to the Hapsburg dynasty and are very central to the Austro-Hungarian empire. The Baron was a highly prized advisor to the Emperor and spent a lot of his time in Vienna over the past twenty years, possibly why I've not crossed paths with him. My last meeting with him was briefly at the wedding to his first wife. My family made this same journey, though it was a lot less refined in those days and took over a week as this wonderful train didn't exist then," he continued.

"You said his first wife," I said.

"Yes. Poor soul died a year later during childbirth. Both she and the babe succumbed. I understand the Baron was devastated, but a few years later married another and not long after that they gave birth to a fine young boy, Frederick. He is now the Baron, I assume."

"What a tragic history?" I said.

"That's not the half of it," Holmes said with a wry grin on his lips.

I waited but nothing came forth, so I decided to nudge him further.

"Not the half of it?"

"No. The Metzengerstein family owns a sprawling estate of thousands of acres on the western shores of Lake Balaton, just to the east of the market town of Keszthely. They are the power in the district but have always been at bitter odds with the other powerful family of that area, the Berlifitzings. Even Mycroft has no idea what started the conflict, and if you ask the families they probably have no recollection either, but the feud has existed for centuries. I can only hope that the new Baron would be of a mind to lay such animosities to rest, but he is only young so who can say what thoughts have been placed in his mind."

"How intriguing," I said.

We passed the rest of the journey in virtual silence. Holmes sat back and stared out the window, I peeked at him a few moments later and he had drifted off. I busied myself with some papers relating to past adventures that I wished to read through and edit, by the time I looked up from my work we were pulling into the outskirts of Vienna.

I nudged Holmes awake and we returned to our sleeper and packed away our belongings.

When planning the journey, we realised that it would be quicker to alight at Vienna and continue in a carriage than to proceed through to Budapest and return. Taking a room in a nearby hotel, we rested before strolling to a nearby stable in the morning after a light breakfast.

Luckily, our telegram had reached the local office, and our request for a carriage to take us to Keszthely was answered. The onward journey across rough and sometimes narrow trails took the best part of the rest of the day and we arrived in the early evening.

Our contact, Istvan Herzog, the Metzengerstein family's solicitor, was still waiting for us at the local inn on our arrival. He was very apologetic about the state of the roads from Vienna and hoped that our journey was satisfactory.

I found him an affable man. He was in his mid-forties, balding and turning slightly too fat. He spoke excellent English with a slight eastern European accent, which to my ears was a blessing.

Holmes regarded him with a wry smile and after our introductions remarked, "I find it interesting that a man whose name translates to Duke would find himself in the service to a Baron."

I was flummoxed. Herzog simply smiled and nodded.

"Yes, I think though you will find there are just as many Herzogs in Austria and Hungary as there are Dukes in Britain. I'm afraid our early lofty origins have been diluted over the centuries. There are only so many Duchy's to go around I suppose," he said.

Holmes chuckled, "Well said. Well said."

"We did have a Count. Count Berlifitzing to be exact. The Berlifitzings have a marvellous historical line stretching back as far as the Metzengersteins," Herzog said.

"Had?" I asked.

"Yes. Sadly, the last Count died in a fire in his stables only a month ago. It was the Count's death, and that of the Baron that has caused such consternation around the region."

"Why?" asked Holmes.

"Well, the Metzengersteins and the Berlifitzings have been arch enemies for centuries, but a level of stability has occurred across both of their lands for at least the last hundred years. With one line effectively ended, and the other with a new Baron, the people are unsure and nervous."

"Interesting," said Holmes, "I presume that's why you would like me to look into the Baron's death then?"

"Yes, a satisfactory resolution would be of great relief to myself and many others."

We checked into our modest, but tidy rooms in the inn and within a few moments met Herzog back in the main bar to take a meal and some of the local beer.

As all three of us tucked into the local goulash with glee, Herzog filled us in on the details for the next couple of days.

"The funeral service is not for another two days, I'm afraid. I hope that doesn't affect your travel plans," he said.

We both shook our heads and Holmes added, "No, we weren't sure what would greet us when he arrived, so have left our departure date open and will take the train that is most appropriate at the time."

Herzog nodded, "Good. We had a small problem with the local Sheriff. He was a little indecisive over the circumstances of the Baron's death and needed to wait for assistance from Vienna. The Emperor himself asked for an investigation and sent his own man."

"And? what were those circumstances? I have only the event of his death, not the details of how he died," Holmes asked.

Herzog took a long draw from his beer, wiped his lip, and continued.

"The Baron and his young wife, God bless their souls, were travelling back from Budapest along the shores of Lake Balaton. They were traversing a rather narrow part of the road that runs along a high cliff when the carriage left the road. The Baron, his wife and the driver all perished in the crash," he said.

His lip quivered, possibly from his sense of loss, and he took another sip of beer.

"How sad and unexpected," I said.

Holmes piped up.

"Would it be possible to visit the scene tomorrow?" he asked.

. Herzog looked pleased. "Of course. I'm glad you are so keen to begin. The Emperor's man ruled it as an accident, but I still don't quite agree."

"I believe it may be prudent to concoct a little cover story. Such as, that in my family we have a custom of paying respects to our lost ones both at the scene of their demise and at their respective funerals. We believe that their spirits may be trapped at the site of their death and can pass on easier if they know they are loved and missed."

Herzog smiled and nodded.

"Of course, that would be a very generous and kind notion. We are an old people in this area and have many similar traditions ourselves. To help you out, I have arranged for a driver to be at your service for the next few days. The two of you are among only a few who come from other countries. Most others will have their own transportation," he said as he turned his attention back to his meal.

***

Late the next morning, Holmes and I decided to seize the opportunity to tour the area and take in the sights along the shores of Lake Balaton, Hungary's largest lake.

After a hearty breakfast, we met our assigned driver, who introduced himself as Zoltan. He spoke no English but had a good understanding of German. Holmes was able to converse quite readily with him, and before long we were soon on our way.

I had managed to convince the Inn-keeper's wife to prepare a suitable repast for the three of us and showed the contents to Zoltan, who nodded very favourably, before ensuring the basket was safely stowed away for the journey.

We set off at a languid pace. The object of the day was more for sightseeing, though there was a specific point of interest we were seeking.

The carriage trotted down towards the lakeshore and turned left to follow the rutted dirt pathway along the northern side of the lake.

Within half an hour we had passed through several villages with a few residents tending to gardens or making their way along the narrow roadway on foot. Long names with many consonants appeared on signboards and passed through my gaze. I knew that when I came to write up this adventure I would probably need access to a map of the area to provide them with their proper spellings.

After about an hour we exited a heavily overgrown forested area and found that to our left there were wide open fields of low-cut grasslands and well-maintained hedgerows. Sitting well away from the road was a four-storey mansion with a wide frontage and several spires that jutted above the main roofline.

Zoltan pointed and said, "Dort ist Schloss Metzengerstein."

Even I could understand that this was the Castle and grounds belonging to the unfortunate Baron whose funeral we would attend on the morrow.

"It is certainly impressive," I remarked to Holmes.

"We are only seeing the rear. The front entrance is something rather stunning," he said.

We continued for another few minutes before plunging back into an overgrown forested area that ran down to the lake's shoreline.

I noticed that the ground itself was rising as we ploughed on through the dark forest. Looking to my right, I found the lakeshore had dropped away significantly, so much so that we were now only feet from a sheer cliff.

The wooded cover broke and we were once again in the open air. Off to our left were more open lands, pockmarked with patches of wooded areas and some low-lying buildings in the distance.

"Was ist das?" Holmes asked Zoltan.

He remarked, "Das ist das Herrenhaus des Berlifitzing."

I understood so murmured, "The Berlifitzing estate."

Holmes nodded then asked Zoltan, "Wo ist der Unfall des Barons passiert?" (Where did the Baron's accident happen?)

Zoltan pointed forward.

"Eine Meile voraus," he said.

I realised he meant about a mile ahead.

As we reached the area, Holmes asked Zoltan to stop. He dutifully pulled across to a small layby. Holmes and I jumped down. Zoltan stayed put, giving us a queer look, and probably trying to figure out what the strange Englanders were up to.

I added up the number of days, and given the time since the tragedy, was curious as to what Holmes hoped to find.

"Holmes, the accident happened over a week ago, there'd be very little evidence left of anything, don't you think?"

He turned and gave me a wry smile.

"I would never think such a thing, Watson," he said.

We stepped around the area, careful to stay on the edge of the track. I kept an ear out for the noises of any approaching carriages, this was a public road after all, but it was quiet. Only the sounds of birds and the odd knicker of our horse filtered through.

Holmes glanced from one end of the track to the other. About a hundred yards ahead, the road came around a sharp right-hand bend, then carried on straight for about two hundred yards before disappearing around another right-hand bend.

"Do you think they took the bend too fast?" I asked.

Holmes simply walked across to the other side of the track and pointed out some broken tree branches. I noticed it was in the middle of the long straight stretch.

"They went off here," he said pointing at several deep ruts that carved through the grassed area on the verge of the trail. Several tree branches had snapped off and were hanging by thin threads of bark or were lying on the ground.

The ground stretched out from the road for another few yards before dropping down to the lakeshore. We carefully stepped through the break in the foliage and peered down.

"Good Lord, the carriage is still there," I exclaimed.

"Interesting," said Holmes, "I would assume that the authorities recovered the bodies, but any thoughts of retrieving the carriage or, indeed, the horse, were abandoned because of the precarious nature."

Holmes looked over his shoulder and strode back towards Zoltan. After a few moments of conversation and hand waving, he returned.

He pointed up the road and said, "Our driver says there is a small track that leads down to the shore just up around the corner."

I stared off in that direction, a faint notion of despair in my mind.

"What do you hope to find, Holmes?" I asked.

"Why answers Watson, answers," he said, striding off towards the corner.

***

The climb down was long and arduous and for the whole time, I felt that I was perched in a more precarious position than your average mountain goat. We finally alighted onto the rock-strewn shoreline of the lake and made our way along until we reached the broken carriage and the bloated remains of the horse.

It was a horrible and sorrowful sight. The poor nag had expired upon impact with the ground. Her head twisted around with her now vacant eye sockets staring at the sky.

Holmes stepped around the carriage, examining the wheels, and murmuring to himself. From my position, I could see that each one seemed intact, remarkable given the thirty yards they had fallen. The horse and front of the carriage had taken the brunt of the force.

Finished with his examination of the carriage, Holmes moved towards the horse. I noticed him take a kerchief from his pocket to block the offending smell of the decaying mare. I joined him, keeping a kerchief over my face as well.

From the cuts and abrasions that ran along the animal's neck, shoulder, and withers, she had dashed through the dense underbrush before her final descent. That accounted for the broken tree branches above. Holmes made his way to her flanks and finally her rump. It was there he stopped and peered closer.

"What do you make of this Watson?" he asked.

Annoyed at the prospect of putting my face closer to the poor putrefying animal, I nevertheless leaned in to find a strange wound sitting high on the animal's rear hindquarter without any evidence of other injuries in the surrounding area.

It was about one inch high and opened to about an eighth of an inch across in the middle. There was very little blood around it, unlike some of the other injuries and wounds.

"Strange. Not made by a branch or twig, I would say. Perhaps it was an existing wound that opened up again when the animal died?" I said.

"Perhaps," Holmes replied, "Perhaps."

He looked around the rest of the area. His eyes intently searching and squinting to focus solely on some object of his desire. After a few moments, he stood up straight, looked towards the top of the cliff and spoke.

"I don't think I'll find much more down here," he said, "It's a glorious day, let us enjoy the rest while we can."

***

And we did. The remainder of our day was rather enjoyable. We found a grassed area down by the lakeside to spread a blanket and feast on the contents of our basket. The landlady had even included a rather nice bottle of local white wine. Zoltan's face split into a wide grin when he saw it. He told us it was from the vineyards on the Northern shores of the lake.

We returned in the early evening after visiting several small towns and wonderful vantage points. The Landlady had dinner waiting for us and Istvan joined us as we sat down to eat.

He reminded us that the funeral service would be held at around eleven o'clock the next morning at the large church in the centre of town. He also mentioned that we had been invited to the memorial at Schloss Metzengerstein later that afternoon.

We all agreed that tomorrow would be a tiring day and shortly after our meal was finished we bid goodnight to Istvan and retired to our respective rooms.

***

After a light breakfast and several fortifying cups of coffee, Holmes and I met in the small forecourt of the inn. We both sported our most sombre regalia of dark suits, vests and tie matched with a crisp white shirt.

The service was to be held at the *Magyar Hölgyünk*, or as Istvan had translated for us, *The Church of Our Lady in Hungary*. I assumed that there were many churches by that name across the country, similarly as there are numerous Notre Dame churches and cathedrals throughout France.

It was not far away, so we strolled through the bustling little town towards the imposingly grand bell tower and found a formidable-looking fourteenth-century church.

A large number of sombre people attired in dark, drab mourning clothes, similar to us, were gathered around the entrance to the church. Their numbers were dotted with the occasional appearance of a more ornately dressed person. I assumed these to be members of the local gentry and soon found myself overhearing conversations involving several mentions of the title *Count*.

I took in the presence of an older gentleman refined in an ensemble of green and white, complete with feathers and medals and assumed this was the object of most discussions. It was at that moment that Istvan found us and provided an explanation. The gentleman was József Horvath, the chief advisor to Count Berlifitzing. He had chosen to wear the Count's own livery for the occasion.

"As would be expected, his appearance here is out of respect to the Baron, even though there still existed much animosity between the two families," Istvan said.

"But I thought you said that the Count had died not long ago, effectively ending the line," I said.

Herzog nodded. "Yes, Mr. Horvath has stayed on to sort out the final legal arrangements. We have been in constant contact as there are some intricacies we are working through between the two families."

"Intriguing, what intricacies?" asked Holmes.

"I may leave that until later," Herzog said, nodding towards the road leading to the church.

I looked in the direction he indicated and noticed a large carriage, drawn by four black horses, arrive and pull up to the entrance of the church.

A young man, dressed in an overtly ornate blue and gold uniform, complete with a feathered hat and gold sword, exited the carriage.

Even before Istvan said, "That is the young Baron Frederick," I knew who it was. He was joined by three other young men who left the carriage behind him. They seemed a little older but had the confident swagger of young men whose life has never seen real servitude. As I watched them move into the church I swear I saw one of them stagger as if under the influence of alcohol.

The service itself was long and unremarkable. Most of the speeches were in Hungarian, so I found myself mostly lost and simply watching the crowd. I was impressed by the gorgeous colours cast on the audience by the sun beaming through the large stained-glass window in the church's bell tower.

I never gained an impression of whether the Baron and his wife were loved by these people or merely someone that must be paid respect out a sense of duty. The latter was our reason for being there, so I wondered how many others were similar.

The young Baron's three friends were especially part of that coterie, as I noticed the staggering youth nodded off several times and had to be shoved awake by the nearest boy.

After the service, we made our way from the church and stood amongst the other mourners outside. Istvan joined us and we observed Frederick as he left. He was somewhat agitated by the youths around him, but when he regained his composure, he slipped into the fugue that besets the recently bereaved. Grief strikes people in different ways and the Baron's actions were in some ways similar to others I had witnessed but in many ways very different. The three youths around him seemed more of an encumbrance than assistance. I sincerely hoped there was someone else that he could turn to in this hour of need.

I turned away as the Baron's coach arrived to look further amongst the crowd. When I gazed back, the coach began to pull away.

Istvan mentioned that Zoltan would be along to collect us in an hour or so. From there we would head out to the Schloss Metzengerstein. As he shuffled off, Holmes and I parted with the idea of observing as many of the mourners as possible.

I walked around the grounds, admiring the beautiful architecture of both the church and the memorial crypts in the graveyard. Holmes went the other way to partake in a cigarette. His was the more interesting stroll.

It seems that as he made his way through the small gardens to the side of the church, he heard voices, one old and gruff, the other youthful, speaking in German around the corner of the church. He stopped and listened, as he is often want to do. Thankfully, he translated the conversation for me.

"Has he said anything about it?" said the gruff voice.

"Not yet. I'm working on him. He succumbs more every day. His mind wanders even as we speak. It is working. He is enamoured with the horse, rides every morning. It won't be long," said the youthful voice.

"Sandor, it is very important that he signs soon, otherwise all will pass to the state," the older voice said.

"I know that. The dosage can't be increased, or he might die."

"True but keep an eye on him and report back soon. You stand to gain a lot out of this yourself, but that can easily be stopped."

"What? I'm doing all you asked. Don't threaten me."

"Then hurry up. I'm already old. I want to see this through before I'm gone."

"Fine. Just don't threaten me again."

Holmes was taken aback as the blonde-haired young man that accompanied the Baron stormed around the corner, looked at him for a moment with distaste and carried on. Holmes steadied himself and took on a casual air. He waited a few moments before continuing around the corner.

There he found Ur. Horvath, sitting alone on a small bench beneath an arbour filled with fragrant flowers. Holmes walked beneath it and glanced down at the old gentleman.

"I do beg your pardon, Ur. Horvath isn't it?" The man nodded. "I was simply walking and thinking whilst I passed the time before the memorial," Holmes said.

Horvath waved a hand at Holmes, "Do not worry yourself. I was sitting doing much the same." Holmes peered around at the surrounding buildings. "Your town is so beautiful and peaceful. It is very rare to find this near my home."

"Your accent. Englander? Yes?" said the other man.

"Why yes," Holmes said, "My family are business associates of the Baron."

At the mention of the Baron's name, Horvath's face screwed up in a grimace. Quickly composing himself, he rose from his seat and looked up into Holmes's eyes, sizing him up before stepping forwards and bowing.

"On behalf of my dear departed friend, Count Gustav Berlifitzing, I welcome you to my country and to my town," he said.

Holmes likewise bowed, "A pleasure to meet you, I am Sherlock Holmes of London, England. If I can ever be of service, I can be found through Ur. Istvan Herzog."

The other man looked slightly puzzled.

"I doubt that I would ever require your service as I haven't travelled to England in many a year but thank you all the same." He trotted off slowly through the gardens and passed out of view.

Holmes regarded him for a while then finished his cigarette and found me to compare notes.

***

Istvan joined us in the carriage as we made our way to the Schloss Metzengerstein. We bumped along the dirt track out to the castle, each one lost in his own thoughts. I was still curious about the welfare of the young Baron and couldn't get the picture out of my mind of the three callow youths that surrounded him.

"Istvan," I asked, "With his parents deceased, does the young Baron have any adult presence in his life to guide him through the next few years?"

Istvan's face went dark.

"No. Sadly, not," he said, "I was one of his father's closest advisors, but Frederick has shut me out altogether."

"The three youths that seem to be his friends, where do they fit in?" Holmes asked.

Istvan almost spat out his reply, the anger on his voice was almost palpable. "Those three useless …," he checked himself before continuing, "They came with Frederick when he returned from school in Vienna last summer. They took up residence in the old servants' quarters above the stables. Frederick was to return to school in the autumn but given recent events, he will stay on here. Those three layabouts moved into the castle the day after the accident."

"The scoundrels," I said.

"Oh, they are more than that. Sadly, you may see for yourself soon," he said as he turned around in his seat.

Looking out of the carriage window, I saw that we had entered the grounds of the Schloss Metzengerstein. The view we had of the rear did not do justice to the magnificence of the place.

The path we were on turned into a wide gravel driveway that ran between beautifully manicured lawns and gardens and ended up in the forecourt of the castle.

It contained three great wings, the main one we had seen from the rear and one on each side. A large number of carriages were arrayed within the forecourt and in areas to either side of the castle.

Zoltan brought us to the front entrance where a footman opened the carriage door and led us up the steps. A doorman took our names and showed us into the castle.

Stepping into an ornate foyer, I noticed two staircases that wound their way to the upper floors, their gilded balustrades glittering in the light filtering in from windows high in the West facing front wall. The foyer was immaculately decorated in expensive furnishings and fabrics. I truly believe that even her majesty would have been impressed by the level of finish.

I looked to one side and could see into the grand ballroom which had been set up as a reception area for the guests.

Istvan was about to lead us into the ballroom when a white-haired servant scurried over to him and began to talk in excited tones, all in German. I managed to follow most of the conversation and was perplexed by its indications.

Miklos, who I found out was the head-butler, was very concerned about the young Baron's welfare. He went on at length to Istvan about how the Baron's mind had become confused and misdirected. Istvan placed a hand on Miklos's shoulder to calm him and continued to assure him that the young Baron was fine, just in grief at the loss of his parents.

Miklos baulked at the idea and said it had all begun well before the accident. Ever since he returned from school, his attitude had changed, and his behaviour had become most peculiar. Some of the servants had seen him wandering the grounds, alone, late at night. When he was approached he seemed confused and lost. Most times he was led back to the castle and went quietly back to sleep. Other times he would run away only to return in the morning, covered in mud, leaves and twigs, as if he had slept in the forest. Miklos went slightly red for a moment when he said that a few times the Baron had been completely naked.

He went on to say that the Baron spent much of his time in the ballroom, staring at the tapestry. Miklos had seen him in there for hours on end.

"It can't be healthy. He needs help," the old man entreated Istvan to do something.

Istvan answered, "I understand your concern Miklos, but to be honest, I am unsure of my own position in the young Baron's life, now that he is an orphan. He has the power to remove me from his service on a whim."

He patted the old man on the shoulder again before finishing, "But I will do all I can to advise the young man. We have known each other for years; I can only hope he heeds my advice."

Miklos nodded, his eyes a little downcast. He bowed and disappeared into the bowels of the castle. As Istvan turned towards us, his face showing signs of concern, he saw our expressions and replaced his own with a happier visage. "Shall we see what is happening?" he said, pointing to the ballroom.

We took advantage of the fair on offer and I noticed many of the same people that had attended the service that morning. I searched the room several times, but the Baron and his entourage were nowhere to be seen.

Istvan introduced us to several guests and we managed to conduct small talk in a variety of languages depending on the level of English of the other party.

From time to time, I noticed Holmes's eyes drift to one end of the room. I succumbed to the same distraction, in fact, nobody could fail to notice the astonishing main feature of the room and be enamoured with it.

At one end, taking up the entire wall between two thin windows, was a large tapestry detailing a medieval battle on wide-open plains that had a remarkable similarity to the castle's estate.

Istvan noticed our attention travelling to the scene and led us across to have a closer inspection. "Wonderful isn't it," espoused Istvan, "This tapestry has been in the family for centuries."

I stared at the intricate detail of the wall-hanging and marvelled at the scene played out. It showed a battle. There were knights in armour on horseback. Two sets of standards accompanied each force. One was bright blue and gold, the other a drab shade of green and white. Immediately it became clear that this was a battle between the Metzengerstein and the Berlifitzing families.

Istvan noticed my expression. "Yes, you have realised Doctor."

Holmes was peering at a startling presence in the centre of the tapestry. An incredibly detailed and life-like horse stood in the centre near the bottom of the tapestry. Its rider, bearing green and white, was pictured losing his life at the hands of a tall, armoured knight trimmed in blue and gold. The horse remained proud and resolute in the midst of what must have been a terrifying ordeal.

"The tapestry shows, what many believe to be the beginning of the troubles between the families. The dying man is believed to be the very first Count Berlifitzing, his assassin the Baron Metzengerstein who then laid claim to all these lands, including a vast area that had once been under the Berlifitzing family's control," he said.

"Fascinating," I said as I stared at the piercing black eyes of the horse.

Istvan and Holmes moved away to mingle with the other guests. I followed for a moment, but my attention was drawn back to the tapestry.

I gasped in shock as I viewed it once more. The white horse's head was now straight on, both eyes staring at me. I could have sworn it was looking off to the side before. I shook my head and turned away.

I must be tired.

I met up with Holmes to find that Istvan had moved away to speak with someone he knew, Holmes took me lightly by the arm and led me across to the doors leading out to the rear area. I tried to gain his attention to look back at the tapestry but failed. Glancing back, I stopped in my tracks. The horse was again looking to the side. Rubbing at my eyes, I heard Holmes speak over my shoulder.

"Intriguing isn't it?" he said, "It's a trick of the light. The weaver has managed to make the horse stare ahead and to the side depending on the angle the tapestry is viewed from."

I looked up at him, an expression of relief came across my face. "I thought I was going mad."

"I would think that anyone who stared at that tapestry for too long may think the same thing." Smiling, Holmes proceeded towards the exit doors, with me following close behind.

Once outside, we found the Baron. He was sitting on a chaise longue beneath a large umbrella to shield him from the sun.

157

His entourage was scattered around him, either sitting or partaking in some archery practice. Several targets had been set up around fifty yards away. A number of bows and quivers stood nearby.

A dark-haired member of the Baron's party was lining up one of the targets. His shot hit the target but well wide of the red centre circle. Two young ladies clapped and cheered. He turned and bowed to them.

I quickly realised that this was not the sort of endeavour I would have presumed would accompany a memorial wake, but again reminded myself that I knew nothing of eastern European customs.

Looking across at the Baron's party, I noticed Sandor, the fair-haired companion that Holmes had described. He stepped across into the path of a waitress who brought a tray of champagne. Taking the tray from the young girl, Sandor leaned in and spoke to her. She tittered out loud before composing herself and withdrew back into the castle. Watching her leave for a moment before turning towards the Baron, Sandor strode over and instead of offering the tray, simply gave a glass of champagne directly to the Baron then the other members of the party.

I saw Holmes wait until Sandor had moved away before stepping across to the Baron. He bowed and introduced us.

"Please let me give you my deepest condolences, your Grace. I am Sherlock Holmes, and this is my associate Dr. John Watson. Your father was a long-time business partner of my family and I bring their sympathy and best wishes for your future. If there is anything that I or my family can do for you then we are at your service," he said.

The Baron regarded him for a moment before speaking. His face retained the vacant expression I had seen earlier, in fact, it looked even more vacuous.

"Thank you, Mr. Holmes. My father spoke well of your family, there was a very healthy mutual relationship between us. I think I may have even met your brother, 'erm Mycrow was it?"

"Mycroft, your grace," Holmes corrected gently.

"Ah, Mycroft. Fat man if I remember," he said.

I smiled to myself at the description of Holmes's brother.

Holmes nodded, "Yes, he has enjoyed life."

The Baron changed the subject completely. "Do you shoot, Mr. Holmes," he said nodding towards the targets.

As Holmes turned and glanced at the targets; I noticed a smile touch his lips. "It has been a while, but I can handle a bow."

Without turning, the Baron motioned towards the blonde-haired man. "Sandor is our best, should give you a run for your money."

I was still flummoxed at such a display on such a sorrowful day, but we were guests. Holmes didn't miss a beat. He took off his jacket, passed it to me and strode over to the nearest bow and quiver.

I noticed Sandor pick up a bow and quiver from behind one of the lounge chairs and walk across to join Holmes. In German, he said to Holmes, "I am the best in these parts Englander, you will not come close."

Holmes smiled and replied, "Fifty yards I make it."

Sandor nodded as he watched Holmes knock an arrow, aim, and let fly. The calm day was split by a high-pitched whistle and thud as the arrow struck home.

I looked over and saw it sticking out of the target just on the edge of the red centre circle.

"Too bad, too bad," said Sandor.

He knocked and loosed the arrow, hitting the target dead in the centre of the red bullseye.

"Fine shooting, Sir," remarked Holmes.

"I am just as good over a hundred yards," Sandor boasted, "In fact, the French man, Baron de Coubertin, has invited me to this competition he wishes to host in a few years, in Greece I think it is."

As he started to move towards the target, Holmes held up a hand. "You won this round, allow me." He strode to the target and withdrew the arrows. His own left a simple round hole, while Sandor's left a long thin cut in the target. Walking back, Holmes examined the arrows. His own sported a simple rounded bullet head, while Sandor's had a flanged triangular head made of iron or steel.

As he handed the arrow back to Sandor, he remarked "Interesting arrow for target practice. Is it for hunting?"

"Yes, I hunt, so I like to use the same arrows. No need to adjust to the different weight," he said.

Holmes nodded. "Another round?" he asked. As Sandor nodded, Holmes stepped back, allowing the younger man to go first. "Winner first."

Sandor knocked the same arrow, aimed, and struck dead centre again. I was sure I could see the original notch in the target sitting just next to his second arrow. As he moved away, Holmes stepped up to the firing line. He knocked, aimed, and loosed.

A loud noise rang out as Holmes's arrow struck the target in the middle of the notch hole made by Sandor's first arrow. Sparks flew as the metal heads struck each other.

Holmes turned to Sandor, who stared in utter dismay. "Must have needed to get my eye in." He put the bow back on the nearby rack, motioned to the target and said, "I'd call that one a draw. Shall I get them?"

Sandor simply turned and walked away, much to the cheers and derisive comments of his friends. I stepped up to Holmes and walked with him to the target.

"What was that all about?" I asked following him towards the target. He pulled the arrows out and showed me the tip of Sandor's arrow.

"When I saw the type of arrowheads I needed to know how good he was," he said, "Now, I know the Baron's death wasn't accidental. I just need more proof."

***

The rest of the afternoon was a long-drawn-out affair, to which we were growing tired. By early evening we decided to return to the Inn and began to say our goodbyes to those guests we had become acquainted with.

I noticed that the Baron had taken up residence in the ballroom once the light began to fade outside. He lounged on a settee and with a glass in his hand and simply stared at the tapestry. His three flunkies were nowhere to be seen.

I moved over to say my goodbyes but was met by a simple swish of his hand to wave me away. I felt slightly offended but hid my emotion, reminding myself that this was the Baron's home, and my feelings were not important in that context.

Holmes noticed and declined to give his own goodbyes. He mentioned that we would return prior to departing for London in a couple of days and make good our farewells then. Returning to the inn, we partook of a light supper and retired to our beds.

In the morning I was greeted by a slightly subdued Holmes, the red tinge to the flesh around his eyes reminded me of many a night spent poring over some arcane volume of forgotten lore.

As I started to quiz him over his obvious weariness, the landlady stepped into the breakfast room and delivered a platter of fresh bread, cheeses, and a selection of cured meats. Within moments of placing the fare down, she returned with a steaming pot of rich, black coffee.

"Eat up Watson, we have a long journey this morning, followed by a return to say our possible farewells to the Baron."

"Where are we travelling?"

"I arranged for Zoltan to take us to the Berlifitzing estate, I wish to investigate the supposed accidental death of the Count."

"Supposed?"

"There have been too many accidents for my liking. Something that our friend Ur. Herzog has questioned as well, hence why we are here."

Upon mention of his name, Herzog burst into the dining room, a wad of papers under his arm and an anxious look on his face. "Mr. Holmes, Doctor Watson, I'm so glad I found you. The most shocking event has happened this morning, I'm still very confused over it, and need to review the legal papers that I leant you last night and compare them to those I received this morning."

Holmes pointed to a vacant chair and told Herzog to sit. "Calm down dear fellow and explain what's happened."

"That young upstart, Sandor Csalas, appeared at my home this morning and woke me up with a loud thumping on my door. Instead of exchanging pleasantries upon entry to my house, he simply thrust these," Herzog placed the papers on the table, "at me and claimed that he was now the Count Berlifitzing, by the fact he was the illegitimate son of the deceased Count."

"Why did Sandor come to you?" I asked.

Istvan replied that as part of a deal struck many years before, between the Count and the Baron, a large proportion of the Metzengerstein estate was to be returned to the Berlifitzings on the death of the Baron.

"I knew about the deal and had informed the young Baron that the legal paperwork was all in order. I have struggled of late to gain the Baron's attention and had been waiting for a more favourable time to press him to sign the final documents," he said.

Holmes regarded Istvan for a moment before speaking.

"This Sandor, is there any evidence to prove that he is who he says he is?" he asked.

"I've only skimmed through the documents, but I would much rather discuss this with Ur. Horvath to ensure he knows about it and can advise. He's much more knowledgeable about the Berlifitzing legalities."

"I imagine that the Baron finding out that one of his good friends is now his supposed familial enemy may be a strange turn of events for him as well," I added.

Istvan nodded.

"It may lead to a more congenial status across the region instead," added Holmes.

Herzog and I both shrugged. To be honest, I hadn't considered that eventuality.

***

The trip to the estate was long and arduous. The roads were quite good, but at the high speeds that Istvan had urged Zoltan to achieve, it became extremely rough and dangerous. We were shaken about as if we were table salt during a banquet, but still, I estimated our journey took us well over an hour.

The Berlifitzing estate was a less sumptuous abode but would befit a minor British royal quite nicely. The stark presence of the burnt-out building in the foreground of the estate detracted from the chateau. The stables had been consumed almost completely by the fire, only the thick skeletal beams of the frame remained. Even the stonework had splintered and collapsed along with the roof.

Zoltan pulled the carriage to a halt near the burnt remains. We all alighted, even the sturdy driver, who after such a drive required a leg-stretching stroll as much as his passengers.

Istvan wandered away, evidently in search of Ur. Horvath, while Holmes and I performed a circuit of the ruins to undertake a cursory examination. Noticing a pile of burnt fabric that was in contrast to the surrounding straw and wood, I stepped carefully into the blackened edifice. Holmes took one look, then moved on.

The heap turned out to be horse blankets that were blackened and charred, but only on one side. When I pulled them away and found the straw beneath to be compressed, but relatively unburnt, I assumed this was where the unfortunate Count had collapsed. The blankets had been used to douse the flames or to protect the poor man from further harm. I dropped my head in reverence for a moment, before stepping out of the remains.

Outside I found Holmes standing by an exterior upright beam that had been severely burnt. The top was a blackened stump, the cross beams burnt through and laying in charred heaps on the ground.

Intrigued, I watched as Holmes leant into the wood and sniffed, before wrinkling his nose and pulling away. "Kerosene." He sniffed lower on the beam, shook his head, then stretched to full height and repeated the action. Stepping around the upright, he picked up a piece of the cross beam remains and held it to his nose. Nodding, he repeated the word, "Kerosene."

"Is that normal?" I asked, "Is it a woodlice treatment or something in these parts?"

"I wouldn't think so, Watson, plus if it were, there would be more on the lower part than the top. Look at this as well." He pointed out a narrow notch in the upright beam that was scorched all around. A small trace of melted metal could be seen on the lower part of the notch.

Holmes held up another small flat lump of cold metal. He handed it to me for examination. It was misshapen after being partially melted by the fire, but the shape reminded me of an arrowhead. I then realised it must have been embedded in the upright beam, the shaft had burnt away, and the head had melted slightly and fallen to the ground.

"What do you think Holmes?" I asked.

He looked grim.

"If I'm not mistaken, that is the remains of an arrowhead, similar to something we saw yesterday. If it were, then the rest was consumed by the flames. It may be nothing or it may be everything," he said, "I have a bad feeling that this fire was no accident." Looking around for Istvan, he saw the young lawyer emerge from the chateau and stride sullenly across the gravel drive, his wad of papers beneath his arm.

I followed Holmes as he paced towards Herzog, but as he started to speak, the young Hungarian cut him off. "Ur. Horvath is in Székesfehérvár visiting the local magistrate." Pulling the papers out and waving them around, he continued, "I believe he knew about this all along, may have even known about this Sandor for quite some time and may have lodged edicts himself in my ignorance. I need to speak to the Baron and advise him on the next course of action."

"That may be out of our hands," said Holmes, snatching Herzog's attention away from his own worries.

"What?"

"I believe this fire was no accident. Which leads me to surmise that our young Baron is in danger and may be the next victim if all plays out as I expect it to."

Istvan glanced around and yelled at Zoltan. "Zoltan, a várba, gyorsan." (Zoltan, quickly, the Castle)

***

The journey to Castle Metzengerstein seemed quick but was possibly due to the silence of all three of us. Each was wrapped in our own thoughts. Zoltan pulled up in the courtyard and we made our way into the foyer.

Immediately, Miklos scurried over, his face a mass of apprehension and fear. I tried to follow along, but Holmes translated for me later.

"Ur. Istvan," he said, "The Baron. I am so worried about the Baron."

"Why?" asked Istvan.

"He has disappeared. He took the new white charger and raced off into the forest," he said.

"What new white charger?" Holmes asked.

"Two of the grooms found a beautiful white horse in the grounds early one morning two weeks ago. I presumed it had escaped from the Berlifitzing stables, such a tragedy that is, but I sent word and they did not know anything about it. The grooms managed to coax the animal into a stall. The young Baron appeared from nowhere, saw the animal and muttered something about the Count returned from the dead." The Butler pleaded with Herzog. "I warned you. I told you his mind is going," he said.

"What happened this morning to worry you?" asked Holmes intent on the story.

Miklos turned and looked up at Holmes with his watery eyes.

"For several days he has walked the grounds in the early morning, but of late he has taken to riding the horse for hours each morning. Today, he strode out before even I had awakened. The grooms said that he saddled the horse and rode off. That was several hours ago. We haven't seen him since. He's not in his right mind. I just hope nothing has happened to him."

Istvan patted the old man on the shoulder, as was his custom and sent him on his way with assurances that we would investigate and find the Baron safe and sound.

"The stables?" answered Holmes when I asked what next.

As we stepped into the Ballroom on our way to the rear exit, our eyes were drawn to the tapestry. A beam of sunlight from a skylight in the ceiling struck the central figure of the white horse giving it an ethereal and almost angelic quality. The effect was incredible.

"Extraordinary," I said.

"You can understand why the Baron is so enamoured with this tapestry, and this newly found white horse," said Istvan.

Holmes wasn't as convinced as the Hungarian. "Or else." Letting his statement hang, he stepped over to the settee on which we had last seen the Baron reclining. An array of dirty dishes and glassware sat on the ground and on a small table to the side.

Holmes picked up a champagne glass and examined the remains in the bottom for a moment before reaching in with his middle finger. Once extracted he rubbed his middle finger and thumb together and stared at the result.

"Watson, what do you make of this?" he asked.

I moved across and looked down at the silver residue on his fingertips. I took the glass from his hand and examined the sediment as well. Repeating Holmes's actions, I extracted some of the remains myself. After a few moments of rubbing the greasy compound around between my fingers, I looked up. "If I was to ponder a guess, I'd say this is elemental mercury."

"My deduction as well," said Holmes.

Suddenly, I was aghast. "You don't think that the Baron ingested elemental mercury?"

"Not only this once but on quite a few occasions," Holmes said, "Possibly for as much as several months."

"Mercury?" asked Istvan joining us at the settee, "What would that do? Is it poison?"

"There have been rare cases of some factory workers in London, where poisoning from elemental mercury caused brain and liver damage. In low levels the victim shows signs of dementia or a continued delirium, higher levels can cause sight problems, muscular atrophy and even liver or kidney disease. Some poor people had died horribly from renal shutdown," I said.

"Horrible," he said, "Would that explain the Baron's mental instability?"

"Yes. I think it would," said Holmes.

"Would it come from the champagne?" asked Istvan, "We import it directly from France."

I shook my head. "No, there is no history of high levels of mercury in champagne, that I know of anyway."

Holmes bent down and picked up a discarded soup bowl, a similar dark silver ring could be seen near the top.

"I would say that the mercury has been introduced into the young Baron's food by a third party," he said. Without a word he disappeared into the bowels of the castle, leaving the lawyer and myself alone.

Carrying on outside, we found the Baron's other two flunkies lounging around near the rear entrance. The number of empty champagne bottles explained a lot about their state of mind. One was asleep, the other one sat on a chaise lounge staring out over the lake. Istvan walked up to the conscious man and spoke.

"Laszlo, wo ist der Baron," he asked.

"Ich habe ihn seit dem Morgen nicht gesehen, jetzt weiß ich es nicht, ist mir egal," Laszlo answered. (I haven't seen him since this morning. Now, don't know, don't care)

"Was ist mit Sandor?" (What about Sandor?)

"Habe ihn seit letzter Nacht nicht gesehen. Auch das ist mir egal." (Haven't seen him since last night, again I don't care)

By this time Istvan had his hands on his hips and was looking quite irritated. He dropped his hands, let out a harrumph and joined me. I could hear him mumbling under his breath. It was Hungarian, that's for sure, and I don't think I needed it translated to understand its intent.

At that point Holmes joined us, he took one look at the recumbent young men and said, "Forget them, I think their time is about to come. Let us check the stables."

Istvan and I both looked across the open fields towards the two-storey stable complex behind the servants' quarters. Holmes strode off. Istvan and I hurried to catch up to him.

When we were still several hundred yards away, a white horse broke from the nearby forest and raced across the field and into the stables. A blue-clad figure rode high in the saddle.

"There's our young Baron now," I said.

"Quite so," said Holmes hurrying up his stride.

Suddenly, a bolt of flame burst from the forest and flew across the open ground striking one of the stable's upper storey beams. Even from that distance, we could tell it was an arrow. The flames licked at the wooden beam which burst into blue and orange flames. Another flaming arrow flew from the woods and landed inside the ground floor; a fireball exploded from within leaving a curling trail of smoke that rose slowly into the sky.

"Kerosene," Holmes said.

Within moments more smoke began to belch out of the upper storey window and through the gap in the stable doors. Bright orange flames began to lick along the wooden beams and the roofline. A loud whinny echoed across the open field and the now riderless white horse bolted from the ground floor and headed towards the forest.

"The Baron," Istvan shouted and began to run towards the stables. I followed in his wake. Turning, I saw Holmes head for the forest, no doubt to apprehend the assailant. It had to be Sandor, no one else we had met could have made those shots with a bow and arrow.

By the time Istvan and I came to the stable, it was fully ablaze. Horses shrieked in abject horror within the flaming building. We, however, could see a pair of legs with riding boots, lying amongst the smouldering straw in the middle of the main area. Covering our faces with kerchiefs we dashed into the smoke and dragged the poor unfortunate Baron out into the clear air.

Once outside, a fit of coughing took both of us a few moments to recover before I was able to examine the Baron. He had as I feared succumbed to the smoke and flames. I tried several methods to revive him, but each failed to draw any breath or heartbeat.

Istvan's face dropped in horror at the realisation. He fell to his knees next to the body and visibly wept for his young charge.

"I failed you, I failed your father," he cried.

I stood and walked away, still suffering from the smoke I had inhaled and found Holmes walking towards me holding a bow and quiver full of arrows.

"No luck," I gasped.

Holmes looked at the body and crying lawyer and said, "Nor you, it seems." I shook my head in remorse. Holmes's face became stern. "Whoever shot these arrows was long gone. I followed a trail of boot marks, but they led to a line of hoof prints. The culprit escaped."

"But we know where," I said.

Holmes nodded. "Indeed. We shall send for the Sheriff and have him meet us at the Berlifitzing estate. I shall prosecute the case as I see it and justice will prevail."

***

"But where is your evidence, Mr. Holmes?" said the blonde-haired youth as he sat on a high-backed chair in the middle of the large room of the Berlifitzing manor house, turning it into a de-facto audience chamber.

"I have presented it as I have seen it," said Holmes, "Everything points to you."

"Even though I am very protective of my bow and arrows," he shrugged, "I admit that I may not have taken as much care of them as I should have. Leaving them at the Castle whilst I delivered my documents to Ur. Herzog, and then moved my possessions to the estate, was possibly a large oversight it seems, but you have no evidence that I was there this afternoon."

"I must ask for more," said the Sheriff, "As of this afternoon, Ur. Csalas, is now legally the Baron and Count of this entire area. A position that holds a great level of honour and power."

Holmes nodded to the Sheriff. "I agree Sir, I agree, and I understand the gravity of these accusations, but you must agree that the evidence presented demands investigation. We have three very high-profile deaths, that have elements pointing to something other than accidents."

The Sheriff nodded. "Yes, I do agree with that point."

"If this is all you have against the Count, then I would ask you to leave your accusations at the door, and withdraw from our presence," piped up Ur. Horvath, standing to Sandor's right.

Holding up a single finger, and wearing a familiar sly grin, Holmes continued. "There is the other matter of the young Baron's mental decline." Holding out a hand towards me, Holmes said, "My good friend Doctor Watson and I found evidence that Frederick had been subjected to a subtle form of poisoning from the effects of elemental mercury being introduced into his food and drink."

Horvath's face grew red as his anger grew. "And you are blaming the Count for this?"

"Yes, yes I am."

"On what grounds? If something was being administered to the Baron, then it could only have been the kitchen staff or that overstuffed butler." Horvath placed a fatherly hand on the Count's shoulder. "Young Sandor here had only been a kind and generous friend to the Baron. Supporting him through his school days and offering a comforting shoulder during the days following his parents' unfortunate demise."

The act was well played, but even I couldn't see how someone who supposedly had only met the newly installed Count in the last day or two would have been able to offer such a character reference.

"Ah, I cannot argue against those points," said Holmes, "As I haven't born witness to the friendship between the deceased Baron and the Count." He stopped for a moment, waiting to see if anyone was prepared to butt in. When all stayed quiet, Holmes began again. "But one could draw a different picture from several facts." As always, Holmes was apt to make a drama of the finale to an adventure. He stalked around the audience chamber and counted his facts off on several fingers as he spoke. "The chances of two strangers meeting at boarding school and becoming strong friends, only to turn out to be the last heirs of two extremely powerful neighbouring families, is quite infinitesimal." Turning towards Ur. Horvath, he said, "I put it to you, Sir, that you knew of the Count's illegitimate son, and managed affairs so that this could happen."

The Count's aide went red with rage once more and started to speak, only to be cut off again. "Remember, I saw you in the Church garden. I also overheard your conversation, which brings me to the second point. Young Sandor, on your instigation, convinced the young Baron to sign documents that would see part of his newly inherited lands handed over to the heir of the Berlifitzing estates. All without the knowledge of his lawyer and confidant, Ur. Herzog. I would also add that the Baron was not of sound mind at the time. If he were, he would have discussed the details with Ur. Herzog. That was the precise reason that Sandor began the mercury poisoning."

"Nonsense," said Horvath, "You have only circumstantial evidence and conjecture. Any documents that have been signed have been legally done so. I have confirmation from the local Magistrate. Ask your lawyer for yourself."

"Well, intriguingly enough, I do have a witness, in fact, several witnesses."

A shocked look came across Horvath's face, his mouth gaped open. Even the young Count sat up straighter at the mention of a witness.

"Who?" he asked, meekly.

"When we were first introduced, I noticed an interaction between yourself and a young housemaid in the Baron's service. It was easy to track down this girl, or Zsófia as she is known."

Sandor's face grew even more horrified. Horvath's returned to anger, with his eyes constantly darting towards his young cohort.

"Zsófia was very effusive about our Count here. She waxed very lyrical about their love and how she would soon hold court in this very building, if not back at the castle itself. Young love is a wonderful thing, not so when it is simply one way though, as I believe your tryst with young Zsófia was." Holmes waited a moment for a reply, but the Count simply sighed. "As I thought. One tiny nugget of information that Zsófia unearthed was the continued assistance that she provided to you to administer the Baron's medicine, as she called it."

Holmes brought a hand out from his pocket. Between finger and thumb, he held a small glass vial with a distinctly silver liquid inside. "This is the medicine in question, I'm sure we can simply test it to verify that it is indeed elemental mercury."

"This girl, she is simply an opportunist, throwing herself at Sandor and leaching off his fortunate circumstance," said Horvath, his face red from rage or embarrassment, of which I was still unsure.

"That may be Ur. Horvath, but would you expect a young girl, born and bred in a region such as this to understand the effects of imbibing elemental mercury, and to what ends would such as she hope to achieve?" Holmes turned towards the young Count. "But you Count, have an intimate knowledge given your studies at the Vienna Institute alongside the young Baron."

"This still seems to be circumstantial, Mr. Holmes," said the Sheriff.

"Ah, you would think, but I have talked to Miklos the butler, who stated he saw the Count and this serving girl on many occasions, plus upon showing him the vial, he stated he had seen it pass from the Count's hand to the girl's. So, we have motive, we have evidence, we have witnesses, to at least impose a deeper level of investigation."

To this, the Sheriff nodded, before expressing his own concerns, "But, under the laws of this region, the Count and the Baron are considered exempt from investigation by virtue of their position. Therefore, regardless of your words, I cannot, in good faith, arrest the Count or even implicate him."

A wry grin came to Holmes's face. I'd seen that grin many times before, always before fireworks. "Yes, I thought that would be the case, but the former Count had been wary of the consequences of such a situation." Turning towards Herzog, he asked, "Istvan, if you will, can you read Clause 44.3 in the edict established by the Count upon his demise."

Surprised, Herzog moved to a nearby side table and placed the wad of papers down. He rifled through them until he came across the required page.

Looking across at Horvath, Holmes said, "These are the papers that young Sandor lodged with Ur. Herzog this morning, so you should have a copy of them, in case you wished to verify." Horvath simply huffed in resentment.

Mumbling to himself for a moment while he read, I noticed Herzog's eyes grow wide in disbelief. "You are right it's all here."

"Well out with it man," yelled Horvath.

"Clause 44.3. To lay claim to the estate of Berlifitzing, the claimant must be of good character and clean reputation. Any action undertaken by the claimant prior to investiture as the Count, that could result in a legal conviction, must be resolved before any claim can be progressed."

"The pertinent word is *could*," said Holmes, "Now, my dear Sheriff, is anything I have said here today given you cause for thought that perhaps Ur. Csalas here could be found to have orchestrated, if not executed, either the descent of the Baron's mental health or, in fact, his unfortunate demise."

"These are very serious accusations," said the Sheriff, "I do not think that anything like this has been seen in the history of this region." Shaking his head slightly, the Sheriff walked across to the table where Herzog stood and read the edict himself, mumbling under his breath as he did so. When finished, he looked back, his lips pursed in contemplation, first at Holmes, then at the young Count, back to Holmes then finally back to the legal edict.

The rest of us held our collective breath as if waiting for some form of judgement to issue from the Sheriff. I spied Horvath's anger seething behind his red face. I truly believe he might have been in serious danger of a heart attack.

After an interminable time, the Sheriff slowly turned to face the collected audience. He shook his head slowly and dropped his eyes. "I have very serious concerns about all of this. It is unprecedented for a Count or Baron of this region to be stripped of a title." Looking up into Holmes's face, he continued, "But if, as you say, Mr. Holmes, any of this evidence you have unearthed does indicate foul play in the deaths of the Barons and the Count, then I am duty-bound to investigate." Looking at the young Count, he said, "I am truly sorry your Grace, but the legal documents that were used to prove your investiture, also state that until this matter is cleared you are prohibited from taking the title of Count. Under those circumstances, you may be found guilty of the crimes of which you are accused. So, I have no choice but to place you under arrest until this is all resolved."

It was the young Count's turn to shout in anger, but his rage was directed not at the Sheriff or Holmes, but at Ur. Horvath. "You said I would be Count. You told me I would be protected by my rightful title." He stood and grabbed the older man by the lapels, pushing him back against a wall. "I killed because of you. I killed my father. I killed my friend."

The Sheriff, Holmes and I rushed across to the two men, dragging the young Count away from the frightened Horvath. His face showed the sorrow of someone who had lost everything in a matter of seconds. The Sheriff motioned towards a nearby doorway and two constables appeared, taking hold of the young Count, and dragging him, shouting, and screaming obscenities, from the room.

All eyes fell on the sad figure of Horvath. "Is he correct? Did you orchestrate all of this?" asked Holmes. The diminished man simply nodded.

It was the stoic figure of the Sheriff who had the last word. "You have brought shame upon the name of this family, and upon our community as a whole. If I do not take you from this place for your own protection, I cannot guarantee your safety."

Herzog, Holmes, and I watched the Sheriff lead the broken man away from the audience chamber, bringing a close to a very strange and wretched affair.

***

During the train journey from Vienna, I questioned Holmes over the next steps in both the houses of Metzengerstein and Berlifitzing.

He pondered for a moment, staring at the scenery rushing by outside before turning to me. "Despite the heard confession from young Sandor, the Sheriff will need to prosecute the case for murder and accessory to murder on both Sandor and Horvath. That may take many months, as I understand it will need to be presented in Budapest or to a Judge from the capital. Once that is finished, then our friend Ur. Herzog will be tasked with executing the final Will and Testaments of both the Baron and Count. Herzog seemed to think that his first steps will be to find a suitable heir to both estates. The families were large so there should be a relative somewhere that is legally entitled to each. There will no doubt be a cavalcade of suitors applying to be the next Baron or Count. I dare say that our friend will be employed on that exercise for some time to come."

"Well good for him."

"Yes, even once all is finished, I imagine Herzog will be kept busy managing the legal affairs for both estates for many years."

I thought for a moment, establishing the train of events in my mind in preparation for documenting the adventure when something occurred to me. "What about the young housemaid?"

"Ah, yes, the young at heart, in love with a supposed Count. I discussed her with Herzog, but nothing in her demeanour indicated she knew what the intention was of Sandor's deception. For all intents and purposes, she was simply a pawn in his twisted game. Hopefully, she will not be disposed of her employment because of it."

I nodded and settled back for the long journey home.

The Case of the Borneo Tribesman

Even though it was heading towards nightfall on that August evening, the dying sun of the day still beat down with a ferocity that had been unseen in London for quite some time.

Holmes and I departed our hansom and stood before the modestly appointed three-storey Kensington abode of our host for the evening. From what I knew of our host, the appointment of the building was more in line with the tastes of his wife, rather than the flamboyant nature of the man of the house. The couple had bought all three connecting terraced houses and made them a single abode, with all décor and modifications left to the wife.

It was two days since the simple but elegant card had arrived, inviting me rather than Holmes to what was coined an "event" at this address.

Our host was adventurer and businessman Sir Tristan Leavins, the head of the London division of the North Borneo Chartered Company. From my reading, I knew that he spent the majority of his time in the East Indies, coordinating the trading of resources and goods between Borneo and England.

A small handwritten note had accompanied the card and told me more than I could have gleaned from the invitation itself.

It seemed that Sir Tristan was to present, to the British Trade Commission, a selection of goods from far-flung Borneo to engender a want within them and secure funds for establishing a series of trade routes between the two countries. The event, as the invitation called it, was a prelude for a small but distinct class of attendees.

How I had been chosen to attend was indicated by the signature at the bottom of the letter. The name was Willard Kesson, or as I had known him Lieutenant Willard Kesson of the Royal Engineers, who fought in the Battle of Maiwand where I was unfortunately injured.

As a postscript, Kesson had noted that he would be delighted to see me again. He also suggested bringing Holmes to add colour to what may be a rather dull affair.

Taking the lead, I approached the door, readying myself to lift the brass knocker to announce our arrival. As I reached towards it, the door was opened wide, and we were met by an incredible sight. Standing in the entranceway was a half-naked, dark-skinned man. He was resplendent in a brightly coloured cloth that wrapped around his waist, with a long section hanging down the front. Upon his head, he wore a feathered headdress, with several beaded necklaces that draped down his chest. I was so stunned by the man's appearance that I simply stood with my mouth open.

A bright white smile split the man's dark face. "Good evening, gentlemen. Welcome home to Sir Tristan's." Holmes bowed slightly to the man and introduced us. "Ah, good, good. Holmes and Watson. Yes. I hear that name." He stepped back and bade us enter.

As we passed by, Holmes stopped and asked the man. "I can only assume you hail from Borneo. Your headdress and loincloth are reminiscent of the Northern area, or indeed from the island of Labuan."

"Yes, sir. We all from Labuan. Many more inside," he said.

"And what is your name?" Holmes asked.

"Jamal. Your service I am," the man said, bowing before us.

"*Selamat Berkenalan*," Holmes said.

"And I pleased meet you too, sir," Jamal said.

"Your English is quite good," I said. "Where did you learn?"

"The sisters at the Mission." His face went dour at some remembrance. "I was many, who no parents."

"Oh, I'm so sorry, my good man. An orphanage." He nodded. I started to speak again, but another couple arrived at the doorstep. As Jamal attended to the new arrivals, we took our leave and moved into the house.

Looking down the hallway leading away from the entry foyer, we found another similarly dressed tribesman. He smiled widely as we approached but shook his head when I asked him a question in English. Instead, he simply held out a hand towards the nearby open set of double doors. Holmes repeated his Malay welcome, to which the man's face broke into a wide smile.

As we stepped through, I was simply awestruck. This would be called a ballroom in a country manor house, but here in a simple terraced house, it was something else entirely. The room stretched from the entrance hallway all the way to the far end of the third house. On one side a series of bay windows looked out across the gardens and onto the street, while on the other a succession of small alcoves had been created, with curtains supposedly hanging in front of doorways exiting the room.

I wasn't an architect by any measure, but I could see that as part of the expansion, the supporting walls between each house had been removed – something that I presumed would be extremely dangerous to the structural integrity of the floors above. "Holmes?" I asked my friend, turning to find him likewise studying the grand room.

"Yes, Watson, amazing isn't it? An incredible feat of engineering. The man responsible must be congratulated."

"I think you are seeing the room differently to me."

Holmes glanced at me for a moment, and upon seeing my slight discomfort, patted me on the shoulder and began to point out certain aspects of the room. "Fear not. If you look along the lines of the original walls, you can see arches built at the extremities, they meet up to sunken iron beams that virtually replace the function of the old bricks and mortar walls." He pointed along the length of the room and I could finally see the series of beams that had been added to strengthen the floor. "It's quite a remarkable design."

"Thank you," came a reply from nearby, "Sir Tristan asked me to help the builder with a new style of design that would enable the virtual disappearance of the load-bearing walls."

We both turned and found my old friend Lieutenant Willard Kesson standing just slightly behind us, a wide grin on his face.

"Willy!" I almost shouted, delighted to meet my old friend.

He stepped forward and thrust a hand out, grabbing mine and shaking vigorously. "John, it's been far too long, so good to see you again." Before I could introduce him, Kesson turned to Holmes and shook his hand as well. "Mr. Holmes, I am so glad you could make it. Even more pleased that you appreciate all of my designs in this room."

"It is a rather remarkable feat, sir," Holmes replied.

"Lieutenant Willard Kesson, here, was with the Royal Engineers at the Battle of Maiwand."

"Willard is fine if you please. John and I met in the field hospital after I succumbed to injuries as well."

"And you've been in Borneo for the last few years?" asked Holmes.

"Yes. I was recruited by Admiral Mayne, one of the North Borneo Company's directors. They needed engineers, and the Admiral wanted servicemen due to their diligence and perseverance. Plus, the warm weather is kinder on my injured leg."

"What have you been doing over there, Willy?" I asked.

"Ah, John, some amazing things. The North Borneo Chartered Company, as it is rightly called, was set up in competition with the East India Company. The Directors have been given the rights to investigate and exploit the resources available in the country."

"I'm intrigued," said Holmes. "What resources exactly?"

"Well to begin with foodstuffs, animal and plant goods, but there are moves afoot to investigate any mineral finds that we can unearth." Kesson indicated the room before us. "That's what tonight is all about. A first introduction to some of the produce, animals, and cultural artifacts that are on offer in Borneo. Sir Tristan has brought some of the local tribesmen with him, and a range of foodstuffs and produce to tempt the British Trade Commission, in the hopes of garnering further financial support and setting up future trade routes."

"Doesn't really sound like any of that is within your area of expertise," I said. "What do you do with your time and intellect?"

"Ah, that's where it is interesting," Kesson said, "The Admiral sent me out to Borneo with the intention of assisting with a way of bringing fresh food all the way from the East Indies to England. My first stop was in Australia where I met with a man called James Harrison, who had invented an ice-making machine. I brought his design and manufacturing techniques back to Borneo and using his initial design, I've improved it to a point where we can install the machine onto a ship and create ice at will, ensuring that any food shipped across the globe will be kept frozen or chilled for the entire journey."

"Marvellous," I said.

Kesson indicated the various displays and offerings around the room with a sweep of his hand. "What is on show tonight are some of the tastiest delicacies and intriguing objects of interest that we've discovered so far in Borneo." We stepped into the room, following Kesson as he led us around the various exhibits.

Following his movements, my eyes fell on several distinct areas around the room. In one small alcove, one of the tribesmen stood with an orange-haired orangutan on a stand. "This is of course an orangutan. We brought in another female as a donation to London Zoo to assist with their breeding program." Nearby was a table with an aquarium sitting on top. Inside, a long blue snake, with black stripes and a tiny swatch of yellow around its mouth, swam around. Its wide black eyes seemed to be fixed on my own as it moved. "This is the yellow-lipped sea krait," said Kesson, leaning in close to the aquarium. The snake jerked back before striking forward and smacking into the glass. "Quite deadly – and aggressive, as you can see. We did bring a breeding pair, but sadly one of them died on the voyage."

Not far from the aquarium was a six-foot-tall cage, with a wide-eyed animal, reminiscent of a small lemur, clinging desperately to a cut-down tree branch. "Ah, this cute little creature is locally called a cuscus. Again, we wanted to bring a breeding pair, but thought best to settle this little one in first and bring another on the next journey."

As we stepped away from the cuscus, we were approached by a tribesman carrying a large silver platter, covered in chips of ice, and topped with orange-and-white striped morsels of prawn meat. "Now this is special," said Kesson, picking one of the prawns from the tray with his fingers and biting into it with pleasure. "These are a large type of prawn caught off the coast of Borneo. We cooked and then froze them for transportation, ready to be thawed and consumed. You really should try some." He waved a hand at some of the other men holding serving platters. "We also have crayfish meat, brought over the same way, and some wonderful fruits, like jackfruit and rambutans. The fruit itself wasn't frozen but stored in a chilled room to ensure that it was kept fresh."

I did as Kesson said and using a small plate and fork offered to me by the tribesman, plucked one of the prawns from the tray and experimentally bit into the fleshier end. The meat was exquisite, the consistency of succulent chicken, but with a saltier, light fish taste to it. The morsel also had a slight smell to it, which remained on the plate afterwards, making me glad I had used the fork. "My word," I exclaimed, "That is indeed delicious."

"So, it isn't just the food that your company is promoting," said Holmes, "but also the freezing technology?"

"Indeed, it is, sir. The modifications I've made to Harrison's design could revolutionise food transport and open up the world."

Just as I was about to ask another question, a tall, immaculately dressed man entered with a much more demure lady by his side. Holmes leaned in and said, "Our host, I think."

Indeed, Sir Tristan Leavins, with his wife Blanche close by his side, made such a grand couple as they worked their way around the room that I almost forgot about the wonderful fare on offer and the fabulous beasts and items on display.

As they finally approached, Kesson introduced us to Sir Tristan and his wife. Usually, upon the mention of Holmes's name, people's faces light up with recognition and begin to deluge my good friend with questions aplenty. Sir Tristan's face was placid and engaging, but it was almost as if he'd never heard of Holmes. Lady Blanche was another matter. She gushed with enthusiasm and asked him all manner of trivial questions about some of his adventures. Sir Tristan moved off, leaving his wife to interrogate Holmes for a few moments before finally signalling her to join him and make the acquaintance of a couple across the room.

Turning to Holmes, I asked, "Do you think Sir Tristan was purposely rude, or actually didn't know who you were?"

"Well, given that the man has spent several years in Asia, building up the presence of his company, he may not have had a chance to peruse *The Strand*, unlike his London-based wife."

Nodding, I retorted, "Well, that would be fair. For a moment, I thought my writing had lost its touch." I searched for Kesson and found him munching on another prawn, smacking his fingers afterwards. I started to ask a question when a young man in his early thirties, with the tanned skin of someone that spends much of his time outside, stepped up beside Holmes and spoke quietly into his ear. Kesson quickly stated that he was needed to see to the ice machine and would return once the problem was resolved.

We amused ourselves by trying the crayfish meat and fruits on offer. Each was a delight and pleasure to the senses. Sating our appetite, we moved around the room and examined the special items that were displayed. Most were collections of weaponry, supposedly from the Bornean tribes during their pre-colonial state. One display contained several long wooden spears, and another a collection of short wooden, stone, and even iron knives. One of the most fascinating was a set of blowpipes, ranging in size and intricacy. There were five in all, starting at six inches in length, and growing to almost a yard.

In a small dish below the rack of blowpipes were a selection of actual darts used in the pipes. They were about three inches long, consisting of a slender needle for the most part and a thicker cone-shaped section at the end. I assumed that the thicker part pressed against the sides of the pipe, with the needle penetrating the skin of the animal or man. A small card explained that the darts were generally dipped in poison to incapacitate or kill the intended target.

I turned to ask Holmes's thoughts but found that he'd wandered away and was engaged in conversation with a couple across the room. Glancing back, I began to examine the longest blowpipe again. I was fascinated by both the simplicity and complexity of such a weapon. As I leaned in to look closer at the mouthpiece, a male voice spoke over my shoulder.

"Pick it up if you like," he said.

Standing nearby was an elderly gentleman. Although succumbing to a slight arch in his back, he stood as ramrod straight as he was able. "There's no mistaking a fellow military man," I said, holding out my hand, "I am Dr. John Watson, formerly of the Fifth Northumberland Fusiliers, and then with the Berkshires at Maiwand."

The older gent took my hand and shook it firmly. A small smile crept to his face. "Rear-Admiral Richard Mayne, formerly of Her Majesty's Royal Navy. Now I simply sit on the board of this damn company."

"Very pleased to meet you, sir. I am a good friend of one of your employees, Lieutenant Willard Kesson."

"Ah, Kesson. Good man, brilliant mind. I recruited him myself, you know. Was in the Royal Engineers. His superiors were very impressed. Sad that he was injured at Maiwand, though. Has been doing some great things in Borneo the past few years. That ice-making machine is a stroke of genius. His ingenuity will bring millions into the company. He'll be well rewarded for his efforts, but," the Admiral's face turned slightly dour, "I'm afraid that he wants more than just money."

"I don't follow, sir."

"Power, my boy! Power. Too many people want power for power's sake. Kesson will go far, but it will take time. This company has been built on reputation more than genius." Turning he pointed towards Sir Tristan. "Kesson needs to build up his own status, like Leavins over there. For the North Borneo Chartered Company to grow, we need people who can present to Parliament and Governments around the world. That requires status. We only put Knights of the Realm or highly-ranked military men in such positions." He stood for a moment and stared at the blowpipes, gathering both his thoughts and breath. "Kesson has time. His brilliance will shine through. He just needs time."

The Admiral reached for the longest blowpipe and passed it to me. "Though genius can sometimes come undone. Even something as elegant and deadly as this weapon is no match for a good soldier with a gun."

Examining the blowpipe, I was still impressed with the design. Looking down its length, I was unsure whether the tribesmen had hollowed out a straight length of wood or used something of a natural occurrence. It was light, and I could only assume that the length gave the projectile a much truer flight. When I turned back to remark to the Admiral, he was gone, almost as if he had never been there in the first place.

Replacing the blowpipe, I moved past the animals again, smiling at the huge eyes of the cuscus, and the ancient-looking face of the orangutan before joining Holmes and being introduced to the couple with whom he conversed.

After a few moments of answering questions, I chanced a glance across the room and noticed Sir Tristan and his wife speaking with another couple. They stood in a small alcove on the other side of the room not far from the racks of weapons. As I turned back, my eyes darted to the sharp movement of Sir Tristan's hand as it slapped at the back of his neck. I could have sworn he mouthed the word mosquito. At the time I thought nothing of it, amused by the idea that there would be any mosquitoes inside a Kensington residence, but I supposed at the height of summer, with Hyde Park not that far away, it was a possibility.

Re-joining the conversation around me, I found myself, once again, plied with questions about Holmes's adventures. I was, however, delighted when Kesson stepped up next to me. He leant in and whispered. "John, can you come with me? Sir Tristan has taken ill." I glanced over at the alcove where I had last seen our host and found it empty.

"Do you know what's wrong?"

"He fell faint, and it was only fortunate that another man caught him before he collapsed to the ground. He's been taken into a nearby room and laid on a settee. When I left, he was unconscious."

Holmes noticed our conversation and made his excuses as Kesson and I stepped away, joining us as we exited the large room and came upon the small crowd surrounding Sir Tristan.

I hurried up to the reclining man and ushered the others away. "Please, I'm a doctor. Give this man some space and air to breath." Kneeling down, I felt Sir Tristan's brow. His temperature was elevated, leading to my first thought that he had simply been overcome by the heat of the occasion. Glancing around, I noticed a maidservant standing nearby. I implored her to retrieve a cloth and some cold water.

"Would ice be better?" Kesson asked.

"Much."

"See to it, Gwendolyn." The young girl disappeared.

"What's wrong with him?" my friend asked.

"I think he has simply been overcome. I do wish I had my bag. I would like to check his heart." Dismissing any propriety, I reached down and undid the neck of Sir Tristan's shirt and tie. Touching my fingers to his neck I counted the rate of his pulse. It seemed to be slowing. I hoped that meant that he was relaxing after a mild case of anxiety.

I was so wrong.

Suddenly, Sir Tristan's body arched from the settee. His arms and legs twitched, his eyes snapped open, with the whites showing. Frothy drool gathered at his lips and streamed from his mouth.

Frantically, I glanced around at the nearby audience. "He's having a seizure. I need something small and hard. A spoon, fork, or knife. Quickly now." It was Holmes that found a letter opener with a thick wooden handle on a nearby desk. Snatching it from him, I tried to prize the man's mouth open, so I could slide it above his tongue, but as quickly as the seizure started it stopped.

It was then I realised the man in my arms was dead.

Checking his pulse again and finding nothing, I dropped my head in dejection. I hadn't realised who was still in the room but regretted my actions when Sir Tristan's wife cried out in despair. "No. No. Tristan. No."

Kesson went straight to the stricken woman and organised someone to take her from the room. My last sight was of the look of hopelessness on her face as her eyes stared at the corpse of her husband. Others were ushered out until it was only Holmes, me, and the corpse.

"If I'd had my bag," I spat, "I could have saved him." A hand patted me on the shoulder. Turning I gazed up into Holmes's stoic expression.

"You did everything you could, given the circumstances. More than anybody else could do." I realised his eyes lay on the corpse, rather than on my face. As always, Holmes was searching for clews. "I have my opinions, but from what do you believe he died?"

Staring back at the poor dead man before me, I answered, "Until a police surgeon investigates we won't have a solid answer. It could have been anything. Heart attack. A stroke. An epileptic fit. Perhaps a reaction to something."

"You may be onto something with the allergy angle." Moving closer to Sir Tristan, Holmes bent over and began examining the corpse.

I must have been weary, as I snapped at him, "Come, Holmes. A man has just died. In all likelihood it was natural. Not everything need be suspicious."

"That may be so, but until everything is eliminated, I will never drop my scepticism." He proceeded to kneel, examining him before gently lifting the man's head to reveal a small, dried bloodspot on the back of Sir Tristan's neck. "Now that is interesting."

Looking with weary eyes, I realised the spot was where I had seen Sir Tristan slap, only minutes ago. "That was where the mosquito bit him." But I was also recalling something else that I'd seen not long before – at the beginning of my conversation with Admiral Mayne.

Holmes glanced around at me, a look of surprise on his face. "Mosquito?" Nodding, I explained what I had seen earlier. His eyes drifted away as some inner thoughts began to run. Reaching into his pocket he withdrew his glass. Smiling at my look of shock, he said, "Always come prepared, Watson. Always come prepared."

I thought his comment a little rough, given my wish to have my doctor's bag at my side, but left it at that.

"Help me roll him on his side." I did as asked and watched Holmes study the small blood spot with great interest. "What do you make of this?" he said. He pulled away, leaving his glass hovering over the spot. Leaning in for a closer look, I noticed the blood spot was a lot larger than a simple mosquito bite. There was also a dried crust around the area. It was difficult to tell colour in the dull light of the room, but it looked cream or light yellow in tone. Definitely not a normal bodily fluid from such a wound.

"I have no idea, but whatever that dried substance is, I don't think it came from Sir Tristan."

"My thoughts precisely. Now, where was he when you saw the mosquito bite him?"

I described the alcove again – and the fact that there were blowpipes on display. Holmes was away within seconds. I was in two minds whether to follow or stay with the corpse until Kesson returned with help. There was nothing more that I could do for the dead man. Since he was beyond help and wasn't going anywhere in a hurry, I rolled him again onto his back and placed his hands on his chest. To anyone else he would look as if he was simply reposing.

Moving into the ballroom, I was surprised to find it empty of people and animals. I assumed that Kesson had sent word throughout the room that their host and hostess were indisposed and informed all to vacate the premises. I noticed that the racks of weapons remained, presumably to be removed at a later date.

I found Holmes on his hands and knees, studying the floor near where I had seen Sir Tristan supposedly bitten by an insect. "What the devil are you looking for?"

"Clews."

Remaining on his knees, Holmes looked at me and held up a small object. "I don't wish to suppose yet, but I'm beginning to paint a picture in my mind."

"Is that what I think it is?"

Holding the object between thumb and forefinger, he looked at it through his glass. "It appears to be small and cone-shaped, possibly made of wood or bamboo. There is a tiny indentation in the centre of the pointed end."

I noted that it very much resembled one of the darts that had been lying near the blowpipes.

"This is where it lay," he said, pointing to a small, discoloured area on the dark wooden floor. From where I stood it was either off-white or a light yellow in colour.

"Is that – ?"

"The same substance as we found on Sir Tristan's neck? It may well be." Holmes leaned in closer with his glass to study the substance again. "We shall need to examine it further, and possibly run a chemical test, but given the colour, consistency, and location, I am fairly certain they're one and the same."

"Any conjecture on what it could be?"

"No, but let us look amongst the weapons. In just a moment, I confirmed that the largest blowpipe was missing.

"The one I picked up and examined," I added.

Holmes gave the vacant spot a cursory glance, before picking up one of the darts and holding both it and his prize next to each other at eye level. The small conical object that Holmes had found was identical, although the needle was missing from the base of the dart.

I commented on that fact. "Do you think that it fell out?"

"I didn't find a needle anywhere." He wrapped the dart in one of the small envelopes that he habitually carried. "I think this is our mosquito."

"Perhaps the needle must be caught in Sir Tristan's clothing or something."

That sly grin grew on Holmes's face. "Perhaps. That would be one answer, but there's another I'd like to investigate."

"These darts are generally tipped with poison. It seems likely that this is what happened to Sir Tristan."

"I'm not prepared to say anything at this stage, but I want to eliminate as much uncertainty as I can." Turning to face me, Holmes asked, "Think back on Sir Tristan's symptoms before his unfortunate demise."

"He fell faint and reportedly passed out."

"Yes, and when you were attending him?"

"He was unresponsive. His heartbeat was slow but erratic, then finally he had a seizure before expiring. Everything happened so quickly."

"Yes. Not the sort of thing I would have thought could be attributed to a simple heart attack or apoplexy."

"True, but poison? Cyanide or even arsenic wouldn't affect someone in that way. Plus, they are much slower."

"What about some poison that attacks the central nervous system?"

"Well, I suppose, but where would someone obtain something so toxic?"

Holmes pointed behind me. As I turned, my eyes fell on the slowly moving solitary sea krait in its aquarium. "Good Lord? But how? I'm not even sure how to extract the venom from such a dangerous animal."

"Ah, but if you recall, there were originally two."

"Of course. If you removed the poison glands, you could extract the venom, and even concentrate it. That would make it deadly."

"Something, I think, that the Bornean tribesmen have been doing for centuries."

"What have the Bornean tribesmen been doing?" asked a voice from behind us. We both turned to find Kesson standing nearby.

"Watson and I were just ruminating on the use of blowpipes by primitive tribesman in Borneo."

"That's a strange thing to be talking about moments after a man died." Kesson's face was stern, almost brimming with anger at our indifference until his eyes grew wide. "You don't think Sir Tristan was killed by poison?"

I chipped in to try and guide Kesson's thought patterns in a different direction. "We were simply passing the time until the authorities arrive."

It was then that my old friend noticed the objects in Holmes's hands. "Those are blowpipe darts." His eyes rose to Holmes's face, and then to mine. "You *do* think Sir Tristan was poisoned, don't you?" Turning his head, he glanced at the empty spot in the rack nearby. "One is missing. Those cursed tribesmen! I knew they were a foolish idea." Without waiting, Kesson stormed from the room. I started after him, but Holmes placed a hand on my shoulder to stop me.

"Stay, Watson. With the Lieutenant out of the way, we can investigate further in peace."

Understanding my associate's desire, a niggle of doubt surfaced in my mind regarding Kesson's possible future actions. Turning those thoughts more towards things at hand, I glanced around to see what Holmes was up to.

He stood, hands-on-hips, near the alcove where the blowpipe dart had been found. As I stepped up next to him, he remarked, "I need you to do something for me."

"Yes?"

"Can you stand as close to the spot that you saw Sir Tristan when he was bitten?"

"Certainly." I stepped back a few strides and studied the area for a moment, whilst replaying as many of my memories of the event as I could. I then strode forward and stood as close to the spot and in the posture of our host as I could remember.

"Excellent," said Holmes, now stay still for me. He was silent for a while as he continued to stare, first at me, then at the small stain on the floor, before I heard him step away across the room. I chanced a glance over my shoulder, to see him searching behind the curtains at the other end of the room. Finally, he expressed an "A-ha!" Checking my position and location, I broke away and hurried to see what had piqued his interest.

There, behind one of the heavy drapes, and propped up against the wall, was the missing blowpipe. I glanced across to where I had previously stood and judged the distance to be some fifteen yards. "That would be a remarkable shot."

"Yes. I can only presume that whoever made it was quite conversant with the use of these blowpipes and had many years of practice."

"Oh, surely not one of the tribesmen?"

Standing, Holmes replied, "I will wait to answer that question." Pushing aside the curtain, he stepped through the doorway behind. Following, we found ourselves in a small, dark anteroom that led further into the bowels of the house. I pushed on and found an exit door that opened into a passageway leading through to the rear of the building.

Returning, I found Holmes holding a small silver dish. "What have you there?"

Pulling the draw-cord for the drapes, parting them to let light from the main room enter, I saw that the dish held two of the cone-shaped darts. They floated in a small puddle of coloured liquid, along with several chunks of ice.

"These are the ammunition for that blowpipe," Holmes said.

"But aren't those simply the larger cones? There are no needles – they simply wouldn't fly."

"Ah, there are needles – or at least there *were* needles, I believe."

"I don't follow."

"The day has been hot, has it not?" I nodded. "There are small bits of ice floating in this dish of water. I would conjecture that originally the dish was full of small chunks of ice, used to keep something cold – the needles of several blowdarts – perhaps formed of ice themselves."

"Incredible."

"Quite so. And quite ingenious. If one could create needles from ice, they would remain intact for the immediate purpose then melt away to nothing more than liquid in a matter of minutes or even seconds. The only remains would be the conical end used to stabilise the dart during flight. Something so small and trivial that most people would dismiss one as merely a piece of detritus and not give it another thought."

"Devilish. If the needles were formed from pure venom, then they would be deadly. The tip would penetrate far enough to break off inside the skin and deliver a dose of poison directly into the bloodstream. Death would almost be a certainty."

"Exactly."

A voice floated to use from across the room. "John? Are you still here?"

I stepped out through the curtains and found Kesson standing in the alcove leading through to where the unfortunate Sir Tristan lay. "Willard, over here."

"Good, good." He approached, his eyes darting to where the curtains were gently moving after Holmes had dropped them back in place. "The police and the surgeon are here. As you were the doctor that pronounced Sir Tristan dead, they would like to talk with you."

191

"Of course, of course." I glanced around before following Kesson, but there was no sign of Holmes.

Behind the curtains, we found a sorrowful looking man in his late fifties and a pair of young bobbies. All were staring down at the reposing form of Sir Tristan. The older man, whom I guessed to be the police surgeon, glanced across at us as we entered. Kesson quickly introduced us, and the man plied me with questions that I duly answered.

"Hmm," he said. "Based on so little, I can only conclude that it was natural, but I will have to investigate further back at the morgue. Thank you for being so diligent and thoughtful, Doctor Watson. Sir Tristan might have been saved if you'd had your medical bag, but given the rapidity with which he passed, I sincerely doubt it. Death appears to have been sudden, and probable."

"One thing you may wish to undertake is an analysis of the blood."

"What am I looking for?"

"A poison."

"What?"

"Possibly from snake venom."

"Surely you're joking! How would this man have been bitten by a snake in this environment?"

"Well, there was a live sea krait in an aquarium, but we do not believe that is how the venom entered his system."

"We?"

"My associate and I. Mr. Sherlock Holmes."

The old surgeon's eyes went wide. "You're *that* Doctor Watson?" I nodded in answer. "Do strange deaths just follow you around?"

"It does seem that way. Regardless, we have no solid proof as yet, but there are indications that this man has been the victim of foul play. The small mark on his neck. The dry crust around it. The seizure he had just before expiring. Holmes is working on other evidence as we speak, but it would add to our store of knowledge if you could undertake further investigation of this poor man."

He nodded. "I thought this would be a simple case, but you're right. I'll do as you say before writing up the certificate."

"Thank you. I'm sure we will be in touch if we have anything more, either directly or through Scotland Yard."

Kesson seemed to have lost all interest in overseeing his former boss's corpse and had taken on an air of agitation. Standing in the doorway, he indicated that I should follow. As I joined him in the adjoining corridor, he turned and said, "I think I have our man."

Slightly stunned, I simply trailed behind him as he wound his way through the house and down into a dimly lit area of the large basement.

There, one of the Borneo tribesmen sat on a straight-backed chair. Another man, apparently some sort of assistant to Kesson, stood behind him, an indifferent look on his face, but bearing a posture said he was ready to pounce if the man in the chair even moved.

The tribesman's face bore all the hallmarks of someone frightened out of his wits. His eyes were wide and darted between Kesson and myself upon our entry.

Taking a long look at the frightened Bornean, I asked, "Why?"

"What do you mean?"

"Why would this man have killed Sir Tristan? Motive is generally the first thing that Holmes establishes when faced with a puzzle such as this."

Kesson stared at me for a moment and then approached the tribesman. Leaning in he asked a question in Malay, which was followed by a fearful response. Standing, Kesson crossed his arms and glared at the man in anger. "I asked why he murdered Sir Tristan. His response was that we British must be killed because we invaded Borneo."

Leaning in close to the man's face, Kesson spoke another long string of Malay, which was followed by an equally long response, the man's mouth turned down in a grimace of absolute fear. "He is part of a Labuan resistance group who have sworn to destroy our company." Turning towards the man standing nearby, Kesson added, "Anderson, make sure he doesn't move. I'll bring the constables to take him away." Without another word, Kesson stormed from the room.

Standing for a moment, I stared at the poor tribesman for a while. Even though he didn't seem to speak English, his face spoke volumes. To me, this man wasn't someone fighting for a cause. He was simply a lone man, a long way from home, in a truly alien world. Glancing at Anderson, I asked, "Do you believe any of what Willard just said?"

Anderson looked my way, shrugged, and said, "I'm not paid to think, sir. Simply to do. If Mr. Kesson believes this man is responsible for Sir Tristan's murder, then I believe what Mr. Kesson believes."

A very convenient way of thinking.

"I personally don't believe a single word of what your friend said," came a voice from the shadows. The tall form of Sherlock Holmes appeared from the gloom. He still held the long blowpipe, and I noticed the shorter form of Jamal, the man who had greeted us at the front door upon our arrival, appear behind and follow him into the light. The Borneo tribesman still wore his ceremonial dress, but his smile had disappeared to be replaced by a dour look on his face. Indicating the seated man, Holmes said, "This man is innocent."

"How so? What further evidence have you found?"

"I'll get to that, but from what I overheard in the conversation between him and Kesson, I'm afraid that your friend is lying."

"How did you understand what they were saying? I didn't think you spoke Malay."

"Well, I don't very well, but I have studied."

"When?"

"The other night, after you received your invitation. Why? Didn't you?"

I gave Holmes a withering look before noticing movement as Jamal stepped over to the man and said, "Lian?" He followed up with a few words in Malay. Lian, the other tribesman, responded with his own string of sentences.

Finally, Jamal turned towards Holmes. "Lian, my friend here, he says that Mr. Kesson asked him to – how you say? – play a trick on Sir Tristan." Lian spoke further, with Jamal simply listening for a moment. "Yes, it was to show how the blowpipes work. The darts were only ice. Harmless. Mr. Kesson made them."

Holmes addressed Jamal, "I assume that Lian here was asked to hide behind the curtains and shoot one of Mr. Kesson's supposedly harmless darts into Sir Tristan's neck?" Jamal spoke to Lian who simply nodded. "The problem being that Kesson's darts were poisonous."

"What do you mean 'Kesson's darts were poisonous'?"

We all turned to the source of the voice. The man who until that point I had thought of as a friend stood in the entranceway, the two police constables standing behind him.

"Ah, just the person, I think," said Holmes.

"Why?" Stepping into the room, Kesson's eyes fell on Jamal. "And what is he doing here?"

"Jamal here has been helping us speak with Lian, your chosen perpetrator."

"What? He can't speak English. None of them can."

"Ah, that isn't quite true, sir," said Anderson, his face a slight shade of red from embarrassment at contradicting his superior. "Jamal's English is quite limited but effective. That's why I placed him on door duty."

"But he's obviously lying, just like this one," Kesson retorted, pointing at the seated man. "They're all in it together. We've been defending ourselves from their type for years."

"What do you mean by 'their type', Willard?" I asked.

"The insurgents. The resistance. They've obviously infiltrated the locals that we employ in the company, to get what they've always wanted. To kill Sir Tristan – or any of us, for that matter."

Turning towards Anderson, I asked, "Is this true? Have you been struggling against these terrorists?"

Anderson's eyes grew wide. They darted towards Kesson, who scowled at his underling, then to the policemen, then to Holmes, and finally back to me. His head began to shake slowly from side to side. A growl rose from Kesson. "Anderson, remember for whom you work." The younger man's gaze rushed back to Kesson's.

"I'm sorry, sir. I cannot lie. Not about this. Not with Sir Tristan dead. Especially if you are involved."

"Anderson . . . ." Kesson's voice rose in pitch and volume. His face flushed red with anger.

"No. I can't. There is no resistance. We've been at peace with the local tribes for years. They've never had it so good. Our company has furnished them with clothes, food, housing, and employment. Brought them out of their primitive ways and into the Nineteenth Century. They love us." His face turned towards Jamal. "Isn't that right, Jamal?"

"Yes, sir. It is. We would never wish harm on the white men."

All eyes turned back to Kesson. His own grew wide. "What? What am I supposed to have done? I have done nothing. If I have where is your proof?"

"Ah, proof," said Holmes. "Let me replay the facts for our constables here. One: Sir Tristan Leavins died earlier tonight, from a suspected heart attack, but more likely from the poison of the yellow-lipped sea krait. Two: This tribesman was coerced to unknowingly deliver the fatal dose of poison, using a primitive blowpipe, armed with darts made from frozen krait poison."

"Ridiculous!" cried Kesson. "That would be impossible."

"Except for the fact that you are a genius at ice-making and refrigeration," answered Holmes, bringing a small metallic object from his pocket and holding it before him. He broke the object apart, showing it to be a solid metal mould. "I visited your ingenious ice-making machine, and the little workspace you created nearby. This was simply sitting on the bench. It is a mould that can be used to create extremely delicate needles of ice." Pointing to a set of small conical cavities at one end, he said, "You can place a cone-shaped dart stabiliser in here, then pour liquid here, ready for freezing. And, *voilà*, ice darts ready for use in a blowpipe. Though you must be quick, or else they melt, as Watson and I discovered, when we found a dish with the remains of two darts and the ice that kept them chilled."

"That could have been used to make ice for drinks," Kesson countered.

"Perhaps, but the other mould I found inside a refrigeration unit upstairs would contradict that. It contained three cone-shaped moulds that still had traces upon them of a light-yellow liquid, seemingly formed into highly lethal poison darts."

"What liquid?"

"This liquid," said Holmes, holding up a small glass vial half-filled with a light-yellow liquid, "It was in a drawer attached to the workbench. I'm sure if we have it analysed, it will prove to be sea krait venom."

"Where would that come from?" Kesson demanded.

"From the poison sac of a certain yellow lipped sea krait that expired on the journey from Borneo most likely."

"But what possible reason could I have to orchestrate all of this? I was recruited personally to this company. I've worked diligently for years. I'm in charge of the entire engineering team in North Borneo."

"I think I can answer that," I said. All eyes turned my way. "I met Admiral Mayne. He was very complimentary of you but was a little concerned about your ambitions – ambitions that he believed might never be realised."

"What? What do you mean? I was virtually second-in-charge to Sir Tristan."

"From the Admiral's words, it seems that the company only promotes self-made men of station or with high military ranks into the top echelon of the company. He suggested that you could gain a higher level if you established yourself outside of the company or gained a title or honour."

"That old fool! When I was hired, he promised me a long and industrious career. I could take them far. My inventions will open new trade routes, bring millions into the company's coffers. But I can't do that as just as an underling, I need the power to direct the operations of the company. Sir Tristan was a blind fool, with no foresight. The company is better off this way."

"Does that mean you eliminated him for just that purpose?"

"What? No. I had nothing to do with this. Everything you have said is just circumstantial. You have no solid proof."

"Oh, I wouldn't say that," said a familiar voice from the doorway. Glancing across, I saw the short frame of a man whom we knew, filling the doorway. "In fact, from what I've just heard, I think the Yard could build quite a case against you, Mr. Kesson."

"Who are you?" said Kesson, his voice rising close to a yell.

"Inspector Lestrade, Scotland Yard, at your service," our colleague said, with a wry smile on his lips. Turning towards the two constables, he said, "You two, take Mr. Kesson here up to the wagon parked outside. Hold him for murder, and I'll interview him when I return."

The constables, each took hold of one of Kesson's arms.

"Anderson," said Kesson, "I need the company's solicitor. They'll have me out in a moment."

"Yes, sir, but I don't think the board will be very happy. They have very strict rules about the consequences of any improprieties of senior staff members – even where the person has only been charged, but the charges are overturned later. They simply do not tolerate any sullying of a person's reputation."

Kesson's face dropped as Anderson's words sunk in. "No. I've done nothing." The two policemen led him struggling and yelling from the room. I could hear his proclamations of innocence all the way down the corridor and up the stairs to the ground floor.

When all was quiet once again, Lestrade turned to face Holmes and said, "I received your message. I'd already heard about the poor unfortunate Sir Tristan, so now you'd better fill me in on the rest of this case."

***

It was several days later whilst I was finishing my breakfast coffee and reading the morning paper, that Mrs. Hudson brought Lestrade into the sitting room.

"Good morning, Doctor. I just wanted to drop by and give you and Mr. Holmes an update on this Sir Tristan Leavins business."

"Excellent," said Holmes stepping into the room. "I'd been wondering how you'd got on." He walked across to the table, sat down, and poured himself a cup of coffee. I offered Lestrade a cup, but he declined.

"It didn't take long, but this Kesson fellow broke down after a few poignant facts came to light. The police surgeon was quick. He found traces of poison in Sir Tristan's blood and labelled the cause of death as such. He also identified the liquid in the yellow bottle as krait venom. That linked to the frozen darts, and a full version of events from Lian, the Borneo tribesman, confirms everything."

"How did you get more information out of Lian?" Holmes asked.

"We only had Jamal to translate, and while his English is good, it probably isn't good enough for that purpose."

"There was a Professor of Asiatic dialects at London University who is fluent in Malay. He was good enough to sit in with us and interpret."

"Has Willard been charged with murder then?" I asked, my heart heavy at the thought of Kesson's imminent fate.

"Yes. I know he was an army friend of yours, Doctor, but murder is murder, and it is especially heinous when the reason is for personal gain."

"He'll hang then, won't he?"

"Oh, yes. I can't see any other eventuality than that. Again, I'm sorry."

When the inspector had gone, Holmes glanced my way and spoke. "I, too, am sorry. We make far too few good friends in our lives. To find one that has transgressed the law in such a calculated way and used the ignorance of someone so innocent as a primitive tribesman is especially galling. You have my sympathies."

"Thank you, but I find that with all that we have found out about this man. I can neither condone his actions nor indeed regard him as a friend after such. My only hope is that the poor tribesmen that were caught up in this are treated properly and taken home quickly and with a minimum of fuss."

"That would be a proper conclusion to this adventure," Holmes said, sipping his coffee.